Praise for Crucial Step

Immersed in the tropical heat of the Malaysian wet season a young Australian navigates his way through the past and the clash of cultures to make sense of the past. Crucial Step is a great mystery story with a satisfying twist.
KEN FISHER, author of Beach Spinifex

What a glorious read! Wow! What a journey! Your vivid descriptions paint a picture more than any postcard or photo could do. Wonderful. I really loved your well-drawn characters – particularly Theo, Jack, Biru, Eric and Franka. Your art with the dialogue was very well done and blended in perfectly for the characters both Asian and Swedish (and, of course Australian!). The tension ebbed and flowed nicely and kept me totally engaged.
BOB GOODWIN, author of Ezekiel, and the Max Justice trilogy

I've just finished reading 'Crucial Step'. Congratulations! It is a good read. Your insights and descriptions of Malaysia bring back lots of memories for me back-packing through SE Asia on the hippie road from Bali to London so many years ago. I like the complications involving the characters, the personal background story of Theo's father with a twist at the end, as well as the book Theo carries on his trip detailing the execution of the Australian drug dealer, that story having so much more of a reach into Theo's own personal life than he first realises. Well done! Thanks for giving me the opportunity to read it.
BEN ARMSTRONG, author of Wasted on the Warrego Highway

Crucial Step, with its well-drawn characters and action-packed story taking place in exotic Asia, will keep you in suspense all the way through.
ROBIN STOREY, author of Murder Undone and Secret Kill

An enthralling journey that brilliantly connects the reader with the heart and soul of south east Asia.
DR BRIAN PURDEY, author of Mindfulness Decoded

UNEASY

IAN LAVER

UNEASY
First published in Australia by Ian Laver 2022
Copyright © Ian Laver 2022
All Rights Reserved

 A catalogue record for this
book is available from the
National Library of Australia

ISBN: 978-0-6451887-2-1 (pbk)
ISBN: 978-0-6451887-3-8 (ebk)

Cover design by Jan Forbes © 2022

Typesetting and design by Publicious Book Publishing
Published in collaboration with Publicious Book Publishing
www.publicious.com.au

Disclaimer
This is a work of fiction and no offence is intended. The story incorporates many true political, geographical and historical facts. All the active characters in the book are fictitious, but the names of politicians and musicians mentioned who existed at this time are true. The geographic locations are basically correct, but some map details have been altered. Key dates have been juggled in the interest of allowing the story to flow for this period in history.

This book is dedicated to my mother
Ina Helena Laver
who just celebrated her 104th birthday

and

In loving memory of my daughter
Nicole Shaneen Ivory

Chapter 1

Fitzy was a cop. He looked like one and thought like one. But not like an ordinary cop, he was a smart cop and he knew it. A career cop, he could not do anything else. Because he was a detective, he did not have to wear a uniform. Some of his mates joked he should work in a long-board shop selling bright beachy surf shirts – if he grew his hair longer. He'd developed a strong liking for this type of shirt, not least of all because he got some free a couple of years ago from a mate called Stewie. These days he checked out the various thrift shops for the odd bargain and just because the style was out of favour did not stop him from liking the shirts.

At this particular moment, he ran a hand through his prickle-cropped brown hair, adjusted his aviator sunglasses, and looked around the Gordon Park Primary School playground which was adjacent to the High School.

He did not object to his partner, Acting Senior Sergeant Lerlene Diplock, interviewing the mothers who were comforting children and talking among themselves. She was dressed for authority; jeans, loose-fitting comfortable blouse and silver badge on her belt. She wore a shoulder holster to keep her police issue Glock hand gun out of sight. Sometimes she wore the firearm on her hip, partly concealed by a light weight denim jacket but on this occasion, she did not wish to up the ante. It was the late 1990's and supervisory positions were no longer reserved exclusively for males and Lerlene intended to make a success of her Acting Senior Sergeant position.

Lerlene said to Fitzy, 'How about you go and have a wander around the crime scene,' as she verbally nudged him out of the way knowing his sometimes abrasive manner would not work very well in a situation like this.

Detective Sergeant FitzMichael's keen vision raked the crime scene area. The police had been called to the school to investigate the attempted abduction of a five-year-old boy, a student from the primary school. Unfortunately for the police, the child had been whisked away in an ambulance just as they arrived so there was no hope of extracting any information from him. The child's mother was evidently distraught, as any parent would be in a situation such as this.

Gordon Park was considered to be a very safe area and the attempted abduction of a child was a serious concern for the local community. It was unusual for two police sergeants to be working together but Fitzy was in the *nether land* of employment, awaiting transfer to Homicide and Lerlene Diplock had been seconded to set up a comprehensive computer network to deal with the ever-growing offences against children. For all intents she was in charge of a new section, which had not been officially named as yet, and she was directly responsible to the chief superintendent, not an inspector as was usually the case. When the duties of the unit were eventually determined, positions would be advertised in the formal way and it was thought that Lerlene would almost certainly be selected. Normally a case such as this attempted abduction would be handled by a constable or senior constable until such time as something more serious was discovered in the investigation.

Fitzy, although unhappy about not being in Homicide, was still very much a professional police detective and was focused on the job in hand. They were as certain as they could be that the perpetrator had already left the area but they had patrols combing the adjoining districts. Lerlene looked towards him, moving her eyes only, so as to not break conversation with one of the mothers. He nodded. Their mental telepathy worked well. She slowly moved her head to signal him to stay away from her for the moment. He turned and strolled over to where the lush foliage blessed the surrounds with some shade.

The remaining area was a typical Australian schoolyard garden, boasting wiry natives and woodchip covering most of the area. He stood and observed the drag marks from the child's heels through the mulchy soil. The two parallel channels about a foot apart showed clearly that the five-year-old tried to dig his heels in which further suggested the boy did not want to go with the perpetrator. Fitzy knew straight away the spot where a deviant would hide because the land fell away to a shallow gully. It provided good cover and an excellent view of the school buildings. It was also out of vision of the admin block and the seats, where the mothers and teachers congregated when supervising children at play. The area was situated between the senior and junior schools. The car park for the senior school was adjoining the scrub.

He lit a cigarette with some difficulty in the breeze, inhaled deeply, bent the match double and placed it back in the box. The action was nothing to do with doing the right thing; he would have just thrown the match on the ground. He did not want to compromise the crime scene, a practiced reaction. Normally he would have used a cigarette lighter, but he was doing his best to cut down smoking and using matches made the habit just that bit harder, particularly in the wind. His measured glance scanned the terrain again, not spying anything of note, so he reverted to the basic rules of investigation and re-examined every inch again. On the ground were the flotsam and jetsam of school life; lolly wrappers, ice-cream sticks, and all manner of plastics, glinting tinsel scraps and a few dead balloons with string attached. There was nothing of obvious significance in his opinion, but being a shrewd campaigner, he never discounted anything until there was sufficient reason to do so.

Fitzy was always very careful when combing a crime scene. Whatever clothing or shoes he had on at the time he would always tread carefully, observe everything, and move slowly. Sometimes he wore trainers – jogging shoes – plain if possible, like Dunlop volleys for cases where he needed to do some running – he hated all the American design and brand naming prevalent on most casual footwear. Most of the time he wore Doc Martin boots, like most police, because of their toughness, and comfort for long hours on his feet. Fitzy liked them also because they could act as a weapon if the need arose. Being kicked by a Doc hurt a lot more than a sandshoe. He preferred Doc desert boots and had burnt a dot on each heel with a soldering iron so he would be able to identify his shoe prints at any scene from others.

After about ten minutes of very slow walking he arrived at the outer perimeter chain-wire fence and was drawn to a section where the bush had been disturbed. He thought about it for a second or two and concluded that it was of no major significance because the fence had clearly been broken for a long time, maybe years. Fitzy wandered along the fence in both directions and arrived back at the original spot. He concluded this was the best, and probably, the only place anyone could get into the school grounds easily. Also, there were trees and shrubs along the corresponding footpath, which was some distance from the last house in the sub-division fronting the park and leading down to a cul de sac. He noted someone could park anywhere here unobserved as the last house was some distance away; also, all the houses in the street were obscured by thick, bushy gardens or timber fences. One large house had a rendered concrete wall with trees overhanging into the Chinese elms and jacarandas lining the footpath. He always measured distances in cricket pitches, and he estimated about three from the path, about sixty metres. There was a thick patch of clumping golden cane palms where he was standing which would allow someone to easily slip in and out of this area unnoticed. For that very reason it was clear street vagrants and school children congregated here as the number of cigarette butts and other rubbish indicated. Younger children obviously played in the area and the older high school youth played and got up to all sorts of adolescent mischief.

Fitzy could not see any point in collecting butts, there were too many of them, but he squatted and examined the area as thoroughly as possible. People walking by could easily flick a butt or throw rubbish into the area just as easily as someone dropping something where they stood. It was a pity the boss had ruled out forensic staff and junior officers to help do this initial donkey work. He cursed. Fitzy and Lerlene had such a good clean up rate, but in reality, it was more because of his unique investigatory skills. Unfortunately, it went against them to a certain extent because the upper management thought extra staff was not necessary.

There were a few used condoms, obviously old and a needle that looked at least two or three days old as it appeared the rain had splashed a few specks of wood chip or dirt on it. The sight of the needle on the ground disgusted him.

'Filthy bastards,' he mumbled.

He wondered how someone could just drop a needle on the ground without any thought or consideration for others. Even though he did not think it was relevant to the case he picked up the syringe in a tissue, then he noticed a plastic cap about a foot away, so he gently pushed it over the needle. Fitzy was fully aware the cap may not necessarily be associated with that particular needle. He also was aware of needle stick injuries, AIDS, hepatitis and other diseases. Wrapping up the syringe in an evidence bag, and then adding a crime scene card, he stood and placed it behind the frangipani flower displayed on the top left pocket of his Bali shirt.

He slowly moved back towards the playground, treading gingerly, doing his best to place himself in the position of someone who would use this path. It was not an established path, but he used his imagination to conclude it was a possible thoroughfare. His vision tracked bent grass blades and slightly disturbed wood chip ... a track, iffy at best. The track took a slight turn and as he methodically walked back to his starting point he saw it.

Movement of a leafy branch in the breeze above allowed the sun to alert his eyes with a split-second metal flash. Lying on the ground was a pen with a gold clip. The sun hit it at just the right angle. He picked it up with his car key and held it up for close scrutiny. The pen was obviously an expensive Parker ballpoint and he grinned, seeing the initials C.A.T. engraved on it in what he knew to be Gothic script. He recently attended a computer course and remembered the exercise they had done on the choice of fonts. Even though he was aware this could easily mean nothing at all, he felt at least he was coming away with something. He surmised it would be unlikely for a student to have a pen of this quality, so it probably belonged to someone older, maybe the perpetrator. Fitzy bagged the pen and dropped it into his other top pocket behind the hibiscus flower.

Chapter 2

'You'd better ring that computer bloke … he said they'd get it to us last week!' bellowed Gretel in her forty-a-day voice.

Colin winced from the tirade coming from the laundry through two closed doors. He turned and did his best to yell back. He did not do a very good job, but she heard anyway because he knew her hearing was as sharp as her tongue when she wanted it to be. Only when she wanted it to be.

'Yyyyyes love, I'll give …'

She barked, 'Now! Bloody well *now*!'

'Um … righto dear, soon, I'm just finishing …'

'Now! Not soon. *Now*!' Her voice cracked like a bull whip over the spin drier and through the doors.

He rubbed his eyes and flopped his short, chubby frame into the office chair. They shared the spare room for office space, her desk by the window, his in the corner … facing the wall. A sign, with flowers stencilled around the edge, was Blu-Tacked to the wall; ***A happy home is a family that pulls together***.

A computer table linked the two, although it was closer to her desk than his. His right hand went automatically to the bottom drawer where he kept a small water bottle - with a few measures of Vodka. It was difficult to sneak a swig when she was around. Colin needed to be careful, but he always managed to. So far. He was aware her inverted pyramid shaped, crewcut head could appear at any time, with her eyes glaring and a voice on the ready to hammer and cut.

'Bugger it all,' he murmured.

He figured a small sip would not hurt, after all it was already afternoon, or eleven something anyway. Just as his hand touched the chrome drawer handle, the door flew open.

'*Now*, damn you, Colin, *now!* I need the computer for work; this nonsense has gone on long enough!'

That was close. 'Yyyyyes dear, I was just about to …' He picked up the phone to show her demand had clout.

The door slammed. He was aware enough for a second to wonder how the door jambs could handle abuse like that.

Now Colin, *now.* He knew there was time. He whipped open the drawer, grabbed the bottle and leaned against the door, rewarding himself with a small hit. Fair enough, more than a slug this time, he deserved it. Liquid pleasure, his first for the day.

The drawer slid shut and with ever increasing increments, the warmth eased his pain as the alcohol filtered into his blood stream. Colin wiped his mouth with his forearm and picked up the card, Galaxy Extra Experience Komputer Services. GEEKS

After three transfers from seemingly busy people he finally reached the person he wanted to speak to.

Colin did his best to be assertive. 'Er … g'day Scott, I was just inquiring about our …'

'What? Who's this?'

'It's Colin, remember, you were …'

'Colin? Colin who?' The voice had generation Y cockiness to it.

'Colin Thistleton. Remember, you were going to send my repaired computer three weeks ago, we've spoken, um, recently and you promised you'd make sure I got it well before yesterday, remember?'

'Thistle … mmmmmm … yeah? Mmmmm, bud, yeah. Aaaarh yeah, got it! How ya doin' bud, yeah. How's ya day been? What was the order again, buddy? Here, I tell ya, we been kickin' butt big time an' haulin' ass here bud, day in, day out, that's how busy we been. So, what was the …?'

'Replacement order J16743. Remember we spoke, in fact we've spoken quite regularly … you said you'd personally, like guarantee we'd have it sort of, uh three weeks ago, and a number of other times we talked, and you guaranteed … We spoke three days ago and you absolutely promised we'd have it er, yesterday.'

'Thistle ... er, what was the number again? Aaaaah! ... Yeah, got it, yeah. Haven't you received it yet, Bud?'

'Er ... no Scott, look we need the computer, my wife ...'

'You sure you haven't got it yet? Look, here ...' Silence for a few seconds and then rustle of papers. 'Yeah, here it is, the boys have made a note here, yeah right, ya didn't answer ya phone, yeah ... note right here in front a me. They said they tried to ring ya ... a few probs with the freight company I think, yeah, says here ya didn't answer ya phone.'

Colin ignored that, thinking about the number of times at school he received the same sort of carry-on from some of his colleagues who were lazy and manipulative, filling the space with meaningless, confusing babble and had not done what was asked of them.

He continued, not willing to be knocked off track. 'Any rate Scott,' he kept his voice under control, doing his utmost to be assertive, 'Um when are you going to send it, I mean ...'

'Right buddy, you better believe it, not a prob, be special delivery, you'll get it, latest, tomorrow ... how's that, dude?'

'Right. Er mate, you sure, tomorrow, I mean, my missus ... tomorrow?'

'You bedder believe it bud, you bedder believe it, done and dusted.'

'So, we're clear, it is tomorrow, right!' Sweat dribbled in Colin's eyes.

'You bet bud, you bet.'

Click.

Colin needed to go to the shed.

Chapter 3

'I'm off to the shed, dear,' signalled Colin, certain Gretel did not pay him any attention.

'Take the bloody shovel with you, I'm sick and tired of you leaving tools lying around the place.'

He picked up the shovel leaning against the house, shaking his head, mindful of the fact *she* was the one who wanted the shovel for some reason or other at least a week before. He thought she had not finished with it, *which* was why he did not take it back to the shed. He usually carried something to or from the shed as a decoy, so his wife would think he was doing some form of work. Colin was convinced, however, she did not even think about anything he did at the shed. She rarely went near his shed, nor did his daughter, ten-year-old Rosa. He was always careful anyway.

At the shed there was an elaborate but simple warning system set up in case anyone should arrive unexpectedly. When he had a swig or two, he was so quick there was no prior warning needed, apart from a quick glance at the door. He generally placed a couple of empty stubbies at strategic locations, all looking innocent if noticed but with a slug of Vodka in the bottom. Gretel knew he liked a beer or two but insisted he drink only low alcohol beer. There was a bar fridge in which he kept a few things when the inside fridge was full. Also, he kept two-pack glue, tinters and wood stains for those times when he restored or repaired a piece of furniture. She knew he liked a drink but had absolutely no idea how much he was drinking. Also, he kept a water bottle on the bench, or nearby always with a good measure or two of the seemingly odourless and colourless spirit.

Colin was an alcoholic.

Alcohol was slowly taking over his life. Whether it filled the void of his disenchantment with the teaching fraternity, or his lack of self esteem, or his poor relationship with his daughter, or his increasingly empty and meaningless situation with his wife, it was hard to pinpoint.

But there was another looming problem rapidly spiralling out of control. It was becoming out of hand like his alcohol abuse. Colin possessed a huge collection of men's magazines, most were available over the counter, some he was required to send away for. Playboy, Esquire, Penthouse and even the Black Label ones were legal via the post. There was Bumfeast, Fun Bags, Bum'n'Burger, and others ... all legal. Looking at legal, 'over the counter' reading material was not the problem; many members of society read all sorts of magazines, but ... Colin was aware of how aroused he became when he looked at these girls. In some of the magazines he suspected they were no older than children. He realised he was increasingly unable to control his desires.

Before Colin pulled out a magazine, he positioned his push bike so it blocked the door. Where he kept the magazines there was no direct line of sight to the door as an old wardrobe obscured the view. The window at his bench provided a clear view of the path to the house. Usually there was one or both main doors open, but like most blokes' sheds, he possessed piles of junk and negotiating through that would slow down any visitor. There was plenty of time to stash evidence, no danger of being sprung unless the visitor was quick.

Colin downed a stubby of beer. The low alcohol had zero effect. He washed out the bottle and poured a Vodka chaser and gulped it. His mind and body badly needed the booster. He poured another vodka, hid the bottle behind a box and whipped the lid off another stubby. The warmth flooded over him as he grabbed a magazine and sat against the wall, with full vision of any impending danger. Colin began masturbating. Those beautiful young nude girls in all sorts of positions sent him just about mad.

The loud wrap of a motorbike down the street jagged him back to the present. Colin slapped his wrist, chastising himself. He needed to be alert.

He felt no guilt at all about fantasizing over women in a magazine. Gretel, although only just thirty, long ago expressed no interest in sex, in fact he could not remember the last time they actually engaged in it. Having sex never really occurred to either of them. *It* had only been almost an accident, the few times they ever did it. They had a daughter to prove it. Now, Colin would not have sex with her, he could not, even if she begged him, no way in a week of Sundays. She repulsed him with her bad breath; always too close when yelling at him. It was like a gust of wind over a sewer pipe. She gave him hell every minute she was near, 'Do this, do that, you useless prick, you this, you that, dickhead this and moron that.' He could not stand the way she yelled and swore at him in her deep voice, croaky as a witch. She smoked more cigarettes every day, yelled louder and more … every day.

Once upon a time, she told him they were going to be married. All his mates seemed to be moving in the direction of marriage about then and it seemed like the thing to do. She proudly told him she was named after a yacht, the beautiful graceful lady, Gretel, which went on several years later to become the Australian challenger in the America's Cup in 1970. Colin had once seen the sleek heavenly racing marvel and wondered if her father would now see the irony in his choice of name. The old man died of cirrhosis of the liver not long after Colin and Gretel married. The young Gretel was chubby but now she was many kilos heavier and fast heading towards obesity.

Colin just shook his head. 'Beautiful Graceful Lady?' He shook his head again. 'Graceful Lady?' he mumbled to the shadow board where his tools hung outlined by white marker so as to know exactly where to return each item. Gretel owned an increasingly pyramid body and an inverted pyramid head. She insisted on having her hair cropped short, flat and wide across the top and with the shape of her face, all he could visualise when he saw her was one pyramid stacked on top of another. Big, nasty and overbearing.

She was bad enough, he knew that alright, but it was his other problem that was becoming hard to handle. The sight of those lovely young things at school, young and innocent. He was a teacher for Christ's sake; he knew it was seriously wrong desiring such things. Sitting at their desks, it was so easy to look up their dresses. It was making him lustful and crazy. They were everywhere, young and beautiful, so young, just kids, there to be … what? What about his daughter, Rosa? What would she think of her father being uncontrollably turned on by school children?

Colin shook his head and reached for the chaser. The spirit mainlined again and he felt a sharp spike of relief for a short time. He put his hands on both sides of his face and leant forward on his elbows. His mind drifted to those gorgeous kids around him at school every day. And next door at the primary school, young kids. He got worked up easily, every day, sometimes having to go for a walk to take his mind off it all. And the drinking? *Phew.* He knew his life was a mess - everything was out of control.

Chapter 4

Most of the day, Colin sweated about the computer and he was definitely nervous and if he was up-front with himself he was also scared. Scared of what he would find out when he arrived home from school. Either way, he knew he would attract abuse from Gretel. He managed to guzzle a decent slug of vodka in the car before walking inside. It was perfectly clear to him the computer was not there; he could feel the heat as he opened the door. Gretel's irritation had gone up a notch. It was her day off; she was washing the clothes and the spin drier was whirring around as well, slightly out of balance. *Whoomp, whoomp, whoomp!*

She wiped the kitchen bench with fury in a circular motion, Colin thought it looked like she was determined to rub a hole in it – all the way to South America.

'Colin, you useless moron, where in the fuck is the computer?' She was geared, as usual, for a brawl. Her boiling, molten question was put in such a way it was clear she was not open to accepting any answer he could give to satisfy her mental state.

'Yyyyyes dear … er …'

'You gutless bastard. Get on the bloody phone and *threaten them*!' The voice cranked up to almost a screech towards the end.

He nodded, mindful of how good she was at transferring the pressure. 'Yes dear, I'm …'

Colin closed the door, not because it would make a great deal of difference when she started really bellowing, a door was no better than a lace curtain.

He picked up the phone and dialled with a hand that had recently developed a slow shimmer, a low-level tremor. He hated the thought of dealing with Scott; he detested the task even more the way some young people like Scott took on American jargon and terminology and just crapped on to you as if you were nobody.

'Umm, g'day, I'd like to speak to Scott Sumich, please.'

'Scott? I don't think he's at work today, can anyone …' a disinterested female voice trailed.

Colin swallowed. He knew it was necessary to stand up for himself. He said in a louder voice, 'This is getting out of hand. I want to speak to Scott, please.' Colin worked hard with the firmness of the statement. 'He said he was going to be there and to ask for him.'

'Riiiiiiiiiight,' smoothed a voice Colin pictured the owner of, feet on the open bottom drawer, filing nails and chewing bubble gum. 'May I ask who's …?'

'*Look!* He almost frightened himself. 'Please put me on to Scott!'

Sweat decorated his brow, but in a deep-down way, he was proud of himself. The shake was giving him strength; there was a reward, just for him at the end of this, in a few minutes, a drink.

'One moment please, oh yes, Scott,' Her voice was away from the phone, 'Hey is that you Scott?' Back to Colin again, 'Yeah, you happen to be in luck, he's just walked in, I'll put you through, just a tick.'

Colin sighed, almost relieved but he was apprehensive about what was to follow. There was a scuffle noise grabbing the phone.

'Good afternoon, this is Scott, how can I be of help to you?'

'Um, g'day, Scott, this is Colin.'

'Colin? Colin? Colin … Colin who?'

'Colin Thistleton, remember we spoke yesterday, you said our computer would be delivered today. Remember?'

'Thistle… aaah yeah, you bet. How's your day been buddy? Right. Yeah, I've got ya. What? You haven't received it? I mean are you sure bud? Says here it went priority freight.'

As if Colin was not sure he had received it. *Christ!* Just then the door flew open like a burst water main. Gretel wrenched the phone from Colin's hand.

She shrieked into the mouthpiece, 'My name is Gretel Thistleton, right? *Right!* Now you listen here you arsehole, we paid our money six weeks ago, *right*? Now, if that fucking computer is not here by noon tomorrow, *right*? I'm not only just gunna take legal action against you and your company, but, right? I'm gunna personally drive down to your place and give you a decent smack in the head, right? And then I'm going to the police and my local MP.'

'Yyyyyye ...'

Colin could just hear the other end of the phone. He could feel the heat coming off his wife.

'Right Mister fucking Scott? Is that clear?' she snarled.

'Yyyyyyes ... er Mrs Thistleton, you bet ... yep, no worries, you got it.'

Her anger remained like soot on the line and in the room. Then the hard voice became a gravelly bark, just as frightening.

'That better be the case you prick. Or I'll come after ya, and you better believe it, *buddy*. Right?'

She slammed the phone down, almost crushing the tips of Colin's fingers. The handset bounced on to the floor.

Her voice dropped to a stern almost reasonable level incorporating a dripping, condescending tone, 'That's how you handle arseholes, Colin, take note. I can't trust you to do any fucking thing around here!'

She stormed out almost tearing the hinges off the door in the slamming process.

Colin mumbled and fumbled the word, 'Jesus.'

He had not felt lower for a long time. A dead wombat was higher in the pecking order than him. He needed to go and get his reward at the shed, a drink and a gawk at his magazines.

~

The next day at school, Colin received a message from the Registrar at school to ring home urgently. He scratched his head thinking maybe something serious had happened. The thought of Gretel leaving him crossed his mind and he managed a small tight smile. It did not last long. He dialled home.

Gretel picked up the phone. 'The computer has arrived, get home as soon as possible to set it up, right? I need it immediately for work things,' she barked. There was an inward breath which sounded like she took a deep drag from her cigarette. 'It's your bloody job to install the programmes so get here!'

As far as he was concerned, she did not need a phone and she barely needed the computer, she only worked part time for the local council and it seemed to Colin that she did not work very hard. He wandered back to the classroom as the last few students ambled past. Colin, bewildered, dejected and depressed, shook his head. He needed a drink, had not managed to sneak one since just after lunch when the other staff returned to classes. After grabbing his bag, he detoured past the staff room to the alcove near the canteen. The guzzle from his water bottle felt good; no one suspected it was vodka, he was sure of it.

When he arrived home the washing machine was surging and agitating out of kilter again and he could hear the vacuum cleaner in the lounge.

She yelled above the din. 'Is that you, Colin?'

'No dear, it's a burglar,' he mumbled, 'Who else do you think it might be?'

'Get the blasted computer organised, I need to run off a heap of copies for work tomorrow. Well, jump to it, I haven't got all day.'

At least he'd just gulped a good slug of spirit, from a bottle he kept under the front seat of the car, before braving dialogue with the Graceful Lady. The boxes had been unpacked but nothing was plugged in, so he opened all the plastic bags and commenced the process of hooking it all up. Twice during the next hour, she bellowed angrily about the state of progress. There was no need to answer; she didn't expect an answer anyway.

During the last few months, Colin's confidence and self-worth were slipping and he knew he was on the edge of a blackness that just went on for ever. He knew it was beckoning and there was absolutely nothing he could do about it. The dark space was there, and he could feel the draw towards the abyss.

Chapter 5

Fitzy edged back to the playground and contemplated the actual spot where Timothy Leak, the five year old, struggled with his abductor and managed to run away. There were scuffle marks where the perpetrator tried to … *tried to do what?* Fitzy figured the child had struggled, managed to free himself and the perpetrator must have made a lunge because there were two heavier indentations which spread the mulch when he gave up and turned to run.

He looked over at the carpark reserved for the teachers from the high school. He noted the lack of cover if someone tried to force a recalcitrant child into a vehicle and he concluded whoever attempted it did not park there. There was a locked gate at the cul de sac end but the track through to the road was undisturbed. Also, the chain-wire fence was two metres high and the gate nearly as high. He checked the gravel roadway, no vehicle had been through there for ages. The main entry at the opposite end was a similar gate and it was obvious people always used that gate.

Acting Senior Sergeant Diplock called him over. She was taking notes as she conversed with a sour looking woman who glanced sharply in his direction. He could feel her man hatred from five metres away.

His partner looked up. 'Ah, Sergeant FitzMichael this is …' she turned to the woman, 'Ms Verona Digweed, the cleaner.'

The woman frowned with indignation and spluttered, 'Custodian, my correct designated title is Custodian of Buildings.'

'Umm sorry, I mean custodian,' continued Lerlene Diplock with a raised right eyebrow and a quick glance in Fitzy's direction, 'has stated she saw a bloke, smallish ...'

Ms Digweed interrupted, 'Well, not really that small ...'

'Balding and slight, perhaps skinn..?'

'Well not really balding as such, you know, a little bit of hair and not that skinny.'

Lerlene's eyebrows went up as she glanced at Fitzy again. 'She says she may have seen him around the place, could be a teacher.'

Fitzy sighed; he had dealt with people like this before. He covered the space between them purposefully and stood in front of the cleaner. It was clear she did not like him, but it was equally clear he was more than a match for her.

'Right Mizzzz.'

Lerlene winced.

He continued. 'It is Mizzzz, isn't it, not Miss? Or is it Mrs?'

She took to it, face tight. 'It's Mz. Orright? She spelled out the letters, eM Zed!'

The controlled smirk on his face radiated his obvious contempt for her. 'Right, Mizzzz.'

Acting Senior Sergeant Diplock flashed a glare at him without moving her head.

Fitzy continued. 'How long have you been working here?' His tone contained the keenest of edges.

Ms Digweed's mouth looked like she had just tasted a lemon. 'Umm, three weeks.'

'Are you sure?'

'Well just over ... about two weeks ...' Her face lost the previous look and she became defiant again. 'Does it matter?'

Fitzy stood straighter and exhaled a loud breath, as far as he was concerned, she was an unreliable witness.

'Well, Mizzzz Digweed, it may, or it may not. We will be in touch with you again soon. May I suggest you think hard about the details when we speak to you next?' He nodded; he was torn between tolerance and contempt as he turned and walked away.

Lerlene was clearly annoyed at his behaviour but she was sensible enough to know Fitzy's crime solving ability had been instrumental and essential to her successful climb up the ladder. She knew the good cop, bad cop dynamic worked well, particularly with Fitzy's arrogant manner and aggression. Other officers she had partnered with did not match up. Male officers seemed to be able to get away with rude behaviour. She was regularly reminded that there was nothing easy about being a woman in the Queensland Police Service.

She turned to the cleaner. 'Thank you, Ms. Digweed, you've been very helpful, we'll be in touch.'

~

Back in the office she verbally attacked Fitzy as he walked in. 'Bloody hell, you can be a prick when you want to be.'

He just smiled below his straight nose and folded his arms, the biceps teasing the stitching on the colourful shirt sleeves.

She continued in a tense but lighter vein, 'She's liable to report you to the local man hater's club.'

'Listen Dipp ...'

Her demeanour changed like a dropped glass. 'No! You bloody well listen to me Fitzy, if you call me that again, I'll ...'

He was tending more regularly towards the habit of calling her Dipstick, a name some called her behind her back.

'You'll what, sir.'

'Sir! *Sir*? You arsehole, Fitzy. You'd better pull your socks up or I'll report you. You'd better show some respect for a senior officer.'

With her blond hair tied back and her tanned face taking on a reddish tinge, ears back, he must have realised he might have taken things a bit far.

'Look Lerle... Acting Senior Sergeant, I didn't mean it the way you took it. I mean ...'

'Listen Fitzy, I'm the senior officer and you are to respect that office, right? It goes without saying but I *will* say it, I don't like it any more than you. It's not my fault that you, you know, *the incident* ... Anyway, I *am* the senior officer. Right?'

He answered, eyebrows forming a straight line. 'Yes, Acting Senior Sergeant.'

It was her turn now. She knew Fitzy had to be handled in a certain way at times. 'That's better, junior officer. The designation is senior sergeant, we drop the acting bit, remember?' It was only then she allowed herself a tight smile, an acknowledgement of victory. 'Now, if you would be so kind as to give me a few minutes to wind up this other rubbish we can talk then, okay?'

Fitzy went outside for a smoke. The crack about the senior officer and *the incident* hit a nerve.

Chapter 6

'Fucking hell,' he said and kicked the verandah post.

He leaned up against the steel railing, noting it needed some rust treatment soon. Typical of the police department, the cops and criminals battled in third world conditions, except for the reception area with coffee table books, where the brass seemed to spend the entire budget in an attempt to make it look to the public as if it was a streamlined, friendly and *extremely* helpful service.

He recalled *the incident* that had marked the down grading of his status from acting senior sergeant to sergeant. How could he forget that?

'Fuck,' he said again as much to himself as the carpark, not game to kick the post again because the last effort hurt his big toe.

The incident in question, about a year earlier, was the result of what often went on in police stations when a questioning officer knows someone is guilty and the person just keeps denying everything *and* making fun of the police. In this case the person in question was a well-known troublemaker and was accused of assaulting an old woman and stealing her handbag, the most clichéd of crimes. Fitzy was not even part of the investigation team but was called in as a last resort by Senior Constable Warren McTavish who knew Fitzy was good at getting results.

Roscoe Bagshaw was a low life criminal who spent a lifetime in and out of reform schools and prisons. He was from a dysfunctional family amongst a brood of eight children, all of whom were either in trouble with the law or had been at some stage. The three girls in the family were pregnant as teenagers and were either married or living with local drop kick bullies or criminals. The boys of the family seemed to be doing their best to follow their father's leadership example by not working, assaulting others, thieving, selling drugs or spending time in Corrective Service institutions as much as possible.

The police in general were annoyed with people like them, particularly because their crimes were mostly petty and it always involved hours of paperwork. In addition, the politically correct lawyers from legal aid not only cleaned up with the fees they billed the government but seemed to enjoy hours of fun putting up every possible hurdle to make the investigator's job more difficult.

Senior Constable McTavish had said, "Hey Fitzy, I'm getting nowhere with this prick. He's progressed from petty crime to downright lousy gutter sniping, now belting old women. I wonder where he will stop. I'm sick of the bastard. We know he did it, he's been identified by photo. We found him passed out sitting in his car with the engine running. Looked like he'd just done a line of speed. The old woman's bag was under the seat. We've charged him but we are waiting for a lawyer. Do ya wanna have a try at him?"

Fitzy recalled laughing, "Yeah Wowzer, I know the mongrel. Leave it to me."

He wished he had not been so blasé about it. The crunch of gravel under the wheels of a patrol car brought him back to the moment. *Don't dwell on it, Fitzy* he thought.

At the time, Fitzy walked straight in to the interview room, glanced at the tape recorder and noted the red light was off. He asked Bagshaw, a cocky, arrogant individual if he had perpetrated the crime in question. Bagshaw laughed. Fitzy remembered the rotten teeth, lined up like dirty pickets in a decaying fence. Bagshaw made some snide comment about Fitzy's shirt and then he made a wise-crack about his nose. Fitzy walked up to him and smacked him across the head, with an open hand, so hard the man fell off the chair. The incident happened so quickly the other man looked up in fright. Fitzy then went around and helped Bagshaw back into his seat.

"Now Baggy, you squirming little cunt, I'm about to do that again, your word against mine, right? Now, again, did you assault the woman and ..."

"Yyyyess ... I did."

Fitzy slid a clipboard in front of him. "Now I'm going to bring in someone to witness your signature."

Oh how Acting Senior Sergeant Rodney FitzMichael wishes he had checked to see if the video camera was on or not, but of course he didn't even know about it. The camera was mounted on the wall, up high. The video camera was new and on a trial run *and* no one told him about it. He found out later that it was perpetually switched on but remained on standby until there was movement within its range of vision. It provided some interesting viewing for the wrong people.

'Bugger me.' He flicked his cigarette butt over the rail and went back inside.

~

Fitzy sat down and shuffled some papers.

Knowing the mood he was in, Lerlene waited a few moments before speaking.

'Righto, let's get back on track here, did you come up with anything during your bush walk?'

She reclined in her chair, hands clasped behind her head, pushing up her blond, tight knot of hair. Lerlene seemed to be able to use her skills just enough to be in charge and keep Fitzy in line. Fitzy slowly spun around in his office chair a couple of times like a child and then stopped, facing her, focused and ready to talk about the case.

Chapter 7

Colin sat in the staff room. His thoughts reviewed the day that had transpired so far. The aggression he copped from home and the unruly behaviour of his classes paled in comparison to the business about the young kid being abducted or molested at the primary school next door. Cops crawling over everything like blowflies around a dead dingo, but he had not done anything wrong. The arrogant bastard of a sergeant with a big nose and a ridiculous shirt was harassing the shit out of everyone; several teachers and office staff were interviewed twice. He was one of them.

And the missus. She had harped on to him about her visit to the psychologist who had diagnosed her with OCD - Obsessive Compulsive Disorder – and how selfish he was for not comforting her and not being considerate to her illness. *Fuck me!* There she was, constantly washing clothes that didn't need washing, cleaning things that didn't need cleaning, almost vacuuming the carpets bare, sweeping and dusting what? And smoking as well as yelling at him. He did not need any doctor to tell him she was as crackers as a box of Chinese fireworks, bloody bonkers.

He knew he had a few problems. Not only personal ones either. It was hard to take pride in his work. The Government in recent years, no matter what colour, was starving the public schools into oblivion to fund private schools; no money for basic repairs and maintenance, let alone new items like science resources, sporting gear and computers. Some of the teachers were heading into the private school system or going off onto all sorts of stress related leave. And now this attention from the police.

Colin glanced around the empty staff room and took a generous swallow from the water bottle on his desk. The alcohol hit his blood stream like an anaesthetic and he felt a cosmic second of bliss. Then reality filtered back, it was impossible to block.

There was a good magazine in the bottom drawer he was dying to read, well not read, look at the pictures. He bought it from the 'Breast of Luck Adult Shop' up on the range. Gretel had no idea he was buying them. Even though she was on medication now it made no difference to how attentive she was, at least as far as he could tell.

He took another gulp; he knew he was drinking far too much. All those young things around the place, at the supermarket, on the street, at school. It was wrong even thinking the thought, desiring them, he knew it was straight out wrong, but he couldn't help it. Maybe he should see someone about it. The horizon loomed closer, lower and darker. He needed help alright, not easy to do though, who do you approach? The doctor, the help line, what help line? *Look doctor, my wife is repelled by* me *but I couldn't touch her with a goal post anyway. Doctor, I see these girls, just kids, everywhere, some really young.* The whole matter was so close to out of hand and Colin knew it.

Chapter 8

'So, you don't think the syringe has any bearing on the crime?' Fitzy ran a hand back over his prickle cut.

'No, I'm pretty sure it was dropped a day or two before because there was some dirt on it, probably splashed by the rain. Rained yesterday but not today, but that pen could be a go-er. I handed it into the lab on my way back here; it has C-A-T engraved on it, more than likely someone's initials and probably belongs to an adult rather than a kid.' He rubbed his jaw, a musing action, 'But that's just a guess too, gut feeling. Looks like it's worth a quid. I'll get Meredith to check out people's initials around the scene. It's handy she's been seconded to assist our new unit.'

'We don't have much to go on at this stage,' said Lerlene. 'The man hater, Ms Digweed, told me she thought she saw someone who looked like a teacher. Even though she's not much of a witness, we'll check her out again but … anyway, as you know Fitzy, I've got all this Q-PED stuff to deal with, so you'll have to take on the main part of the leg work.'

She turned to her computer screen.

'Right, we've got our three regular paedophile suspects; none of them have initials C-A-T. First up we have Tim *Tugger* Morton, records show he's in London but I've got Meredith checking it out. Secondly, Devon *Sailor-Boy* Swanson. Right as we speak, he's in Long Bay, it's confirmed. Been there for eight months and isn't due for release for, let's see, yeah two years at least anyway, hasn't had parole or leave or anything like that. We've also got our local regular child botherer, Glen *Stink Finger* Hewitt. He's been out for six months or so.'

Fitzy helped one of the undercover officers, Hugo Firsch, put him away some time back. He knew Hewitt alright, a slimy little mongrel if ever there was one as far as he was concerned. At least he fitted the suspect's profile, slight with a pot belly, balding, short, with a ruddy complexion.

She continued, 'You never know, with this Q-PED set up, we might even find something related to this case, boss thinks so, I mean, children, paedophiles … never know.'

Q-PED, Queensland Paedophile Enquiry Database, was the special initiative Lerlene had been assigned to set up within the police service to document the increasing growth of child pornography on the internet.

'We've started to confiscate some suspects' computers and we're examining the hard drives; finding all sorts of stuff. You know Hazza Harrison, don't you?'

Fitzy nodded, he'd met Senior Constable Harold Harrison, sometimes known as *Hazza Hard-Drive* Harrison, on a number of occasions at various courses but didn't know him well. As far as he was concerned, Hazza was not a real cop, Fitzy saw him as a computer smart arse shunted up the ladder for his geek expertise, not for hard core police work.

She continued, 'Well, his specialty is obviously computers in general but for me he's sniffing around the internet and combing hard drives for incriminating info, reckons even if data has been deleted, it can still be retrieved.' She leant back in the chair. 'Rightee-ho Fitzy, go and give Stink Finger,' she stifled a giggle, 'a bit of a shakeup. I've requested the Electoral Roll, both State and Federal, we've got Meredith looking at that side of things, never know, it might throw something up. Also, if you get a moment, scan the phone book, or get her to, shouldn't be too many people with the initials C-A-T. It's all hands on deck, do what you can, just let people around you know what you're doing, but mainly, Fitzy…?'

'Yes?'

'Keep me informed, okay?'

Fitzy stood up, stretched and nodded.

She directly glanced at him. 'I don't want to harp on this, but I know how you feel about me being your supervising officer, I didn't ask for it. If you want to know the truth, I'd be as shitty as you, but this is the way it is. So, keep me informed.' She wanted an answer, not a nod. She continued the stare.

'Yeah. Bugger it all, yeah alright,' he responded with a slight testy edge, moving from one foot to the other wanting to change the subject. 'Yeah, alright. What about the kid who was the subject of this attempted abduction, and his mother for that matter?'

'Nah, not first up but very soon, the kid's distraught and she won't let anyone near him. She's pretty agro – was when I spoke to her for a fleeting couple of minutes. I hope she has calmed down when we, you and I, go to interview them both, we need to know as much as possible. But, the young victim, only five, did say it was a male, short, with thinning hair, bit of a belly and smelt funny, perfume but not like grandma or mummy. Also, I suppose you could go and interview Mizzzz Digweed again, if you can be trusted not to antagonize her.' She smiled at her impersonation of Mizzzz.

Fitzy lit a cigarette. Her smile faded into a glare and she pointed at the *NO SMOKING* sign on the wall. The action was intimidating enough for him to put up his hands in defence.

'Alright, Senior Sergeant Dippy, alright, I'm on me way,' and he walked out.

She spoke firmly at his back and challenged, 'You prick, if I have to tell you my name again there will be trouble.' She followed with a grumbled, 'Arsehole.'

~

Half an hour later Fitzy knocked and was just about to knock again. The door opened, just enough for Fitzy to identify the acne scarred, sun-damaged face.

'Yeah?'

'You probably don't remember me, Stink Finger, eh? Open up, I want to talk to you.'

'I don't have to open up to no-bloody-one, mister.' There was a cocky edge to the statement.

Fitzy held up his identification.

'Aaah heck.' Crestfallen. 'I remember you, sir. Look ... er Mr Fitzgerald.'

'FitzMichael, Sergeant FitzMichael, pinhead, get it right or you'll be whistling Waltzing Matilda through a split lip.'

'Sir, sorry. I've done nothing wrong, sir, I'm clean. Did you know, I pray every day, sir?' retorted the short man standing up straight and puffing out his chest.

'So fucking what, Stink Finger, so probably did Captain Fairy-floss, means bugger all to me. He's still in Boggo Road Prison as far as I know. You bastards never change.'

'But sir, Sergeant FitzGib ... er FitzMichael, I've been cleansed, I went to confession earlier and I prayed with Father O'Neill, he just left, just then, only less than ten ...'

'Like I say, means nothing to me. You're in strife Stink Finger, where were you on Monday morning eh? Between ten and noon.'

'Ten and noon? I ... I can't remember, sir. Hey, what is this?'

Fitzy edged past the short, tubby man, walked into the house and turned. 'I'll play along. You were at the Gordon Park Primary School, that's where you were, you miserable speck of fly shit.'

'Whaat? But ... mister ... sir ... I ... no sir, I wasn't.' His memory seemed to kick back in. 'That's right; I was with Father O'Neill, praying at Saint Christopher's Cathedral.'

'Likely story, mate,' sneered Fitzy, glancing around the room; the place was clean, neat and seemingly tidy, no dishes in the sink, no clothes strewn around like many of the people he visited. It surprised him somewhat. He turned. 'Two witnesses said they saw you, or someone answering your description, hanging around the school at the time.'

'At the time? Time of ... er what, sir?' inquired Glen Hewitt. Beads of sweat glistened on his forehead and threatened to congregate into a blob and run down his bulbous nose.

'A child was molested.' Fitzy's statement was delivered hard and his probing stare bored into the smaller man, searching for anything that might betray signs of subversive behaviour.

'What? Sir, no, it wasn't me, talk to Father O'Neill; he was with me, we pray, regular as clockwork. I'm cured sir, I'm not like I was, I don't do those sorts of things anymore; God has shown me the way to salvation.' His eyes appeared to grow with enthusiasm. 'I've left that life behind, and,' as if an afterthought, 'I have been keeping up my appointments with Doctor Goode, you know, the psychiatrist I've been told to see, haven't missed one appointment.'

'I'll check with your case officer about the doctor, but I intend to have a yarn with this Father O'Neill, Stink Finger. I intend to, don't you worry about that.' Fitzy leant even closer and cocked his head. 'Have you been drinking?'

'Y..yes, I did have a small nip, but sir, it's not part of my release conditions, no alcohol I mean, I sometimes feel under enormous strain.' His eyebrows bunched in the middle.

'What have you been dr...?'

'Gin, sir, gin, Father says a small nip every now and again is beneficial to my wellbeing, you know, sort of help me cope with life outside.'

'People like you don't change Stink Finger, especially kiddie tamperers. I've got my eye on you, orright?'

'But sir, I'm innocent! Sir?' He dabbed sweat from his scalp with a tissue. His thinning brown hair matted in strands and was almost like the clichéd comb over.

'Yeah?'

'Um sir? My name's not Stink Finger, I left those type of things behind when I changed my ugly ways, when God showed me the path to salvation and how to take responsibility for my previous life. Sir, Mr Fitzpat ... um ... Sergeant, I find the name very offensive, my name is Glen Hewitt.' The last part of the statement was delivered with a tightening of the mouth and a slightly upward slant of his jaw.

'Glen? Glen. Ha, what a laugh,' mocked Fitzy, 'you'll always be Stink Finger to me, you little slime ball. Now don't move out of the district, remember your release conditions, I'll be in touch.'

Fitzy wheeled around and strode out, lighting a cigarette on the way and chucking the match on the doorstep.

Chapter 9

He decided to go to the cathedral and have a chat with the Father O'Neill whose name had just cropped up. After he parked the car, he noted the orphanage was next door and it occurred to him that if Hewitt was coming to the church, he may not be honouring his bail conditions. Fitzy knew his conditions of release did not allow the offender to be within coo-ee of any such place but if he was under supervision it would probably be deemed to be acceptable. Just. He made a note to check on it later. He rolled names and words around in his head. Paedophiles, Hewitt, Father O'Neill, orphanage, children …

Fitzy made his way up the stone steps, hewn and scoured in unmeasurable amounts over many years by sinners of all shapes and sizes. Fitzy knew he was a hell of a sinner and smiled at the fact; he was damn proud of it. On the top step by the massive doors, a man in his late seventies, cloaked in priest garb, with thin grey hair bade goodbye to a young couple. Before going back inside he turned and acknowledged Fitzy with an engaging smile.

'I'm Father McFarlan, welcome, can I help you my son?'

Fitzy noted cobalt blue eyes as he held up his badge. 'Sergeant FitzMichael, I'm looking for Father O'Neill.'

'He's about the place somewhere. By the way young man, nice shirt. Has anyone told you that you look like the actor, what's his name, Bryan Brown?' He smiled broadly. 'He was in, let me think, yes, A Town like Alice, with Helen someone or other, wonderful film it was and let me see, he was also in …'

'Right, yeah.' Fitzy inclined his head. 'Father O'Neill?'

'Oh yes, of course, if you would follow me; I hope he's not in strife again, is he?'

It took a couple of seconds for Fitzy to get back on track after the comments about his shirt and Bryan Brown. He had often been kidded about both of those matters.

'Strife?'

'Yes, he has a radical way of dealing with street kiddies; some people disapprove of his methods.'

'Radical, what do you mean?'

'Mm well, he meets them at their own level, if you know what I mean.'

Fitzy didn't really, but he slotted in the remark for future reference.

'Also he does wonderful work with those poor unfortunate sex offenders in jail, and of course, some who have been released as well. He's a real saint is our Father O'Neill, a real saint.'

Fitzy was unsure if this was an attempt at humour. They arrived at a plain, heavy-looking wooden door.

The old man knocked. 'There he is.' He raised his voice. 'Father O'Neill? There's someone to see you.' He ushered Fitzy through. 'I'll leave you to it. Nice to meet you, Sergeant.'

The old Father shuffled off, obviously skilled at filling his day with helpful public relations tasks.

'Sergeant?' inquired the other man, who could easily have passed for Robin Hood's offsider, Friar Tuck. Chubby without being obese, a ring of short hair surrounding his otherwise bald head, like a halo.

'That's correct, Father, Sergeant FitzMichael, I'm here to speak to you about Stink Finger Hewitt.'

'Sergeant,' he declared with tightened brows, 'that's a disgusting name. He is a changed man; he's seen the error of his ways and has turned his life around. He has accepted the Lord into his life, turned from wickedness; he prays regularly, you know, attends confession every day, and I'm helping him to … adjust. It says in the bible a man should be given the chance to turn from sin and …'

The priest held up an index finger to emphasize a point. Fitzy was not really sure what point the man was making as there were several to choose from.

The detective held up his hand like a stop sign to regain higher ground. 'Father?'

'What is the problem?'

Father O'Neill's brow tightened. He sighed, turned slightly and fussed with his hands in a, *let's move along I'm a busy man, get to the point,* fashion.

Fitzy's nose tweaked. He sniffed … aftershave? Mouthwash? His alert button piqued.

'What were you doing between ten and twelve on Monday morning, Father?'

'What? What is this?' he retorted and turned back towards Fitzy, eyebrows now a hard line. Outrage hovered.

'You heard the question.' Fitzy held the priest's stare.

The dumpy little man adjusted his cassock. 'What is this about, am I … am I a suspect for something? How dare …' His eyes narrowed.

'Please answer the question, Father.' Fitzy noted the reference to the word suspect.

'If I must, I was with Glen, firstly in the confessional over there.' He firmly pointed, as if identifying the confessional booth would prove his story. 'And then into the congregation area praying. We knelt side by side and brought God into our hearts, if you must know. Now what is this all about Sergeant?' His demeanour still exuded a testy if not arrogant manner.

'We are investigating the molestation of a minor.' Fitzy continued to stare straight into the Father's eyes.

'What? Am I a suspect? You cannot be serious!'

Fitzy needed to remain in control. As a police detective he knew it was important to make this man sweat. Fitzy held a very low opinion of some people, mostly men, in positions of responsibility, often in religious intuitions, who abused that trust. Some, who knew how many, were sex offenders themselves and were able to hide behind their various organisations with impunity. In his experience as a police officer he often found many so called pillars of society were hypocrites and criminals of the worst kind.

'Everyone is a person of interest until such time as they are eliminated from our inquiries, Father.' His stare finally forced Father O'Neill to look away. 'How do you recall exactly what you were doing?'

The priest cleared his throat, a sure sign to Fitzy that he was flustered. His voice took on a slightly more amiable tone.

'Well Sergeant, that's easy, every Monday I'm here at the Cathedral, I'm on duty if you like, I take confession and I'm here for Bible study and, from time to time, other group activities, and I ... er supervise other, you know and ... um, yes, naturally Father McFarlan will, I'm sure, support that ...' The last part of the sentence, words tumbled over each other.

Fitzy narrowed his eyes, wondering if the older priest would support ... what, and in what way? Would the confirmation be support for the office of the church, to retain status quo, or the truth?

'I see.' Fitzy moved slowly from one foot to the other and looked deadpan for a moment. He said in a measured tone, 'That will be all for the moment thank you, Father.'

He turned and walked away. It was one of his tactics to show certain people who was in charge. After five or six strides he turned, Colombo style and lifted his index finger pretending to remember something.

'Oh, by the way, keep up the good work with the street kids, Father!'

The last remark was delivered with a slightly acid edge. Fitzy glared at him. The holy servant was left standing, contemplating the extent of the matter. He turned towards a crucifix on the wall and Fitzy could hear him mumbling something probably to do with forgiveness. He crossed himself.

On his way out, Fitzy wondered if the priest was asking forgiveness for himself, or Fitzy. He smiled, sure that he was well and truly too sinful to be forgiven. He stopped and asked a woman, who was sweeping between the pews, the whereabouts of Father McFarlan. She smiled kindly and said he was out shopping and was not due back for some hours. She offered to give him a message but he declined and thanked her.

He ambled down the stone steps into the early afternoon, noting it was still quite warm for May. The sun was bright, so he pulled out his aviators, gave them a cursory clean with his shirt and put them on. His feet hurt from his long run on the weekend, and his head felt tight, not because of a headache but because there was so little to go on. Like many cases in the early stages, there was plenty of circumstantial evidence but nothing solid. He sat in the car for a few moments rolling over information in his mind. This Father O'Neill could also be in the frame. Unlikely but … short, balding, a whiff of something on his breath, a link with an orphans' home, or similar, work with street kids with drug issues, sex offenders … it went on.

Fitzy had made balls-ups before in his career by jumping in too soon but now he was wise enough to know real evidence was essential; hunches were okay and sometimes paid off, sometimes not. He felt very strongly about getting the right person and not framing people just to get results.

He was also aware of the power of the Church and their unwritten doctrine to deal with unlawful issues within their own establishment. Having senior police officers, politicians and judges as members of the church certainly helped to allow matters of criminality to be swept under the rug. Church officials would discourage people from pressing charges in cases of assault by priests with the assurance the matters would be dealt with in house.

Fitzy figured things would become apparent in this case and lead them to the perpetrator and he would deal with things as required according to law. If anything pointed to the church, the police hierarchy would not be pleased because in recent times many public institutions had come under scrutiny for hiding abuse of children and investigations were often pushed by those who were now adults and had been abused. So, these matters were now more likely to be tried by the justice system.

However, Fitzy's preference was for crimes where people bashed and murdered and robbed others, violent stuff, not the sick child abuse muck he was confronted with at this stage. Deep down though, he knew he would love to get his hands on the perpetrator of this crime, and all his associates, and belt the living daylights out of them. He viewed paedophiles as deranged, sick people, not worthy of being allowed to live and he reflected angrily that judges always seemed to let them off lightly, allowing them to re-offend and continue to waste police resources. He boiled at the thought that these bastards who abused children were given far better treatment than the average criminal, having a separate section of jail where they could continue to swap disgusting stories and plan ways of beating the system when they were released. He was all for the death penalty for the mongrels. Most of the police service felt the same.

He once again reflected on *the incident* which robbed him of his acting senior sergeant designation and landed him back doing this second class policing. *Bagshaw was as guilty as buggery, Fitzy. Alright, you did what you did but next time, if there is next time, don't bloody well get caught.*

'Fuck,' he said, bouncing the heel of his hand against the steering wheel. He lit a cigarette and started the car. 'Fuck.'

Chapter 10

He reined in his temper, and his thoughts, and went to the address given to him to interview Ms Verona Digweed. He figured she would be home because she was not due at school until 3.30pm. Even if she was not at home Fitzy did not mind taking these opportunities to see how people lived. It often gave him a clue about them or opened up a door to something relating to the case, or even another case. Fitzy was aware that he was not in the best of moods, so he focussed to hold himself in check and to not stir her up negatively. It was clear she was an unashamed and committed lesbian with an obvious dislike of males, and it would seem, types just like him, male or not. He was not anti-gay and associated with several gay people, including a close friend. Fitzy simply did not like gay people who took a stick to straight people and assumed before they even spoke to them that all straights were bastards.

He tried to be polite and friendly. It started off badly when he referred to her as a cleaner.

She corrected him, 'Custodian, I'm a Custodian of Buildings, Grade Two! I've already made that clear.'

He felt like pointing out to her she was a cleaner and just because she gave herself an up-market, politically correct, title, as far as he was concerned, she *was* a bloody cleaner. Fitzy did his best not to draw out the Mzzzz too much, but she still regarded him with drawbridge eyebrows and a lemon in the mouth look.

As to the subject of the person she thought she knew, she said with purpose, 'He looked like one of the teachers here, I think his name's er

Thornton … er maybe it's Thistlewaite … or, no, yes, it's Thistleton, yes, no, yes, that's him. I think, yes that's him, I'm positive.'

She nodded up and down, no hint of a smile. Prune mouth.

'Are you sure now, Mzzzz Digweed? Thistleton?'

'Yes, of course I'm sure!' She gave him the battery acid, facial look again and then eased off a little with a mischievous head curtsy and added, 'But I wouldn't want to accuse someone of something, I'm not like that.'

Fitzy smiled thinking she was exactly like that and would love to accuse someone, especially if it was a bloke. He kept her gaze until she broke contact.

He said flatly, 'Fair enough that will be all for the moment thank you, we may need to speak with you again at a later time.'

He continued to stare at her a bit longer. Being a policeman allowed him to do it, a learned behaviour from training school. *Keep 'em guessing what you are thinking.*

The glare she flashed was serious and then she glanced at his short-sleeved, surf and palm tree shirt. Fitzy thought he could detect a slight easing of the mouth.

'Do you always wear second hand shirts?'

She turned and ambled off.

He stood watching her retreat in a round shouldered orangutan style, showing an ample backside forced into ex-army drill combat strides. He was convinced this woman was at best an unreliable witness.

She had a chip on her shoulder as big as a sleeper. He surmised the lump of wood weighing her down was more than just about men. She was a confused and troubled woman and it made her unnecessarily aggressive. His profiling training suggested she was perhaps emotionally damaged by some experience in the past and further questioning was a waste of time.

~

Fitzy had one more visit to make before heading to the office. He wanted to speak to Kathleen Crier, a teacher-aide. Lerlene rang him just after he left Hewitt's place, to ask him to go and speak with her on the off chance she could add to the picture.

The woman was at the school in her staff room when he arrived. Originally she stated that she saw someone at the High School who looked similar to the possible perpetrator. At the time she appeared confused and flustered and Acting Senior Sergeant Diplock let her go with the idea they would check her details later.

Fitzy introduced himself and asked a range of generic questions, hoping to glean something positive.

'I have given the matter some thought and it was just a fleeting glance of someone that day … in the general area. Only a split second and really, to be honest, I can't say.'

Fitzy was astute enough to realise the woman was balancing just being helpful with saying something she genuinely was not sure of. He needed to probe further.

'Could you describe who you saw, or how about what you saw?'

Kathleen Crier grabbed her long dark hair, made a ponytail and secured a black, elastic band around it. She was a well-rounded twenty five year old, with curves in all the right places.

'This is difficult for me, Sergeant.'

She looked directly at him and gave him a gentle smile which turned nearly into a grimace. Clearly she was conflicted about her situation.

'Look. Ms Crier, I promise to keep what you say confidential, or I should say truthfully, as confidential as I can.'

'But what if I identify this person? And as I said I'm not sure who it is because all I really saw was someone outside down the street when I came back from closing the gate. The person was 30, maybe 40 metres away.'

'Was it the cul de sac or the main entrance road?'

'Main entrance, there is a gate to the cul de sac but it is always locked, no one seems to use it.'

'Who was the person you saw?'

She shook her head and was clearly uncomfortable with stating the name of a colleague.

'Ms Crier,' began Fitzy in his best practiced good cop voice, 'you don't want whoever perpetrated this crime to go on to do worse things, do you?' She shook her head.

He could not help staring at her attractive ears. Dangly silver earrings swayed. He noticed there was a thick silver ring on the middle finger of her left hand.

'No, but what if I'm wrong and I ruin the career of a teach…'

'So, it *was* a teacher?'

She didn't respond.

'Ms Crier, I know how you feel but any help you can give us would be of enormous help. Who was it?' He concentrated looking into her eyes.

'Sergeant, I really don't …'

'I hate to have to say this but if you don't tell me you may be charged with withholding information. Do you understand?'

She sighed. 'I've only been here at this school for a short time and I don't really know the teachers very well.'

'It's alright, Ms Crier, believe me I do understand but please, anything you say will be confidential.' Fitzy splayed his hands and gave his best understanding smile.

'Well, Sergeant, I think it could be a teacher.'

'Well?'

She gave the name, 'Colin Thistleton.'

'Thank you, Ms Crier. As I said I will treat the matter delicately. I respect your professional attitude.'

On the way back to the office, Fitzy smoked and thought about the teacher-aide with the silver earrings, green eyes, tanned shoulders and lovely curves. He slotted her details into his memory bank as well as his notebook.

Fitzy was always careful about dating women who were part of an ongoing investigation after a rev-up he received from his senior officer when a constable. He almost compromised an investigation by dating a female who turned out to be lying by providing an alibi for a criminal who just happened to be part of her extended family. He managed to scoot free from it but had learnt his lesson.

Being a police officer had definite advantages in meeting women but it seemed to have as many disadvantages in equal measure. Things like a life of violence, bullying and arrogance that could appeal to some women but was a distinct turn off for others. Not that all police are the same but to be an effective cop you had to have a certain amount of authority and toughness to survive. In addition, a police officer needed to be tough enough to cope with arresting someone in the middle of a brawl and be tough enough to defend themselves from someone bigger and stronger, and sometimes armed.

Fitzy forced his mind back to the job and chewed over the name he just received and the other facts they had put together. It was just a name but better than nothing, the description fitted but there was far too much misty detail around it all and not enough real evidence. He had interviewed Thistleton on the day, twice, and although he did not particularly like him, he did not think Colin was their man. The presence of the pen with CAT inscribed on it crossed his mind and he would check that out next. The man had an alibi, verified by another teacher during the time the crime took place. He needed to have a talk with Lerlene, to formulate a plan and also see if anything from the Q-PED investigation might be relevant to this case.

Chapter 11

Fitzy's comfortable desert boots decorated the desk and a cigarette smouldered away in an ashtray, or more correctly in an aluminium pie base seconded for the purpose, when Lerlene Diplock entered. There was no need for to her to sniff the air, she jumped to it.

Fitzy pushed his luck. 'Mornin' Dippy.'

'Right, Fitzy, your attitude towards me and this office has to change. I'm not to be referred to as Dippy or Dipstick, understand? Anymore! Right?'

'I haven't called you Dipstick for ages.'

'Stop it!' She almost yelled and slung her shoulder bag on a wooden chair alongside the immaculately tidy desk. 'Now look here Rodney FitzMichael, I'm sick and tired of your disrespect for me and this office. It's no smoking in here. There's the bloody sign, see?'

She made a big show of pointing, jabbing several times in the direction of the sign, and him. He looked at her and it was clear he was about to say something sarcastic. She glared at him and held up her hand in a stop sign.

'Now I could report you for a number of misdemeanours. The way you spoke to Ms Digweed for instance, your disrespect for the office of Senior Sergeant, your disrespect for *this* office; no smoking, it's a health and safety issue in case you hadn't noticed. And…'

'And what Super Senior?'

'Jesus Christ!'

Lerlene placed her hands on her strong hips and her face took on a bull terrier look, ears smoothed back like her blonde hair.

'Well I could make all sorts of smart arse comments about your big nose, eh? How about a few of those Rodney FitzMichael and Michael FitzRodney jokes, eh? And what if I joked about those out of date shirts you insist on wearing, but I don't, right? You look like a dickhead, but I keep that to myself. So how's about some co-operation Fitzy. Stop being a downright prick - I'm well and truly past it!'

She threw out her arms in exasperation.

Fitzy's eyes widened. It was obvious he thought the comment about his nose was bad enough but what was wrong with his shirts? *Dick-head?* It floored him. He knew Lerlene rarely hit below the belt.

He went crimson and it took nearly a full minute for him to respond.

'Oh,' he said and gently butted out his cigarette.

Lerlene was smart enough to realise she needed to show command, no point in getting physical with a male. She had to use female tricks, there was no choice. He looked vulnerable for a couple of moments, eyebrows showing concern.

She followed up, 'Alright, Fitzy, I know that was a bit low, but, well, you make it so difficult at times with your attitude. You can be such a miserable bastard at times. Whether we like it or not, we have a job to do and we have to respect each other.' To lighten things up she added, 'Rightee-ho Sergeant FitzMichael, let's get on with it, but before we do, white coffee with two thanks. I'm sure you were just off to get one for yourself, weren't you? And dispose of the stinking ashtray while you're at it.' Almost with a pout she added, 'Thank you. Rodney.'

She wanted to give the impression she was one up, top dog, even if only for the time being.

~

Fitzy placed a mug of coffee at Lerlene's elbow.

She smiled a fixed knowing smile at him. 'Thanks, matey. See? You can be decent if you want to be.' She leaned back and exhaled loudly through her nose. 'Now what do we know? Firstly, I haven't come up with anything of interest from the Q-PED investigations as at this moment.'

Over the next twenty minutes they reviewed what Fitzy had done, the interview with Hewitt and his suspicions in relation to Father O'Neill's alibi which still needed to be verified. They discussed the proximity of the orphanage. Lerlene made several calls and established it was mainly used for emergency housing for families these days. However, there were ten children housed there currently but that number rose and fell by one or two depending on foster care placements.

Fitzy noted, 'I've left a message with, let me see, Louis Bormann, to ring me back. He's Stink Finger's case officer and I have to check in with Doctor Goode, his psychiatrist.'

They talked about Father McFarlan and both agreed he was not a person of interest but Fitzy said he would keep the pressure up on the old man. Father O'Neill was worthy of scrutiny, his links with street kids and sex offenders and other criminals were considered. Lerlene clicked away on her computer through her Q-PED access to see if the good Father's name had cropped up, but it was a negative.

Fitzy spun around on his office chair and flicked through some notes. 'Can we get some help?'

'We might get Hazza to dig around a bit more; at least we are allowed to use him on a needs basis, meaning an hour or two here and there,' she said picking up the phone and instructing Senior Constable Harrison to further investigate more broadly, internet, email and any other computer usage and social media in general from the rectory, the orphanage or any personal connections that he could see fit.

Just after she hung up the phone rattled again. When she replaced the receiver, she procrastinated for a couple of minutes.

'Hey Fitzy, Meredith was just reporting in. Firstly, Tugger Morton is confirmed as being in London, in fact he's on remand for being at it yet again, over there.' She shook her head and grimaced. 'They just can't stop themselves – should be put away for life – so, anyway, he's out of the picture. Secondly, the Electoral Roll, both state and federal, came up with hundreds of people with the initials C-A-T. She also scanned old phone books for this area and came up with twelve names. At present she has excluded females, so amalgamating both those sources she's come up with fifteen.'

She looked at Fitzy who was tapping a cigarette against the pack.

He smiled sheepishly, 'I'm not lighting up, alright, it just helps me think, orright?'

'Now, those fifteen she has been able to reduce to eight by careful elimination, for example, people in hospital, deceased or moved since the phone book was printed, etcetera. She has pruned it down to eight names.'

Lerlene handed Fitzy a sheet of paper.

'Now, there's more, she got the uniforms to visit and pretty well exclude, not absolutely, but exclude for the moment, more who were away at the time, or don't fit the description, which leaves us with three. See there, Clive Andrew Timmins, Cedric Alan Tarcoola and Carson Albert Torrens. I want you to check those blokes out if you wouldn't mind.'

'Yeah, no worries.'

Fitzy stood up and paced, unlit cigarette behind his ear. His ego was still tender from her earlier comments.

He continued, 'I also want to return to the scene, see how McTavish is going with the door-to-door check and also have a chat with our man, Colin Thistleton.'

'Right. I'd like to join you later and we can have a talk to the teacher who provided the alibi that Colin was in the staff room during the time the crime took place. By the way, Meredith has checked most of the prisons for escapees and new parolees and there's nothing of interest there … so far. We are still waiting on info from three States as well and both of the Territories. Same old story, state government bullshit, never keen to part with anything, especially data on pedos. She's also onto mental institutions, hospital psychiatric wards and the like. I've got some more work to do on Q-PED, so let's keep in touch. Righto, you do that and we'll get together later and interview the victim and his mother.'

Just then Inspector Deaver tapped on the door.

'Lerlene? Looks like you and Fitzy have got bugger all to do. Would you deal with this? Theft of valuable orchids. Old Triple Chins is breathing heavy down my collar as well as Jacko about this crap. It's a nothing case, pretty well solved for yas, but I haven't got time to fuck about chasing burg-u-lars.'

Lerlene rolled her eyes at his colourful way of mispronouncing words. The boss of the station was William David Wills, who everyone called Old Triple Chins, or Old TC because of his triple chins.

'Good, ta, love yas all,' he said in Jeff Fenech style and smiled brightly with a pout intended for them both.

He dropped the file on her desk and with a swish of bright tie, white shirt, pressed slacks and polished shoes he was out the door in neat, quick steps.

Fitzy and Lerlene looked at each other, deadpan.

'Devious Deaver's not only a brown-nose, he's a lazy cunt as well,' said Fitzy.

She sighed. 'Well I guess if we have to do it, we have to do it. That's what being a junior officer is all about. Old TC said we would have to take direction at times from Deaver. Bugger. And, Fitzy, please don't use the C word in front of me, alright?'

'Well you call people dickheads, don't you? What's the difference?'

She shook her head.

'Um …' About to debate but decided against it. 'Gawd, let's not discuss it now,' she replied, slightly exasperated. 'I'll have a look at this file so you may as well buzz off, check out the scene again, see how Wowzer McTavish is going and then have a chat with Colin. It should keep you from dozing off, eh? Ring me, if I don't ring you.'

They were both good at arrangements from previous working protocol and generally they stuck to them.

'Very good, ma'am.'

She looked up, began to scowl and then said, 'Get!'

Chapter 12

Fitzy returned to the Gordon Park Primary School playground, the scene of the botched abduction and sat down on a seat nearby. Fortunately, there was some shade and although nearing mid-winter, the sub-tropical Brisbane sun had plenty of strength.

The area was deserted, just what he wanted. He considered himself good at reconstructing things in his head, positioning the known players, speculating on the perpetrator, shuffling around clues, trying to put himself inside the head of the criminal and the victim; painting a picture and then transferring it all to the scene where he was sitting. Fitzy needed a break in the flow of continuous negativity of evidence piled up before them. He was well aware of the clichéd saying that they had to nail something within the first 24 hours because every hour after that the task becomes doubly harder.

He lit a cigarette, noting he seemed to be smoking a lot these days. Fitzy smiled, pretending to think Lerlene was driving him to it. He felt that she was a little nasty with those cracks about his nose and shirts. What was the problem with his beaut colourful shirts?

Fitzy admitted to himself, she wasn't too bad to work with and he further conceded he did stir her up a fair bit, often more than need be at times. Her level headedness was an essential element in their success working together, and she was the best partner he had ever worked with. Fitzy would not let anyone else get away with any smart-arse personal comments.

The main issue he could not cope with very well was that she was now *his* supervising officer and it was mainly his crime solving skills that had put her there. He used to be *her* supervisor. Regardless, he was big enough to admit, the reason he had been demoted was because he often took things too far with what the Chief Superintendent, Old TC, called his rude behaviour, overzealous treatment of suspects, criminals or not, and his tendency towards strong arm tactics to solve problems.

The incident with Roscoe Bagshaw meant Fitzy was on his last chance to shape up, or be transferred, as far as the Chief Superintendent was concerned. Fitzy remembered the conversation clearly.

The big man with the wobbling neck, leaned back in the chief executive style chair, steepled his fingers and spoke, as he always did, with an almost growl.

"Fitzy, basically you're a good cop, right? You would have been a hero 20 years ago, things were different then though, old mate. But, and hear me good and proper, the good old days of clouting suspects and in most cases, arseholes who you know have done the crime or straight out deserve it, those golden days are over. No more verballing when you can sign *your* name to say the crim actually said *he* did it. Over. Get me? Over. Belting some cunt across the back of the scone with a phone book or a decent whack across the kisser was alright twenty years ago, well so long as you never left any tell-tale signs; but that is past tense. The era of paper bags full of used notes bandied around between cops and politicians – is all over. Right? These days, people have rights and the mongrels who least deserve to exercise those rights are the ones who make a welter of using them."

Old TC glared at Fitzy with his classical unwavering stare from shiny, blue-black eyes that made him the hard, uncompromising campaigner everyone knew he was. He commanded his reputation as one of the toughest detectives around in the late seventies and early eighties. In his prime old TC was 16 stone of solid, rugby league muscle and any criminal who thought he could get the better of him never did. Some may have thought they had for a while but it was short-lived because somewhere down the road they got hit from out of the blue. These days he was several kilos heavier than his best detective fighting weight and now had a generous girth from too many counter lunches and beers and as a result he sported a couple of extra chins.

The old professional was always just under the surface and he was never to be taken lightly.

"For Christ's sake, man," he continued, waving his finger, "these low life bastards have lawyers, publicly funded ones who absolutely wipe the floor with us, defending the bastards and because of the money for jam they enjoy sinking the boot into us in their training run to be top line barristers acting for the big end of town. Us, the clean living, fair minded protectors of the public through neither fear nor favour. Us, you and I, the Queensland Police Service. Remember that. You have to realise the politically correct have got their dirty little hands all over this one and you are in shitters' ditch right up to your nuts."

He shook his head slowly. It took a mini second for his chins to catch up. "Now, Fitzy, the Disciplinary Discretionary Board is looking closely at this and I'll let you know how it pans out. Be prepared for, at the very least, a serious boot up the Khyber. You must realise the only reason you will be disciplined is because you got caught, you stupid cunt. Right? You're an acting senior sergeant, man, you should know better. You were in the seat for inspector and now see where you are. Now get the fuck out of my office and use your nouse when dealing with the public."

"Yes, sir," Fitzy remembered saying quietly, and he tried to hold his head up high, walking from the Chief Super's office to the lifts, past the desks of staff of various police designations pretending to be busy. He knew they all knew he had been a naughty boy and was clearly in the brown, stinking stuff.

~

Back at the crime scene, Sergeant Rodney FitzMichael shook his head. *Thinking about it isn't going to change anything, just don't do it again! Fancy not checking the recording equipment, Fitzy, you clown, Christ! Okay, you hadn't been briefed about the video camera but still. Come on, mate, job at hand.*

He stood still for a few pondering moments and glanced around at the dry sparse bush. Standing still sometimes helped him to remember something, trigger a thought. As no one had been actually injured seriously - not of course counting emotional turmoil - or abducted, the brass decided on-site forensic staff was not required, although services were made available for any particular items required for testing at the lab. He wanted to feel that the perpetrator was a local, someone close by and possibly someone who observed the young children regularly, or just observed children in general, regularly. But, he had nagging feelings, the thought of a local male, and it had to be a male, faded. There were no custody battles associated with the case so far according to Meredith's research and it did not seem like a female way of going about taking a child anyway. He began to slowly put one foot in front of the other.

He could be convinced it was a random attack but, he knew other factors, whatever they were, should not be ruled out. Fitzy unconsciously tapped his nose. When he became aware of it he smiled because one of his supervisors, during his training deciphering details of a mock crime scene, told everyone in the group Fitzy possessed a good nose for sniffing out detail, a cop's nose.

Another cadet, who constantly stirred up others with sarcastic remarks, said Fitzy's nose looked like a skeg sticking out of a surfboard. This trainee had been annoying Fitzy for most of the course and a comment like that was all he needed. Fitzy flattened him and it took two others to drag him back from probable suspension. Fitzy tended to lose all reason when his temper got the better of him. That is why he had taken up boxing to try to control his volatile temper. He was reminded once again of this fault which got him into strife many times in his life. Temper, temper, temper.

The crime scene was old now and he ground out his butt in the sawdust before slowly heading in the direction of the administration block. He glanced at his watch and flipped open his new mobile phone. Three thirty pm.

'G'day Wowzer … any progress?'

'No Fitzy, no one saw anything. Still, you did say that'd be the case. That's the trouble with being in uniform, I have to do all the hard yards, not like you.' Senior Constable Warren McTavish chuckled down the line.

Fitzy allowed himself a smile.

'Watch your gob Wowzer, I'm the senior officer here!'

They were mates, had gone through basic training together and regularly worked either as a pair, or as part of a bigger team. They had been known to share a few quiet beers at various times as well.

'Yeah, alright, sir. But still, you're only a Sergeant, Fitzy, and my promotion's up in front of the board right as we speak … so, old mate, soon we'll be equals, right?'

'It may be the case now, but I'll be back Acting senior, and inspector on top of that, sooner than you can have a leak. But right now, I'm the biggest swinging sausage in the area, get it? So, I want you at the admin building at the high school in five minutes, we're gunna have some fun.'

'Yes sir, sergeant, oh man on high, over and out and up you too!'

Chapter 13

Colin guzzled four vodka chasers in rapid succession and was in a dazed state. His vodka chasers were serious sized gulps, probably twice a proper bar measure. He certainly was not relaxed though, not with all the pressures squeezing his brain, his feelings and his nerves.

At a casual glance he may have looked tired; his eyes had a glazed sheen with redness around the rims. He waved a manila folder in a fanning fashion as if it would cool down his state of mind. His red chequered casual shirt showed dark, damp triangles under each arm and a damp patch sat just below his collar at the back.

On the day of the crime he was interviewed twice and allowed to go home. However, several of the other teachers were interviewed twice so he was not particularly worried, but still ... why him? Today he was instructed to stay behind after school by the rude cop with the big nose and the ridiculous shirt.

'Just routine, sir', Sergeant FitzMichael said crisply over the phone. *Bastard*.

Colin's brow felt clammy; he had not done anything wrong. He ran a slightly shaking hand over and through his thinning hair.

'Come on, you big nosed oinker,' he mumbled under his breath.

He was keen to look at the pictures in the new magazine he had just purchased called *Big Boy* which lay on his desk. A file and some loose sheets of paper were strategically placed on the top so casual visitors would not notice. Innocent enough, no-one came near his desk anyway. Colin figured there was nothing wrong with a peek at a magazine every now and again. *Nothing wrong with it all ... those lovely young bodies. No, nothing wrong with that.*

Where was the arrogant prick with the big hooter? He wanted to go home, not to see that horrible, miserable missus of his, no bloody way, he just wanted to get out of school, go home to the shed. Colin was just in the action of lifting a sheet of paper from the top of the magazine when a bolt of colour flashed before his eyes. *Phew! Nearly caught out.* He had not heard anyone come in. He looked up quickly.

'Mr Thistleton? We'd like another chat with you!'

Fitzy covered the distance between the door and the desk in three quick strides, glancing everywhere, strong arms straining the colourful short sleeves. He stopped, placed his knuckles on the desk and leaned forward, well and truly in Colin's shocked face.

Colin flinched again when he noticed a uniformed officer slowly ease into the room behind the big-headed cop with the big nose.

'Um ... yes of course, what can I ...?' stammered Colin, hands open in a gesture of innocence.

Fitzy looked like a pillar of concrete, expressionless, emotionless as he continued to look directly into the other man's eyes.

'... I've told you everything I know.' Heavy, humid silence demanded he continue. 'Am I a suspect or something? What's going on?'

Colin felt a blob of sweat trickle down his back. He knew he had to stand up for himself, but this was not the time to be cocky.

'Well, Mr Thistleton, with all due respect, I don't think you've told us everything, now have you, eh?' Fitzy glared harder, always searching. 'Several witnesses have said they saw you in the area at the time of the assault. What do you say to that?'

Colin knew the policeman was fishing, probably an exaggeration to try to scare him into confessing something.

'But I was in here during that period, Susan told you I was.'

The uniformed police officer moved his solid six foot plus frame forward.

'Would you please stand up.' It was an order, not a question.

Fitzy stepped around the desk and stuck his nose in Colin's face.

'Mmmm. Do you use aftershave sir?'

'Aftershave. What? Aftershave?'

He shook his head genuinely not understanding. 'No, I don't.'

Fitzy looked down and moved several items on the desk.

'Aha! Senior Constable McTavish, what have we here?' he said in a musical, scolding voice.

He picked up the magazine and flicked through a few pages.

'Oooo, look here, not a bad pair of silicon fun bags Colzee-babe, eh? Hey! Crikey, have a gander at that!' he added holding it up.

McTavish leaned forward, fired a quick glance at the raunchy display, smiled, rolled his eyes at Fitzy in *an ease up signal* and then fixed his iron gaze back on Colin Thistleton.

Fitzy dropped the mag with a loud plop.

'So, we like to have a bit of a Micky Merve, eh Colin? Jerk the gherkin, eh?'

'Sir, those magazines are legal, anyone can get them from newsagents, off the shelf ...' Colin wriggled in his seat looking visibly uncomfortable, sweat glistened on his forehead.

'That may be so but at *school*? Does the principal know about this?'

Fitzy knew it was a strong point, useful for leverage, judging by the reaction of Colin.

The uniformed McTavish butted in. 'Right, you may sit down now in that seat over there, sir.' He pointed to the chair alongside the desk.

Colin did as he was instructed, shuffling and glancing everywhere.

Fitzy said nothing and just continued to stare at the sweating, seated man. Colin could not hold eye contact with either of the police officers and he looked away nervously to stare at anything else, anywhere, nowhere.

McTavish sat down at the desk and began to open drawers. He stopped.

'Ah ha! Sergeant, look what we've got here.'

He held up a half empty bottle of vodka.

Fitzy butted in. 'For medical purposes only, Mr Thistleton?'

Colin's forehead popped a loose bead of sweat, which started to dribble down his nose. He needed a drink now, more than ever.

'Ah! More supplies?' teased Wowzer, holding up an unopened bottle of vodka in a paper bag. 'And, lookee here.' He produced four more magazines from a folder marked *Exam Papers*. 'I wouldn't mind having to study for this exam, sir!'

'B-but ... they're all available over the counter, all legal,' protested Colin.

'You're in strife mate,' interjected Fitzy. 'Dirty mags, booze, and at school too! Naughty little boy, Colin. What *would* the principal say, eh Colin?' Fitzy leant forward, upper torso intimidating. 'What about little kids? Do you get turned on by their little nude bodies? Eh?'

Colin Thistleton just sat there, clearly bewildered, looking at the wall behind the two officers, eyes red and glassy.

'You ... you don't think I had anything to do with ...?'

'Did you?' probed McTavish, leaning back in the office chair and linking his hands behind his head.

'No! Absolutely not! You cannot be serious. Look officers, this is not right, I was here during that time, in this office. I'm not into kiddie porn!'

Fitzy fired an electric glance at McTavish, not moving his head. Mental telepathy.

'Right, Colin, you can go for now, but as they say in the westerns, don't go leaving town.'

The teacher sat there with a blank stare.

Fitzy thought maybe he had not heard.

'Sir, you may piss off.'

'Um ... yes. Look, you won't ... won't say anything to the principal, will you, I mean ... put them back in the drawer ...'

'You're not in a position to bargain anything, Mr Thistleton, now, away you go. We'll be in touch.'

Colin stood up slowly and shuffled his tubby frame across the staff room, darting glances in every direction like a frightened puppy.

'Hey,' said McTavish after the other man departed, 'He's a bit of a troubled bloke, isn't he, eh?'

'Yeah, but somehow, I dunno about him. Seems as if he's a piss-pot as well as a bloody perve, but let's be realistic, so are most blokes; give us a gander at those mags again Wowzer,' laughed Fitzy.

He turned serious, 'Dippy spoke to a teacher, Susan Dettman who was working on a play at the time. Now, she confirmed he was in here from ten to midday but I'm going to go and speak to her again with Dippy. Also, I had a chat with Cathleen Crier, a teacher-aide and she said he was sort of in the area, that's about all, nothing definite, but ... anyway, mate, I'm not sure about Colin at all. We've got plenty of suspects and tons of circumstantial evidence here, but nothing really solid to go on. The whole thing is a pain in the arse, if you ask me.'

McTavish sighed heavily. 'Yeah, I haven't turned up anything either from the door-to-door stuff in all the streets surrounding the area. There are a couple of houses where people weren't home. I'll check on them later, don't expect much though. We got a Hep. C reading and blood type A from the syringe, but Doc Moynihan says it's definitely prior to the crime, in other words, not worth a pinch of saw-horse shit to us.'

Fitzy leant against the desk and folded his arms.

'You may as well go. I've got to head back and do a bit of report work. I've been trying to get this Susan Dettman on the dog-and-bone but she's not responding, wanted to find out what her plans are for tomorrow. I've got a meeting with Dipstick early tomorrow, she's pretty touchy at the moment, up to her you know whats in the Q-PED thing. They should make me Acting Senior Sergeant again and put me in charge of this and leave her to the other stuff. I feel uneasy about this whole case though, mate, there's bugger-all to go on.'

'Just as well Dippy's in charge after all then, eh … er in case everything goes down the dunny, my old soon-to-be-re-instated senior sergeant mate?' He winked.

Fitzy smiled. 'Yeah, ha-ha.'

He unscrewed the lid on the opened bottle and sniffed.

'I thought I could catch the slightest of whiffs on his breath, it's almost odourless, hard core alkies drink it, hard to detect.'

He put the bottle back in the drawer with the magazines and closed it. He hesitated for a second.

'Righto Fitzy, I'm off.'

'Yeah mate keep in touch.'

'Yep.'

McTavish turned just in time to see Fitzy slip the unopened bottle of vodka into a plastic bag, along with the first magazine they saw on the desk.

Fitzy noticed him notice.

'Evidence, Senior Constable, crucial evidence!'

'Absolutely sir, absolutely! Very thorough of you, sir. That's at least a couple of beers you owe me sir, isn't it? Wouldn't want a senior constable wandering around saying a certain recently demoted senior sergeant was, you know, stealing evidence …'

'Shut your gob, Wowzer, and get stuffed.'

They both laughed and went their own ways.

Chapter 14

The next morning when Fitzy ambled in, Lerlene Diplock was already there. Her palms gripped her temples with fingers splayed towards the back. It looked as if she was trying to squeeze all her blonde hair into that tight bun, but her hair was already tied into her regular practical bun. Minimal makeup always went well with her. She was one of the lucky thirty-something-year-olds who looked good without dolling up.

The air was piano wire tight.

She looked up. 'G'day Fitzy.' Deadpan.

'Well good morning to you, acting, sorry, Senior Sergeant!'

It was not said sarcastically but her gaze found his eyes like an arrow.

He continued quickly. 'How's the Q-PED stuff coming along?'

She leant back in her chair and stretched.

'Driving me mad, since you ask. Also there's this other little case that our loving Inspector Devious dropped in yesterday.'

Fitzy needed to talk and it was clear she was as frustrated as him because things were going nowhere.

'Well, I haven't got anything much to report that stands out, but I'd like to run through what I do know, maybe something will hit you. Anyway, what about Inspector Devo's case?'

'It involves a number of thefts of rare orchids, petty stuff probably but could be part of something bigger but let's forget that for the moment and talk about what we've got on the attempted abduction case, or should I say, what we haven't got.'

'Right.'

They regularly revised seemingly irrelevant information together and sometimes one would pick up or link something the other may have overlooked.

She stood. Her strong figure in sensible clothes, jeans and a dark blue blouse, had a shapely female frame to it as she stretched.

'Righto Fitzy, what have we got?'

'Well.' He stroked his chin with a pincer movement and his eyebrows bunched up in concentration. 'We've got two suspects so far, not real good ones mind you, but I'd like to add one more. By the way, has anything come up with Father O'Neill?'

'No, but we're still prying.' She sat down.

'Anyway, I'd like to add him to the suspects. I've been thinking about him, he's about the right height, balding, has an aroma, aftershave I think, paunchy. So, I know he's least likely, but we still have to substantiate his whereabouts at the time. He comes across as a slime, he's got access to young children at the orphanage, he is closely tangled up with Stink Finger, he's involved with sex offenders in prison, and out of prison as well I understand. He evidently has some programs with street kids *at their own level*, according to Father McFarlan. He takes confession from Stink Finger, they pray together, I'll bet, probably in search of prey together.'

She strained a smile at his attempt at humour. 'What was his alibi?'

'Well, he said he was on duty that morning at the Cathedral but I was unable to catch Father McFarlan again after, but I bet he would confirm. I wouldn't suggest the old bastard would lie but, you know, I reckon they'd stick together, we all know what these priests are like.'

She sat up abruptly and wagged her index finger.

'Ease up Fitzy, I'm a lapsed Catholic, alright? Don't think for one moment child abuse is restricted to them. After all, there are many good people who work very hard across all religions. Yes, of course there are some rotten mongrels, but I believe the overwhelming majority are good people.'

'It's unnatural for males not to have sex, that's what makes the Catholic priests so bloody dangerous. I haven't met a priest I'd trust yet. And nuns. Married to God, can't have sex so they love to clout kids around the head, and cane them as well. The nuns are legendary abusers.'

'What the … where do you get all this stuff from Fitzy? Bloody hell. Okay, okay, don't answer that but answer this. What about

Brother Dominic? Eh? You are always crapping on about what a great bloke he is.'

'Oh. Orright, orright!'

He held up his hand, remembering well, a sparring mate he knew at Basher's Gym who gave up much of his time and money working with troubled youth and others at the lower end of the social scale.

'He's different …' in apology Fitzy conceded, 'yeah, but this whole kiddie thing really makes me angry. Anyway, Dommo is a brother, not a priest.'

Lerlene was not going to let it go too easily. She gave a quick half smile and a nod at Fitzy's skill of picking minor points so as not to be wrong.

'Ha bloody ha, just 'cos you were brought up in a different church … hey in fact, what about the Church of England Boys' Society, eh?'

'Well, I'm not a practicing Christian, haven't ever since I worked out what a load of tripe it all is. It's widespread, the Christians, the Happy Clappers, the Muslims, they're all at it, chockers with rock spiders, chockers. Sick bastards hiding behind religion, always on the hunt to tamper with innocent little kids.'

'Jesus, Fitzy that is rank. Ease up on that sort of talk around here; why do you have to revert to such abusive language? Anyway Fitzy, you've said yourself how much you admire those blokes from the Salvos, picking up street kids and attending to the down and out. They do it because they believe everyone needs love and understanding at some time in their lives, and to be there to help and not judge, no matter who you are. They make our job easier. You get good with the bad.'

'Yeah, alright, anyway … yeah, yeah, yeah,' he said irritably and threw a balled up piece of paper in the direction of the waste paper basket. 'So, Stink Finger and Father O'Neill are in effect each other's alibis, so we need to look more closely at them. I spoke with Colin Thistleton, he's got an aroma about him too, he's a bloody alcoholic I reckon, drinks vodka, hard to detect. That's my three.'

She mused, 'Yeah, I had an uncle who was a screaming alkie; he used to take frequent nips of vodka. No one really knew or suspected anything until he got crook, then they found bottles all over the place, hidden everywhere.'

Fitzy turned the conversation back on track.

'He reads sheila mags too, all available at your favourite newsagent, fair enough, not really porno, or hard core, but well, he's a strange little bloke. I spoke with Meredith re C-A-T initials for all and sundry and

Colin's initials are C-J-T, so the pen isn't his, his middle name is James. I also checked family members, no C-A-T there. Could possibly be a relation, or something? Anyway, these mags, here have a butchers at one of the mags I confiscated for evidence; nice looking sheilas, eh?'

He stood up and dropped the magazine in front of Lerlene.

'Look here Fitzy, I don't need to see this sort of chauvinistic crap, put it in the case file.'

He slumped down and lounged in his office chair. After a couple of minutes, he picked up a packet of smokes and opened it. She glared at him. He closed it and put his feet on the desk. Then he became all business again.

'I'd like to speak to the teacher, Susan Dettman, who claimed Colzee-babe was in the staff room during the time of the attempted abduction. I got hold of her a while ago on the phone, she's a relief teacher. I, us are going to see her this morning. She sounded like a bit of a space cadet.'

'Yeah, came across to me that way too. So,' said Lerlene, 'let's look at Devo's case. We have to find the thief who has been stealing orchids around the area, Kedron, Grange and Windsor. The jobs seem to be run of the mill. The perp targets people who are away; so it says here anyway in Devo's report – seems he hasn't strained himself checking anything much. Okay Fitzy, the only thing pleasing to me about this is the fact I'm getting you to handle it. She's all yours.' She gave him a pouty sarcastic smile.

'Hey? But Lerlene, I'm flat out on …'

'I've got no one else at the moment.' She looked at him hard. 'All yours, mate, and keep me posted.'

'But … what happened to the *we* bit?'

'That comes in later when you solve it and *we* take the credit, right? Now, speed read the file and familiarise yourself with it so we can say we're moving on it. You can deal with that after we go on an outing.' She dropped the file on his desk.

'An outing?'

'Yes Fitzy, maybe the church first, definitely Mrs Leak and her son – the boy who was almost abducted - seems like they're having a bad time of it, then maybe a teacher or two. I've got to see Meredith again; she's taking over more of this Q-PED stuff for me. There is so much stuff to rein in from so many places it's unreal. I'll be back in about half an hour and we can go together.'

Fitzy stuck his feet on the desk and opened the manila folder.

Chapter 15

'We could try him out on a smell test; aftershave, vodka, gin, perfume… just an idea?' said Fitzy

Lerlene returned and plonked herself into her office chair.

'No, not at the moment, his mother wouldn't have it. We still have to speak with …'

'Aaaaaah, it reminds me,' said Fitzy touching his forehead, 'Wowzer has spoken to Cedric Andrew Tarcoola, C-A-T. He's a farmer at Jacob's Well, claimed to be on his tractor all day. The blokes in the shed, farm workers, one a welder, the other a mechanic were pretty sure he was on the tractor on the morning in question but not absolutely certain. He does in fact fit the profile, but probably a bit fat. He does have an aroma about him, but the aroma is whisky. Stinks like he fell in a tank of it evidently. He brews the stuff. Wowzer nearly arrested him for driving a vehicle whilst under the influence, but he was on private land and it was a tractor and the only person he could hurt is himself. He's an alkie too but has no history of kiddie stuff, unlikely I'd say, nowhere near Kedron that day. So it leaves us with Clive Andrew Timmins and Carlson Albert Torrens. I've asked Wowzer to take Torrens. Torrens has a record, rape, and his physical fits to a degree. Wowser's going to take a couple of rugby league officers with him just in case, should hear about that today at least. Hard to believe Torrens would have an expensive engraved ballpoint pen though.'

Lerlene yawned. 'Yeah, looking for someone with initials C-A-T, someone who is a visitor to the area could have dropped it. The pen probably has nothing to do with the crime, and with the physical description we've got, it's hard to pin anything down. Maybe Parker have a record of who purchased it – another job for Senior Constable Meredith.'

Fitzy added, 'We've got a big day then, Timmins, Crier, McFarlan and maybe O'Neill, the kid and his mother and any others who might pop up.' He made an attempt at easing the load. 'Maybe Mzzzzzzzzz Dick-weed as well, she hates men and a boy is just a small version of a man, eh?'

Senior Sergeant Diplock struck a small smile as she grabbed her bag. 'We need a break of some kind or other here Fitzy.'

He nodded, 'You can say that again!'

The crack about Ms Digweed reminded him he had not so far considered her as a suspect. He slotted the information into the scramble of data whirring around in his head. *Ignore nothing until you prove it is not connected.* Fitzy did not see the need to mention the full bottle of vodka either. He did in fact wonder why he confiscated it.

'Now, boss, what about this outing?'

He placed the orchid folder in his Pending tray. She slipped the bag over her shoulder and gave him the thumb up and nodded towards the door. They walked out.

Chapter 16

Colin had the depressing black dog hanging all over him; fortunately, he was at the shed, away from the Graceful Lady. After the humiliating episode with those cops, particularly the arrogant mongrel with the floral shirt, he badly needed a drink. The bastard pinched his magazine and a full bottle of vodka. The cop was an arsehole and Colin could not help feeling he had it in for him. *Prick*.

Gretel was being more of a bitch than usual, too. Did she bellow at him? Through doors and walls. Her washing and cleaning fetish made it unbearable to be around the house; washing machine grinding away, vacuum cleaner screaming, and commercial talkback radio hammering out meaningless, mind-numbing adverts full bore. House full of smoke too. They had both given up smoking two years ago, but she'd started again recently, blaming him because his behaviour had driven her to take up the habit again. *Bitch*. He thought she was really inconsiderate smoking inside. Colin managed to get some computer time in, fortunately, to sort out some of his school lesson plans, before she stormed in and demanded he go to the shed because, "Didn't he know she had work to do on the computer!"

She well and truly made the house a place not fit to be in. Even his daughter Rosa hardly showed her face, except to dump her school port and rush out to play. She was a primary school child and spent most of her time watching TV and playing but lately she was rarely around with many sleepovers at friends' places. Since Gretel could not yell at Rosa, "Clean ya room, make ya bed, don't be late, I don't run a fucking hotel here!", it just left him as the focus for the abuse. No wonder Rosa did not come home much.

Colin sat at the bench and downed another slug of vodka. He could not stop himself becoming aroused again because he'd treated himself to a gawk at a new magazine he picked up from the adult shop after the humiliating time with the cops at school. The cops were giving him such a hard time. Why? He had an alibi. Thank Christ Susan was around the staff room on that particular morning. It was a rock solid alibi. No worries, so why were they persecuting him? He had done nothing wrong!

He opened another stubby. Colin's life was a mess. Thoughts drifted to the situation at school. No one cared anymore about education; students seemed to do whatever they liked, teachers went off on stress leave and various scams. At home, his missus was out of her brain, driving and hammering him into the ground. Pressure, squeezing, pushing, harassing every possible moment. He knew his life was approaching a precipice.

'Shit.'

Colin remembered something! He hoped the cops would not tell the principal about the magazines, or the vodka. It did not look good but then, after a minute or so, it seemed maybe it did not matter anymore.

He took another nip, by now he was drunk enough to think anything. Colin knew he was no longer rational. He toyed for a moment with an idea. He would just say he confiscated the magazines from some students. Yeah, that would do; it was a reasonable explanation, no problem. Then he remembered he had not denied the drinking or the girlie mags to the police, he realised now he should have.

'I should have told them,' he said to the shadow-board, 'that I confiscated it from a student. Bugger.'

Colin knew he should have done plenty of things, the first one, not marrying the Graceful Lady. He was always slow off the mark. Maybe Gretel was right.

He said aloud, 'Weak as piss!'

He sat there looking out at nothing thinking about a life in tatters. He realised he was being boxed in, no choices up ahead, others held his destiny. Colin Thistleton was hovering in a vacuum where he did not care about anything anymore, least of all himself.

Chapter 17

Fitzy and Lerlene walked up the steps of the cathedral. Father McFarlan happened to be standing at the door, or pair of doors which were four or five metres high. The doors were made of hardwood slabs with some carved petals around the perimeter. Steel straps ran horizontally, punctuated by an old black bolthead at regular intervals, solid trade work by a carpenter and a blacksmith from a bygone era.

He ushered them through a smaller door which was an inset in the right-hand door. It was so well made it was not really noticeable from a short distance away.

The door croaked rather than creaked as they entered into what felt like an enormous cave. The dark interior of the cathedral introduced them to echoes of voices, the smell of furniture wax and candles and the crisp click of shoes on the hard, cold palfrey stone floor.

'Aha, Sergeant, nice to see you again, maybe we can talk you into a small donation towards our Save the Children Fund?'

Lerlene nudged her partner and whispered, 'That'll be the day, eh Fitzy, you tight arse?'

Fitzy was equal to the task.

'Father, we are not permitted to make donations for fear of corruption, sorry, um by the way, is Father O'Neill around?'

'No, he's visiting the sick today, does the round of hospitals once a week, like I pointed out to you last time Sergeant, our Father O'Neill is a tireless worker, a real saint. Is there something I can assist you with? By the way, ripper of a shirt you have my son, wish we were allowed to wear bright apparel like you, you lucky fellow.'

Unlike the other day, the elderly priest was dressed in a white shirt with priest's collar and grey pressed trousers rather than the traditional cassock. He had shaved badly, as old men often do and the collar seemed to have rubbed a red mark around the front perimeter.

Fitzy puffed his chest out and winked at Lerlene saying, 'There, you go, other discerning people can appreciate quality apparel.'

'Mm, okay then, we may as well have a short chat with you if you don't mind. Is there somewhere private we can talk?'

'Yes, of course my son.' His eyes narrowed, still retaining a mischievous glint. 'Are you going to introduce me to your lovely lady assistant, Sergeant?'

Fitzy cut in quickly, 'This is no lovely lady, Father, this is a Senior Sergeant of the Queensland Police Service!'

Lerlene elbowed Fitzy aggressively in the kidneys, stepped forward and held up her badge.

'Senior Sergeant Diplock at your service, Father.' Her smile was forced. 'Now, after you boys have had a good laugh at my expense, let's get on with business.'

Father McFarlan's eyebrows went up.

'Of course, Senior Sergeant. By the way you are allowed to be a lovely lady and a police officer you know, and you are also allowed to be in charge rather than be an assistant. Please forgive an old man for an unintentional blunder,' and he bowed slightly. 'Please follow me; we can have a chat in the vestry room.'

They followed him into the cathedral and down one side, his footwear a soft shuffle, their shoes squelching and echoing.

'In here,' he gestured with a Shakespearean flow of his right arm. 'Please sit.'

He directed them to chairs alongside a well-worn red cedar table with hymn books stacked haphazardly at one end.

'Now, what can I do for you?'

His expression was far from confrontational; it seemed like a genuine offering.

Senior Sergeant Diplock was all business, gaze direct.

'Where was Father O'Neill last Monday between ten and twelve?'

The old man looked slightly confused.

'Er, Monday, he's always here on a Monday, on duty.'

Fitzy prodded. 'Is there anyone here who could verify it?'

Lerlene interjected, perhaps sensing the need to ease up a little; the old man's fingers jittered slightly, he appeared flustered. '… just routine, Father, we need to compile facts, eliminate …'

'Aah, just like Homicide, the police show, used to be on TV, *Dah facts maam, nuttin' but dah facts.* No, not Homicide, Dragline. We had a TV set at the orphanage; Mr Clunies-Ross bought it for … that's it, Dragnet, *nuttin' but da facts, maam* …Friday, no not on Friday, *Joe* Friday, he's the cop in the show, you know … was in black and white, my favourite …'

Fitzy shot a glance at his partner and then back to the priest.

'Father McFarlan,' he said quickly to get the conversation going again, 'we are interested to know if anyone could confirm the whereabouts of Father O'Neill?'

'Sorry. Father O'Neill of course, well, I was here on Monday morning.' He mused, glance drifting to the ceiling, doing his best to remember.

Fitzy tried again to get things on track.

'Did you actually *see* him between ten and twelve on that particular day?'

'Well,' the old man's eyebrows seemed to harden in concentration, 'I remember seeing him here, but … I'm sure he was here. Ah! The roster book, it will show us, yes, there it is!'

He pointed to a book on the table adjacent.

Fitzy looked at Lerlene. Just because the good Father was supposed to be on duty, unless someone could verify he was actually physically there, it all meant nothing.

There was a pleasant aroma of beeswax polish in the room and the faint scent of snuffed candle smoke. The priest dragged an enormous book, bigger than an ancient Bible, over in front of him. His glasses glinted coloured light from a stained glass window high above.

'Ah yes here we are. See!'

Fitzy spun the book around and ran a well bitten index finger nail down the column. 'Looks like the initials O'N, is that Father O'Neill?'

'Yes, always here on a Monda…'

'Well, between ten and eleven, who's this? F S?'

'Oh, that's Father Sheridan, fine man, beaut fellow.'

'So here it says Father Sheridan was here, not Father O'Neill?'

'Oh yes, he was, that's the time he, Father O'Neill, that is, takes a cup of tea in the tea room, down the back. But he's definitely here in case Father Sheridan; he's very young you know, has something he can't handle. There's always a senior member here in case there are more people in for confession, or someone needs help of some kind, that's where I come in …'

Fitzy looked at the ceiling, an eye roll difficult to hide. Lerlene exhaled. It was close to a sigh.

'Father, would there have been anyone else around the place who could have seen Father O'Neill here on Monday morning?' She slowed down her speech on the last four words.

The old man's brow tightened, his demeanour went quickly from dithery to firmly unhappy about the way things were going. *Questioning one of their own?*

'Well, Senior Sergeant, Mrs Grimshaw would have seen him for certain.'

'Mrs Grimshaw?'

'Yes, she does the flowers; um she's here now if you really must speak to someone.' The latter part of the sentence was slightly crisp.

'Thank you for your help, it's only routine but we have to go through the process? Father, could you please take us to Mrs …?'

The two police officers stood up, indicating now was the time. They followed him out into the main body of the cathedral to another alcove with a small door leading out to a courtyard.

'Aha, there she is! Mrs Grimshaw, these police officers would like to ask you if …'

Fitzy butted in. 'We'll ask the questions Father. That will be all for the moment. Thank you for your help, Father.'

Fitzy eyed the old man, it was essential to keep some level of authority. He didn't like possible witnesses like Mrs Grimshaw, put in a compromising position. Father McFarlan looked quizzical, turned and shuffled away. The police officers introduced themselves.

Lerlene took the initiative. 'These are just routine questions. Were you here on Monday morning between ten and twelve?'

Mrs Grimshaw smiled and patted her bouffe of grey hair.

'Yes, Monday is one of my days, I arrange the flowers.'

'Now this is important, did you see Father O'Neill here then?'

She pursed her lips. 'Yes, it's his day on duty.'

'We know, but did you actually see him during that period?'

'Yes, I spoke to him several times. There was a Mr Hewitt I think his name is with him too, if I remember right, yes, Glen, lovely man. None the less, I'm in and out and I did go down to the orphanage to pick flowers, we have a beautiful garden down there - in fact we are not supposed to call it an orphanage these days. It's the Community Building, hard to change old habits isn't it? You must see it sometime … umm yes, anyway, I did see him, but I certainly couldn't verify every minute of course, no more so him verifying me being here. May I ask, is he in some sort of trouble? He always seems to stir people up with his creative ideas with those kiddies who are homeless and live on the streets, and those with social difficulties.'

'Okay, thank you for your time, Mrs Grimshaw, that will be all,' offered Fitzy.

An organ cranked out a few bars and the sound of shuffling and hymn singing tickled the extremities of the cavernous cathedral.

They walked towards the front alcove and entrance doors, the sound of their footsteps joining the other echoes trapped twenty metres up among the ornate plasterwork where De Vinci style artwork, and leadlight windows captured and coloured the rays of the midday sun.

'The old timer didn't seem too happy about us not taking his word for Father O'Neill being at the church, did he?' Lerlene said as she slipped her sunglasses on.

'No, for sure.' Fitzy looked at her. 'That's what I mean about the boys sticking together …'

She nodded, 'Yeah, yeah,' and steered him towards the car, 'Come on you, let's go.' She wanted to avoid another anti-religious rant.

Chapter 18

Their next stop was to interview Susan Dettman, the teacher who originally stated Colin was actually in the staff room for the period in question. They pulled up in front of an untidy house that looked like an unloved rental.

'Mower must have broken down,' declared Fitzy and nudged her, as they made their way along an overgrown path to the front verandah where an old barbecue with a rusty lid leaned to one side on a broken wheel. The front door was open behind a half open insect door with flapping strips of screen, a poor man's pet entrance moving gently in the breeze.

He knocked. A dog barked somewhere but seemed to be too lazy to investigate. Just as he lifted his hand to rap the screen again, a long-haired, alternative type with bleary blood shot eyes, Rasta tangled hair like a root-bound tree with beads intermittently peppered through it, stumbled and grabbed the wall. His demeanour changed quickly when Fitzy flipped open his wallet, showing his identification.

'Is Ms Susan Dettman in?' he queried, glaring at the young man.

'Er … what?' He looked at his bare feet for a second. 'Oh yeah, no worries, just a sec.' He disappeared yelling, 'Kate, the … um *police* are here to see you.' He emphasised the word police slightly louder.

There was an audible shuffle and rustle like mice scurrying. The distinctive aroma of marijuana was obvious and Lerlene gave a wink and did a quick imitation of taking a puff from an imaginary joint as she glanced at Fitzy. Undoubtedly a bag of marijuana, a bong, or other drug paraphernalia was being hidden in a panic. They both knew the value of keeping that information to themselves for the moment, handy to have in the back pocket for later.

Susan Dettman appeared in front of them, slightly flustered, with lazy eyelids, obviously stoned.

'Yeeeeees? What can I do for you?'

Senior Sergeant Diplock took the lead.

'We'd like a word with you, Ms Dettman. We need to recap on the morning of last Monday. Now, exactly what were you doing between ten and twelve?'

The attractive but grubby young woman, dressed in thin, loose fitting cotton pants, no underwear and a silky see through blouse, appeared to think for a moment.

'I was working on a play a colleague asked me to simplify, er shorten, so he could condense it down into one lesson, a one act play.'

Lerlene's eyebrows hardened slightly.

'This is important, Ms Dettman, you have already stated, Colin Thistleton was in the staff room during that period. Correct? Now I'd like you to think carefully, was he there for the full period?'

'Yyyyyyyes.' She rubbed her face with a hand with rings on all fingers.

'He didn't go out of the room, to the toilet, the library or the canteen?'

'No, he was there all the ... hang on, come to think of it, he, I think, yes he did pop out for a few minutes, only a couple of minutes though, to his car, he said ...'

She slowly moved her hand over her short blond hair. Each ear sported a cluster of fine silver earrings.

Lerlene looked at Fitzy. Her eyes rolled, acknowledging the fact they were receiving a lot of ambiguity in this case.

'Were you there all the time, Ms Dettman?'

'Yes, of course I was!'

The statement was delivered with a knitted brow.

Fitzy interjected, 'Listen Miss Dettman, you need to think clearly about exactly what you were doing, or we might go inside and have a bit of a look around for the dope you stashed in a hurry a couple of minutes ago. Now, were you there all the time during those two hours?'

Her fingers fidgeted. 'Er ... umm ... I was there in the staff room at

Brian Chippendale's desk. Oh, that's right; I did pop out to the supply cupboard … only once, no, just a few times …'

'For how long each time?' probed Fitzy, his voice betraying mild anger.

'Only a couple of minutes, although hang on, yes, once for about ten minutes. Yes, ten minutes at most.'

Condensations of sweat glistened on her forehead.

'So, for the record, Miss Dettman, you could not confirm Mister Thistleton was in fact there for the full two hours on Monday. Correct?'

Fitzy moved his shoulders back and forth in a rolling, massaging fashion. The label inside his collar felt as if it was stitched on with nylon fishing line and it made his neck itch. He only ever remembered after he'd had the shirt on for a while and he always forgot to remove the label when he got home. Many of the shirts felt as if a grass seed or a piece of fibre-glass cloth was lodged in his collar until he unpicked the label.

'Yyyyyyes true, although he was there for most …'

He held up his hand.

Lerlene exhaled a full-on sigh.

'That will be all for now. You may be advised to be more careful with your statements in future, Ms Dettman. And other activities too. You are lucky we are not interested in drugs at this point.' She stared at the teacher aide for a long moment. 'Here's my card if you remember anything else.'

The teacher-aide nodded sheepishly; the two police officers turned and walked away. Lerlene nudged Fitzy to make sure his gaze did not linger on the young woman.

They pulled up at a park down the road. Livistona palms fluttered in the breeze and the buzz of insects added to the sub-tropical feel. Children yelled with excitement in a playground far off in the distance.

'Now Fitzy, back to the job matey boy. How many unreliable witnesses can we score in one case?' growled Lerlene, shaking her head, not requiring an answer.

Fitzy smiled to himself as he climbed out of the car and lit a cigarette. Fitzy paced on the passenger side of the car. Lerlene lay the passenger's seat back a couple of notches, rested her head and pushed her sun glasses up into her hair. They needed to talk through the information they had to find a positive path through this investigation.

Fitzy said, 'The stupid bitch, now Colin's alibi goes to the dingoes, but it still doesn't prove, disprove or give us a lead or anything either fucking way. I reckon, to work out a reasonable time frame to go from the staff room, lie in wait, select a target, try to abduct or maybe inappropriately touch up a child, try not to be seen, discard the child and dash back and sit at his desk and make it look like he hadn't done anything; it would take more than ten minutes.' He drew hard on the cigarette. 'And what about a plan, eh? Drag the child to his car, which incidentally was parked in the school carpark, or hide in the bushes and think he wouldn't be seen or missed? Doesn't gel with me. If Colin's car was parked in the cul de sac, well maybe we have something there ... I don't know ... I mean ...'

She interrupted, eyebrows firmed, on a new tack, almost as if she was not really concentrating on what he was saying, but on something she had been thinking about.

'I wouldn't mind betting the time frames might be up the creek, I mean what say Colin went missing for an hour? The time lines seem to be wishy washy. With this Q-PED investigation, I'm in a position to confiscate anyone's computer if I think there's a reason to do so. I'd have to get a warrant but Old TC would do anything for me.'

Fitzy looked at her closing one of his eyes in mock understanding and he followed with a sneaky smile.

'Stop it! Drop the sleaze, strictly business Fitzy, you know me.'

She gazed at him with hooded eyes and a small lifting of the corners of her lips. It was general knowledge Old TC had a bit of a thing for some of the more attractive, young, female police officers, especially Lerlene. Fitzy was sure she was too smart to get involved with anyone in the force, but he was also astute enough to know she was capable of milking a situation if given the chance. In fact, Fitzy was sure her promotion to Acting Senior Sergeant had received more than a little nudge from Old TC.

'I'm thinking we should confiscate Colin's home computer, that's if he has one. I reckon he's our number one suspect at this stage.'

Fitzy said nothing.

She was clearly looking for him to add to her last statement, to verify the direction she was heading.

'Fitzy?'

'I dunno, I've got an uneasy feeling about all of this. I'll admit he's the best suspect we've got, best out of almost nothing, but …'

He ground out the cigarette under the heel of his hard wearing, leather desert boots and walked to the driver's side of the car.

'Let's go and have a gum session with Mr Timmins.'

Fitzy was still thinking about Colin, the nothing bit, and no plan.

~

'We're here to see a Mr Timmins,' said Fitzy.

The small Asian woman looked a little suspicious, or perhaps frightened. Definitely defensive.

'Who won to see him okay?'

They had already introduced themselves and she told them she was married to him, it was also clear they wanted to speak to him.

Lerlene interjected, 'Look Mrs Timmins, it is in relation to finding the owner of an item we have located.'

'Oh, I unnerstan.' She turned and yelled, 'Ay Andy, there some cop here to spea' to you okay?' Her look still balanced between suspicion and fear.

The moment Clive Andrew Timmins appeared, they realised he was the most unlikely suspect yet. He was about eighteen stone and only had one leg.

'What can I do for youse?' he exclaimed in a humourless voice, wheezing from the effort required to get to the door.

Map of India stains decorated the underarms of his grubby, work shirt. Fitzy thought he had the aura of wife basher about him and his body odour and the stale cigarette smoke in the house did not reduce the overall impression.

'Sorry to bother you, sir but we are looking for the owner of a pen with the initials C-A-T on it. Have you lost a pen like this?'

Lerlene showed them the photo.

'Nah, sorry, don't own no pen like that.' His eyes narrowed. 'What is all this? Seems like a lot of trouble to go to about a lost pen, two bloody cops.' He rubbed his bristled chin and stared with unfriendly, hooded eyes.

'Do you have a son or a relative with those initials?'

'Nope.' Said with deadpan lack of humour.

Thank you sir,' said Fitzy. 'For your info, it is in relation to a more complex matter than just a lost pen, but anyway, sorry to bother you.'

He nodded to Lerlene and they departed. Another dead end.

Chapter 19

Lerlene placed her mobile on the dash board.

'She's home and the boy is in his room, still distressed it would seem. Let's go and have a chat with them.'

She told Fitzy, she assumed Mrs Leak was on some sort of drugs or tranquillizers, judging from what she said when they spoke earlier in the day but Lerlene hoped the boy was not drugged. It was important to obtain clear information.

They pulled up at a large well maintained house with two modern vehicles in the driveway, a top of the line BMW rag top, two-door, and the latest *with everything on it* Landcruiser Station Wagon. Deidre Leak was at the front door when they arrived. Her black hair made a statement in a page boy style and her glasses dangling on a chain around her neck would have made Dame Edna envious. Several large circular gold earrings adorned each ear and clinked every time she moved her head.

Fitzy looked up at the blue sky chasing clouds, or the other way round, far too nice a day to perform the next task because his experience in judging body language told him they were in for a savaging. He knew he would much rather sit in the car and leave it all to Lerlene.

The woman was well and truly on the front foot and attacked whilst they were three metres away.

'This whole thing is sooooo distressing. Doctor put me on medication, I hope you're going to be quick, he's most upset and we don't want him disturbed anymore, what do you want anyway, you police take your time, don't you, I suppose you think this is low priority, a young innocent child, I mean to say, terrible, absolutely disgraceful and what do you do? Eh? Amble over here when you feel like it. You better have news for us …'

Lerlene mumbled to Fitzy, 'I wonder how aggressive she'd be if she was not on some sort of medication?'

Fitzy was about to react to Mrs Leak's pushiness and unnecessary aggression when Lerlene gently touched him on the forearm. It was clear she knew Fitzy would make a mess of this interview so she took the lead quickly.

'We're extremely sorry to bother you Mrs Leak, we understand the trauma you and your son have had to deal with but, as I'm sure you appreciate, we really need as much help as we can to apprehend the perpetrator.'

'You mean to tell me you haven't caught the … the … filthy animal who molested my son? What the hell have you been doing all this time?'

Fitzy was about to gently point out that it was an attempted abduction, not a molestation, when he felt a slight nudge. Lerlene delayed her reply to establish the voice of patience and reason.

'We are doing absolutely everything we possibly can. We have a number of leads …'

'Leads? Leads?'

'… Anyway, Mrs Leak, it's imperative we speak to your son, may we?' Lerlene indicated by rolling her hands outwards and smiling.

'Well, if you absolutely must, you may do so but if there is any sign of distress I'll terminate …'

'Of course, I understand, shall we do that …um now?'

The woman spun on her heel and led them to a spacious rumpus room where Tim was reading a book. Her vicious bombastic attitude changed like a snapped twig as she looked at her adored son.

She said gently, 'Timmy dear, there's some people here to have a word with you about …' She wrung her hands and dropped her head in a sympathetic pose.

'About the pedda-file man who tried to …'

'Don't upset yourself dear.' Mrs Leak replied.

Lerlene stepped between them. 'Mrs Leak, would you allow me to chat informally with Timmy, maybe you could you please wait outside? No offence is intended, I just think …'

Her façade changed again. 'What? Outside?' Outrage boiled in her reply.

Lerlene held up her hand and continued in a hushed tone, '…Yes, it's alright, he may open up a little if you aren't here.'

'Not here?' The woman almost shrieked.

Fitzy's Adam's Apple bobbed, reluctant as he was to deal with her, he knew he had to step in with diplomacy.

'Yes Mrs Leak,' he said as gently and as kindly as he could possibly muster. 'Maybe whilst they talk, we could have a chat too.' He struggled to pretend his genuineness. 'Please, let us go back into the kitchen.'

He guided her back through the archway, making sure not to touch her, into the ultra-modern kitchen leaving his partner to speak to the little boy. Lerlene gave Fitzy a stern *I'll have your you know whats if you misbehave* look as he departed.

Deidre Leak frowned, placed her ample bottom on a bench stool, not offering Fitzy a seat and spoke, as if he wasn't there, in an indignant tone.

'I knew he shouldn't have gone to that grubby public school, they have nothing but riff-raff attending there, a lot of the parents are criminals and drug addicts. He's enrolled in St. Leonards Private School at Kelvin Grove, you know, but they can't fit him in until next term.' Her nose screwed up as if someone had broken wind.

Fitzy struggled to not show contempt towards her, even though he certainly held sympathy for the young child. He was more than aware incidents such as this could have a lasting effect on the boy's life. He was no stranger to lasting damage as he recalled the years when his father was drinking heavily and the abuse he and his mother were forced to put up with. He quickly pushed that subject from his thoughts.

Fitzy took a few deep breaths and asked some generic questions about Tim's background, how he got on with others at school and whether the child had mentioned anything further about the incident. Deidre Leak said she did not want her young son ever having to talk about the wretched incident again.

He looked out at the swimming pool and the sprinkler system

which formed a rainbow in the mist. Deidre Leak babbled on about her obviously precious little child and how this would now affect his interaction with others, how degrading it was for her because of what the neighbours might think and how they may now have to move addresses. She ranted on about how difficult it was to find housing in the areas she thought were suitable and how, when her husband was made a partner, they would then be able to afford to live where they deserved to reside.

Fitzy looked out at a golden Labrador chasing the spray and he hoped the dog would rip the hose to pieces or jump into the swimming pool and cause a commotion, anything just to shut the woman up.

She blew her nose, bringing Fitzy back momentarily so he could tune out again as she waffled on about how Brisbane had been taken over by the lower classes, drug dealers, addicts and dole bludgers, and how the only hope for Australia was the return of good, old fashioned, family values only the Liberal and National Parties could deliver. Fitzy could think of nothing of any consequence to ask the opinionated know-all and was on the verge of going outside to have a smoke. He erred on the side of caution because he could imagine the nasty woman in front of him complaining to her local Member of Parliament, or the Prime Minister, about the filthy habit of one of the most inconsiderate police officers she had ever encountered, meaning him. He gently drummed his fingers on the marble-top kitchen bench as Deidre Leak banged on as if he was not there. He hoped Lerlene would make some headway with Tim. After about ten minutes of her whingeing about the fact they were not giving her little Timmy the priority he deserved, Lerlene emerged from next door.

Fitzy was convinced he would not be able glean anything further of value, so he decided to interrupt and end it there.

'Right, Mrs Leak, that will do us for the moment, if he happens to remember anything more, please give us a ring.'

He gave her Lerlene's card. Lerlene stepped out of the playroom and nodded to Fitzy.

'Thank you for your co-operation Mrs Leak, if we need anything more, we will be in touch.' She went to hand the woman her card.

'I've already got one of those,' she snapped.

Lerlene looked at him for a second and Fitzy winked. They hurried out the front door and down the driveway. Fitzy lit up. Clearly both of them were eager to get out of there. When they were back at the car he sucked a couple of quick drags and threw the butt on the front lawn. He jumped in and hit the steering wheel with the heels of his hands in mock rage.

'Fuuuck, I hope we never have to speak to someone as up themselves as her for the rest of our careers!'

Lerlene laughed dryly, 'You managed to restrain yourself very well, Fitzy. I guess you learnt as much as I did. The poor kid is about as reliable as the rest of the witnesses. At least we know the boy was grabbed from behind, he wriggled and fought back and wasn't touched on his … er… private parts. It's always difficult with the very young to get precise information and Tim was attacked from behind. We need another witness so at this point we're still looking for the same shortish, maybe plumpish or skinnyish, baldingish suspect who has a slightly perfumerish aroma to him.'

'There's a few ishes there, Acting Senior Sergeant,' retorted Fitzy in an attempt to put a positive spin on the situation.

'We could charge Senior Constable Steve Brookes.'

'Why?'

Lerlene started to chuckle. 'Timothy picked Brooksie from the photos I showed him. From now on this case could be referred to as the unreliable witness case. Nice touch to give her my phone number too, eh. You'll pay for that, Fitzy.'

She looked out the window, either exhausted or deep in thought but still almost smiling. They drove back to the office in silence.

Chapter 20

Back at the station Lerlene picked up a note lying on her desk right where she could not miss it, asking how things were going with Inspector Deaver's case.

'Bugger,' she said and politely showed it to Fitzy and handed over the relevant file. 'Sorry to do this but away you go, comb through it over the next couple of hours – and when you get sick of that there is other stuff as well - and we'll meet back here and talk. I have got a few other things to sort out here.'

Fitzy grabbed the folder and went to the lunch room, made a coffee and pulled the file apart. There was not much useful information, and he did not think there would be, because Inspector Deaver spent as much time avoiding work as he did actually working.

The crime scene reports for each of the eleven robberies were attached.

Fitzy scratched his head. 'All this trouble for stolen orchids?'

He rang Inspector Deaver. 'G'day Devious, Fitzy here.'

'Hey there, Fitzy, how about a bit of respect. I'm Inspector Deaver, get it?'

'Alright Inspector Devious, how's that for ya? I need to talk to you about these orchid thefts.'

Fitzy was not in the best friend's category with the inspector but they had managed to tolerate each other over the years. They worked together on a few cases but the relationship was strained at best. Eric Deaver was junior in years of service, and age, and that was why Fitzy was allowed to get away with a certain level of familiarity and disrespect – even though there was a mutual underlying dislike between the two of them. Deaver climbed the ladder quicker than most other officers. Many people around the corridors thought Fitzy should have been promoted to inspector before Eric Deaver. Then came, *the incident,* and Fitzy was anchored for the foreseeable future, advancement on hold. Everyone else knew Deaver was only good at looking after himself but he did present a good clean-up rate to the hierarchy. However, he was always conning others to do the work for him as well as not being shy in claiming credit for the work put in by officers junior to him.

'Jesus you're cheeky, Fitzy, I should report you to the disciplinary committee for lack of respect for such a nice bloke as myself. Anyway, the Orchid case is a piece of cake and I just wanted you and Dippy to get the credit for it, that's all.' Semi jovial tone with a hint of acid.

'Pig shit, Devo, that'd be the day, letting us take the credit. Ha - ha, ease up on the jokes, mate. Anyway, what can you tell me about what you know so far?'

'Well, after extensive investigations I put the file together.'

Fitzy sighed. 'So you didn't visit the individual crime scenes and you didn't speak to the victims but you *did* speak to the officers who made the reports, Right?'

'Well, sort of but not in an actual first person kind of contact.'

'So you spoke to no one and you did fuck all and you know fuck all, right?'

'Jesus Fitzy, not sure I like your tone but I guess you are close to correct.'

'Well, Devo, you must know something?'

'I do as it happens. The orchids are valuable, well not real valuable but probably worth about one to two hundred bucks a pop and as you can see the overall value keeps mounting.'

'Well I can see that because the info is written in the file. So is that all?'

'Yep. Look, mate, Superintendent Jackson just dropped it on my desk, I'm far too busy to dick around with this, that's why I selected Dippy, and you of course.'

'Of course. Can't tell you how honoured we are!'

'But you have to get your finger out of your quoit because Jacko's missus is in some orchid club and she's pissing in his ear like mad, and guess what? Jacko's pissing in my ear like a waterfall to get it sorted out. And Old TC's missus is pissing in his ear because she's in some orchid thing as well.'

'So, should I now be prepared for you to piss in my ear?'

'Well, you only get half 'cos the other half goes into Dippy's ear, so win-win the way I see it.'

'For you maybe. Anyway Devo, you should be careful calling her Dippy and I'd be super careful calling her Dipstick because she'll rip your nuts off if she catches you. In fact, I've got a good mind to tell her.'

'Oh, come on, Fitzy, we're mates aren't we, and we are a team as well?'

'Better go Devo, don't get your tie dirty or dust on your shoes, eh? We'll keep you posted.'

Fitzy went back to the office and booted up the shared computer. He was not a natural with computers but had completed a couple of courses and could at least turn one on. He hit Google and looked up the names of the orchids and from a sales catalogue established that all the orchids stolen had a retail price of between one and two hundred dollars.

He leaned back in the chair and rubbed his chin. He knew he would have to speak with the officers who attended the eleven robberies. He noted, fortunately, there were only two officers involved. Also, one of the officers was a woman, Constable Pauline Kaplan and Fitzy was keen to see more of her, so that was at least a bonus. He bumped into her a couple of weeks earlier at the Gordon Arms Hotel, known as a place where local police gathered. He had not seen her there since and was wondering how he could formulate a meeting. Now, maybe, there was a chance in sight.

Lerlene walked in. 'Any clues?'

'Nothing much, other than, on one hand you could ask why in the hell are we bothering about eleven orchids, with a total value of less than two grand, on the other hand I get the feeling there might just be bit more to this. Old TC is probably brown-nosing the Big Shots to get in favour for a medal or more funding or something. He's always on the make and all the big end of town know each other. The Big Shots' wives know each other and Old TC is pandering to that.

'There is a pattern of regularity with these thefts, about a month apart which could indicate the perp might be thinking no one would take this seriously and not bother to investigate, or it may be a well-planned thing that could go on for ever; which means we could be talking about fairly big money after a while, particularly if whoever it is moves on to steal some really valuable ones.'

'Right. Maybe you can at least speak to a few people later on just to show we are doing something.'

'Ah, there's the word *we.*'

'Well Fitzy, we are a team, aren't we?'

'That seems to be a very popular saying these days.'

'Okay, in the meantime we can chew over what we know and then I'm going home. You may do it too, Fitzy.'

'Gee thanks boss, very big of you.'

She gave a forced smile.

'Now first up tomorrow we are going to confiscate a few computers. Colin's first up, also we should double check the computers from the church, orphanage, Father O'Neill if he has one; definitely Stink Fi.... , gee that's a disgusting name, Fitzy.' She giggled again. 'Anyway, him, Glen Hewitt and we should look at the school system as well.'

Fitzy said, 'This morning Meredith told me she had details from nearly all the state's prison systems and no one who was classified as a kiddie fiddler has been released recently, other than two probables – one from Victoria, who is in a care facility and from reports confined to a wheelchair, and the other is in hospital dying of cancer. The Northern Territory and ACT are transferring all records to digital and from what I hear it's a mess. I told Meredith to keep at them. She's working on the electoral rolls, phone books, newspapers and rate notices, you name it, for CAT, and anything relevant. Both of us should check with her regularly.'

'We, it means you and I, are personally going to deal with Colin at home and grab his computer. Good chance he's our man.'

Fitzy fingered the cigarette packet in his top pocket and placed his size eleven-and-a-halves on the desk. He needed to think out loud.

'That's jumping in a bit quick, isn't it? Anyway, we still really haven't cleared Stink Finger or Father O'Neill. They are alibis for each other; mind you, I don't think they're top suspects. O'Neill has access to children all the time, the orphanage is next door, sure, but if he was to tamper with kids' bottoms, why would he hide in the bushes at school? Priests are smarter than that, eh? But still, we shouldn't discount either of them.'

He tapped out a cigarette, looked at it, looked at Lerlene, rolled his eyes and stuck it behind his ear and continued.

'Anything could be going on in and around the orphanage and that doesn't necessarily mean the church and if there was some evidence you would think someone would know something. Mind you, if it *is* the church and if anything was going on, they could probably suppress it with the brass by saying, "We will be diligently looking into these serious matters and will deal with them in house so there is no need for any police action".' He sighed. 'We've got nowhere with the syringe, dead end; nowhere with the pen as yet, not even sure it has any bearing on the case at all. Wowzer rang and said Cain Albert Torrens is an arsehole, violent and unco-operative but he's got a rock solid alibi. He was in hospital with a broken nose after he managed to get in a fight at the Morningside Football Club on Sunday night. The hospital said he's the worst patient they've ever had, wanted to bash the doctor and anyone who came near him. Evidently, he was still pissed the next day from the all-night binge. So, he's pretty well out. Wowzer checked his family, no males, or females for that matter with the initials CAT. I'm going out for a smoke.'

'I'll ring Hazza.'

Senior Constable Harry Harrison, with a certain amount of charm and wangling by Lerlene, was now officially seconded to the Q-PED unit for certain duties. She wanted to get things going in relation to checking on the computers of these key people.

~

Outside, as he smoked, Fitzy rested his foot against the rail and looked out at the police vehicles, parked with parade ground order. He needed a few rounds with his mate, Fridge, down at the gym; he'd go there later on after work. When he got frustrated or angry with things a good boxing session was a great release. It allowed him to cut loose and try to belt the daylights out of someone who could handle it but stay within the rules. The way he felt at the moment, his mate, the cold calculating bouncer, Fridge, would be advised to wear a protective helmet.

Fitzy's mother, Lois, lived in a unit at Sandgate which was on the way to the gym. They got on well and he generally liked to visit her once a week and she was comfortable with him dropping by for a few minutes anytime. She used to harp on about the dangers of his job but in recent years she had resigned herself to the fact that her little boy could take care of himself.

Fitzy's mother and father had separated over twenty years ago when Fitzy was twelve. After many years of emotional and sometimes physical abuse, she kicked her husband out, or more correctly, Fitzy did. It was a stage of his life where the young Rodney FitzMichael had to grow up quickly. These days Lois was a fitness fanatic often competing in triathlons.

Fitzy flicked his cigarette over the rail thinking he should get a move on if he was going to see his mother, belt Fridge about the ropes and then, yes maybe, go to the Gordon Arms Hotel for a beer after that. He made a phone call first.

Chapter 21

'Ah, Constable Pauline Kaplan, fancy seeing you here.'
'G'day, Fitzy. Seeing me here would have nothing to do with the fact you rang me and said you wanted to meet me here. Strictly business you pointed out.'

She smiled, showing the white teeth of a teenager, even though she was in her late twenties. Fitzy struggled for a moment because the last time he saw her she was dressed plainly in a dark dress and blouse with her hair up. The only other times he had seen her she was in uniform and she looked fairly plain with her hair pushed mostly up inside the police issue baseball cap or plaited hair sticking through the gap at the rear of the cap. Her uniform hid her slim, attractive figure but not very well. This time she was more striking in blue jeans and a light cotton blouse with the top two buttons undone, showing off well-developed breasts. Her black rimmed glasses were not convincing in making her look like a geek but they accentuated her straight, blood-red hair combed to about eight inches below her shoulders.

'Well, good you could make it. Isn't your hair redder than last time I saw you?'

She smiled as if it was a game. 'Well red is my natural colour. A man is not supposed to ask questions like that.'

'Umm ... right, what can I get you to drink?'

He ordered a couple of beers and gently ushered her out the back into the beer garden. Fitzy had not thought about it before, but he was glad none of his mates, police or otherwise were in the bar. He realised he should have suggested somewhere else because the rumour mill would be humming at the station as police station gossip was as bad as any workplace. She offered him a cigarette and he lit them both up.

'Right, Fitzy, what's up? By the way has anyone ever said you look like Bryan Brown? Younger version of course.'

He could not see her eyes because light glinted off her glasses.

'All the time.' He took a drag. 'Right, business. I've been handballed the orchids case by Inspector Deaver and I need to find out some background.'

She laughed, shaking her mane and her hair gently billowed back to its original place.

'I don't really know much; Devo said he was going to get one of the detectives to look at it. Seems like you are it.' She took a draft from her beer.

'From what I gather you attended nine of the burglaries, right?'

'Yep. Someone else attended the first two. You wouldn't think anyone would get upset about someone pinching a pot plant, but I can tell you they all seemed to be not only pissed off but quite emotional. I don't know anything about orchids, so I spoke to a friend, who is an amateur collector, to get a handle on orchids in general, even though I wasn't to be the investigating officer, you understand?' She fingered a delicate silver choker around her neck. Mumbling noises drifted from the bar.

'Well then Kappo, you could always assist me, sort of in an off-duty fashion, couldn't you?'

She smiled again. 'No, best left to you but I don't mind helping during office hours. My round, same again?'

Fitzy's glance followed her shapely behind as she headed to the bar next door. He was not sure if her answer was meant to discourage him or not. He mulled over the training session he had attended at the gym prior to coming to the pub. Ron Bleeker, known as Fridge, gave him a decent run for his money. Ron was a big man, ex Olympic weight lifter and these days instead of lifting weights he boxed to keep fit. He was nowhere near the size he was when in training because these days he ran, swam and boxed, as well as keeping a tight rein on his diet but he was overall bigger than Fitzy. He was a natural athlete and Fitzy was no match for him in a technical sense, but Fitzy was a dangerous opponent because he was a street fighter. With his strong upper body and wiry strength, he often got the better of Ron Bleeker but by the end of the rounds, Ron could pound Fitzy into submission simply because he knew how to punch in a calculated way. Fitzy tried to do the same but often his temper took over and he became a dangerous windmill, leaving key areas of his anatomy wide open.

He also had a chat to Brother Dominic to see if any light could be thrown on any of the people Fitzy was investigating. Dominic was guarded, as Fitzy expected, on any discussion regarding Catholic priests but the good brother said he would tweak his ears and sniff around.

Drinks arrived.

They talked over the case; Pauline explained to him that the orchids stolen, from her research, were rare and reasonably valuable but not top shelf. In her opinion it appeared as if the thief was putting together a collection of rare orchids to sell on the black market. Her friend had asked around discretely and had suggested an extensive collection like that, if the person continued in the same vein, would be worth a considerable amount of money after a few years, particularly if the stakes were upped and the thief began to collect rarer plants. She was not an expert but she thought the orchids could be split and separated, like one parent plant to have many pups. That could open up a possible lucrative industry.

Pauline added, 'My opinion only but I guess the theft of semi-valuable plants doesn't raise as much suspicion as top line stock. I mean, the police would only give this case lip service to make everyone think they were doing something but would pretty quickly drop the whole thing if they, meaning us, couldn't solve it within a short time; not enough money in it.

'If the collection, on the quiet, slowly grew over time, rare legally purchased orchids added and the collection made available to overseas buyers, well, who knows. From what we dug up it seems there's huge money in collections, more so than the individual plant, even though there's certainly big bucks in that but more internationally than here. Wealthy people love statues, paintings and anything considered arty and most certainly collections of all kinds and will pay mobs for it, just to bloody well show off to their mates. Also, as you would be aware, some wealthy collectors have been caught buying and selling stolen paintings, originals, and other things too, and these people know they are stolen and cannot display them in public, can only hang them in secret rooms that only a few trusted friends, by that I mean fellow criminals, can view. What's the value of that? Paying a mint for an item you know has been nicked and not being able to show the world?

'Seems to me that this would just be a minor case if it wasn't for Old TC's wife, and other so called prominent people. I guess the people who have had orchids stolen from them are more concerned with the invasion of their private lives, you know, having criminals going into their house and nicking things.'

'How much would the collection come to, did your friend say?' queried Fitzy.

'Oh, probably tens of thousands if there were enough orchids to make an exceptional collection … and throw in a few really rare and valuable ones. Maybe the perp plans to add some really valuable ones to the collection at a later date when everyone has taken their eye off the ball, or maybe even purchase the rare ones legitimately and therefore make the collection legal in a sense. Yeah, how many is a collection, Fitzy? All subjective.' She splayed her hands.

'Any tips?'

'The only suggestion I can make, and my friend said the same thing, we can expect more thefts but not many and not often. The person or persons doing this clearly don't want to put this on the radar. Also, I suggest you have a word with Steve Brooks; he was the officer who attended the other robberies.'

'Right. Looks like I've got a bit of leg work to do. I was going to see Brooksie tomorrow some time anyway, spoke to him earlier.'

'Do you surf?'

'What?'

'Every time I see you, you have a bright surf shirt on. I just thought you, you know?'

'Nah, I don't surf like surfy guys do but I often go out with the surf ski. I just happen to like these type of shirts, not for everyone, I know. What do reckon?' He straightened his collar in an exaggerated fashion.

'Suits you. Right, Fitzy, I've got to go, nice meeting you for a drink.'

Fitzy made an exaggerated balk. Her wind up of the meeting seemed a bit sudden. 'Don't suppose you'd like to …?'

She lowered her dark rimmed glasses. 'Like to what?' She put him back in his box.

He had the feeling she was playing hard to get. He couldn't be totally honest about his intentions.

'Umm, maybe go somewhere else, have a drink, dinner ... my place, you know?'

'Sorry Fitzy, I'm tired, I've got a big day tomorrow.' She smiled.

'Fair enough,' he said and stood when she stood. She held out her hand and they shook. Her grip was firm but not tight. He did not think he was on a winner.

At the door she turned and said, 'Maybe some other time, dinner? Bryan Brown never wore shirts like that, though.' She winked. Her hair swished and she was gone.

Rodney FitzMichael wandered back into the buzz of the front bar to have another drink before going home to a TV dinner. An early night was not such a bad idea and he could think about what might have been tonight but also dream of what might transpire if he was to ask her out formally. He convinced himself tonight really was strictly business, cemented by the fact she shook hands with him but maybe on another occasion things could be different.

Fitzy spent a pleasant evening thinking about Constable Pauline Kaplan. He drifted off remembering the smell of her feminine perfume.

Chapter 22

'We'd like to speak to your husband please Mrs Thistleton,' said Acting Senior Sergeant Diplock flipping open her identification wallet. Fitzy stood passively alongside her mechanically holding his wallet open, still thinking of last night.

'Why!' snapped Gretel. A statement not a question.

'Is he at home? We'd like to speak to him, please.'

'Yeah? What do you want to see him about?' she barked and finished with a cough.

'Mrs Thistle…?'

'Yeah alright.' She didn't bother turning, just continued to yell in their faces as if her husband was behind *them* out in the driveway. 'Hey Colin, there are some cops here to see ya! What the hell have you been doing, you little twerp?'

Fitzy looked away for a second and held back a smile. He thought some of the female officers in the police force could be quite aggressive at times but they were lambs compared to some of the females he had met recently on this case.

'Can we come in, please?' persisted Lerlene.

'Why?' barked Gretel.

Fitzy interjected firmly, 'Mrs Thistleton, if you continue in this way, we may have to take other measures. Now, may we come in, please, much easier to do it this way?' He towered above her, arms straining the stitching on his surf shirt.

'Suit yaselves! Wipe ya feet, eh!'

She coughed again, inhaled on a cigarette, stoking a glowing coal, and stormed off in the direction of the whirring spin dryer out the back in the laundry. The two police officers walked in and had to duck and weave through the maze of hanging ornaments, just as Colin appeared.

'What can I do for you?' he stammered, his glance darting like a startled animal.

They both showed their identification. 'I'm Senior Sergeant Diplock; do you have a computer, sir?'

'Um, yes, of course, what is this ...?'

'Could you please direct us to your computer?' said Fitzy as the bulk of their authority forced the smaller man backwards into the office.

'It's only a few days old, it's new, or most of it, why do you want ...?'

'Is this your desk?'

Fitzy sat down and started opening the drawers. He could see nothing of interest in the top two but when he came to the bottom drawer, he said, 'Aha Colin, we're at it again aren't we, eh? I bet this isn't water.' Fitzy held up a water bottle, removed the lid, took a sniff and smiled sharply.

'Please, Sergeant,' pleaded Colin, hands splayed, looking urgently in all directions, especially the doorway, obviously frightened in case his wife should come into the room. It was clear to Fitzy she had no idea about his drinking.

'What ... what do you want? I've done nothing wr...'

Lerlene sleeked out of the room and headed for the source of the spin drier noise, which indicated the machine was unbalanced and was beginning to thump. She glanced around; the house was crowded with lacy doilies, ornaments, small statues and family keepsakes. She had never seen so many pictures and photos on any walls in any house, ever. Dogs, cats, horses, children, people, monuments, and more. Clinking mobiles and crocheted hangings forced her to dodge and weave and do the limbo, through the lounge and passage. There was no space left anywhere to put anything. The house reeked of stale cigarette smoke, fighting for precedence over cheap perfumed disinfectant, reminding her of a smoker's room in a low budget motel. The crowded, unhappy place made her insides contract, particularly her heart. She found Gretel hauling sheets out of a laundry basket.

'Can we switch the washing machine off for a moment, please?'

Lerlene reached across and turned it off at the wall.

Gretel looked up almost as if she did not know where she was. Her eyes were red and had a lost look. Her skin was a grey-white pallor.

'Are you alright, Mrs Thistleton?' Lerlene was no medical genius but she could tell the woman had serious mental and physical health issues.

'Alright? Yeah, why wouldn't I be, eh? What the hell's going on, what's 'e done?'

'Mrs Thistleton?' Her police experience told her to come straight out with it. 'Does your husband have any pornographic material?'

'Pornographic what? What the bloody hell is this? He's too piss weak to do anything, I tell ya, just too bloody piss weak.'

'Mrs Thistleton, has he?' Lerlene opened her eyes wide and inclined her head with the last part of the sentence.

'No, absolutely not, why would he? I can bloody well tell ya, I'd know.' Gretel lit up a cigarette with shimmering hands. It took at least six clicks with the lighter. Her lips were dry and cracked and there were tiny flecks of white mucus in the corners of her mouth – custard corners.

'What the hell's going on?'

Lerlene's insides cringed again as she looked at the poor creature in front of her.

'An attempt was made to abduct a child at the primary school on Monday, your husband is someone of interest to us. Is there any explicit material on the computer?'

'How the hell would I know? It's only new, the old one crashed and we got it reconditioned.' She almost kissed the cigarette with a prune mouth as she snatched sharp, shallow draws.

'Where is the old hard drive?'

The woman tried to think. 'Probably the repair people, dump, don't know, why?'

They were interrupted by Fitzy who was carrying the computer tower and modem.

'Senior Sergeant, I don't think Mr Thistleton will object to us borrowing his computer.'

'What the hell is this,' barked Gretel, 'You can't just walk in here and …'

Lerlene held up the warrant and then gave it to her. 'Your copy. I'm sorry we have to do this but it is necessary. You'll have the computer back within a short time provided everything is okay.'

Gretel Thistleton looked at the paperwork but Lerlene could tell she was not taking it all in. The police officers edged their way out, dodging hanging objects, leaving the husband and wife standing there. Lerlene clicked the front door behind them.

~

Gretel looked blankly at Colin. 'What the hell have you been up to?'

Colin turned on his heel and went straight into the office. He grabbed the water bottle Fitzy left on the desk and guzzled half of it. The vodka went straight into his blood stream. He lidded it and dropped the bottle in the bottom drawer.

Gretel's pyramid head appeared in the doorway, framed by the afternoon light.

'What the fucking hell have you been up to? You didn't molest any kid. Did you? You're too piss weak to do any bloody thing.' Her voice went up into a shriek. *'Answer me!'*

He could not see her features clearly, just the outline of the inverted pyramid, angry and full of doom. There was no time for an answer, she spun around and stormed out, slamming the door so hard it bounced open again.

Colin was dizzy from the enormous hit of vodka, he sat down, almost missing the chair, totally bewildered and dejected. As far as he was concerned, he had not done anything, let alone anything wrong. His depression was almost total, like freefalling in a vacuum to nowhere. He did not even hear the washing machine had been turned on again and the thumping was vibrating the walls.

Chapter 23

'Well, they've checked the computers at the rectory, orphanage and the one Father O'Neill and the other staff use. The orphanage computer had a lot deleted, wiped off the hard drive but Harry was able to retrieve it, nothing of any substance, just church stuff. The other two are clean, nothing incriminating there. Wowzer and Josie gave Hewitt's place a good going over, clean as you like. No kiddie stuff at all. Maybe he is clean after all but, you know.' Fitzy delivered the last part with a raising of the eyebrows and a shrug.

Lerlene stood up and ambled over to the window. She turned and folded her arms and leant against the jamb. The light behind her highlighted her strong, female figure in jeans and fashionable military style light blue shirt.

'I've got to give Old TC a full report today, he's edgy 'cos that horrible woman Deidre Leak has gone to her local Member of Parliament and complained we were insensitive in our interview techniques and were not doing enough to catch the culprit. What a bitch, I should have let you loose on her, Fitzy, to make our reprimanding worthwhile.'

Fitzy leaned back; the chair creaked. 'I'll be, I sarcastically thought to myself at the time she would go to her MP – or the Prime Minister. What a pretentious harlot, people like her should be locked up just because of how they are.'

She gave a tired smile, 'I don't know why Old TC just doesn't tell the minister to get stuffed, this has top priority, we've been working hard on it and this is all the thanks we get. It'd be good to have support from the top once every now and again rather than criticism. Old TC, and the rest of the management, in the main, used to be rank and file police officers and you would think they would realise that it takes time and just hard grind to get results at the coalface. They seem to have to brown-nose big shots above them in the pecking order. Always the way, eh?'

'Spot on,' said Fitzy. 'We've not much hard stuff to go on, have we? All junketty evidence. What do you reckon?'

They both knew they just had to keep wearing it down, checking, rechecking and following up even the most tenuous links.

'Well, there's not anywhere near enough to link Stink Finger to the crime and Father O'Neill seems most unlikely. I did a bit of general asking around in relation to his reputation with the street kids. He ruffles a few feathers, more with the hierarchy in the church because he doesn't push a Christian agenda, doesn't force the down and outers to embrace God, he simply helps in a non-judgmental fashion. From what I gather there are no rumours hovering around about any malpractice at the orphanage – they don't call it that these days by the way, community centre or some such politically correct title – anyway we probably wouldn't hear about rumours because they'd keep it under wraps. Bearing in mind, eh, there are only a handful of children there at the moment and the number changes regularly.'

She leant back and looked at the ceiling.

He shrugged and pursed his lips. 'Hate to admit it but aside from both of them being arrogant cunts, they're probably alright.'

She frowned in his direction at his use of the C word. 'Meredith's not making much headway with her research but she's keeping at it. NT and ACT are still transferring to digital. Hazza said he'd get back to us in relation to Colin's computer, maybe we'll find something there. He did say after a quick squiz there was something deleted. He thought that strange, because it is supposed to be a brand new hard drive but of course Colin could have deleted something.'

She walked over and stood looking at the police notice board. Tom the Cheap stared down at them, the most wanted criminal of them all. Still not apprehended.

At the top of the notice board was a faded newspaper cutting showing Tom the Cheap of the late 1950's to the 1970's, the legendary chain store grocer from Western Australia, wearing striped prison clothes and a dark mask hiding his eyes. He was called a *naughty boy* and declared a comic strip criminal by the press because he deliberately undercut his opponents and slashed prices. He was against price fixing, said he was prepared to do time keeping wholesalers honest and looking after the mums and dads out there in the suburbs. Fitzy had pinned the clipping on their noticeboard to remind them of who they, the police, were serving – the populace, not the big end of town.

Lerlene's phone interrupted the almost tranquil scene; it was Senior Constable Harrison.

'Hey Lerles, Thistleton's computer has a mountain of kiddie porn …'

'Hang on Hazza,' she said quickly, 'Fitzy's here, I'm putting you on speaker phone. Right, repeat what you just said and go on.'

Harrison did as asked and continued '… absolutely chockers, it had been deleted. Real hard core pedo stuff, like I mean seriously disgusting photos, probably the worst I've ever seen. If it was him, or whoever it was, he was pretty good at hiding it. It wasn't straightforward to find. Pretty good chance your Colin rushed home after school and deleted the lot. If anyone looks good for it, you would have to say he is well and truly in the frame.'

'Nice work, Hazza,' she said, eyes bright and excited looking at Fitzy. 'Any news on the other computers?'

'Yeah but really no … not really, we've been running checks on the school system, haven't come up with much but we did find a small number of shots of little children in bathers and a kid's birthday party. At a stretch could be seen as possible pedo stuff if it was among more graphic material but it's pretty harmless; he would have access to it, could even be his, there's a C in the data box at the top, and could easily be him. But the shots are pretty tame, no nudes, could even be someone's kids, innocent snaps. Anyway, the school stuff in relation to Thistleton is at best circumstantial, but, fact is - he has access to it. However, with his personal computer, no doubt about it, it'd be him in that household from what you have told me, unlikely to be his wife or daughter. I've got a written report and the disc is on the way for you, Wilson will drop it off to you when he drops off some files to registry, could be half hour or so. I thought I'd better let you know, orright?'

'Well done Hazza, well done!'

She clicked the phone off, stood up and punched the air.

'Right, now Fitzy, this is what we've got the way I see it. Point one, Colin has no alibi, point two, his physical fits, point three, he was in the proximity of the crime, point four, his computer is chockers with kiddie porn, point five, he has porno magazines and point six, he has an aroma about him. Vodka whiffs like perfume, it's faint but, you know, an aroma. He's our man Fitzy, I just know it.'

She kept strolling with purposeful steps, like a professor nutting out a problem, stroking her chin. He didn't respond other than pull out a cigarette and tap it on the desk. He pouted his lips and closed one eye as if in deep concentration. It seemed as if she did not notice his lack of enthusiasm.

She continued, 'We've got enough evidence to get him on, porno material of that nature, he's gone for all money. I'm going to arrest him on those charges and with a bit of luck he'll confess to the attempted abduction once we get him in the station.'

She stopped pacing, sat down and looked at him, face aglow, possibly expecting an accolade. Her demeanour changed.

'You don't seem too keen, Fitzy?' Her brows knitted.

Fitzy dropped the unlit cigarette on the desk, stood up, his turn to pace. He took a few steps; hands hooked in his back pockets and then stopped. He then crossed his strong sinewy arms and leant against the two tone, pea soup green wall.

'Well, there's a lot of circumstantial evidence, that's all, I'm a little shaky about it all. I'm not really convinced he *is* our man for the attempted abduction. Kiddie porn, well yep, looks awfully like it. Granted, Colin is probably the best we've got, I'll agree with you there but …'

He shook his head slowly from side to side. Light from the window highlighted the colours of the beach scene on his shoulder. Umbrella and beach ball, bright as.

It was clear Lerlene was convinced of her theory and did her best to not really hear the essence of what he was trying to say. She was the senior officer after all and had to make the decisions, also there was the gut feeling.

'I'm going to look at the stuff Hazza is sending over and then you and I are going for a drive, Fitzy, it is what you and I are going to do.'

He picked up the cigarette and smiled.

'Senior Sergeant, may I go and have a fag first?'

The tone was not sarcastic, just tension breaking.

'You have time; Wilson could be a while.'

For the first time in a week, Acting Senior Sergeant Diplock was able to relax, if only for a moment. She made a cup of coffee, grabbed one of the newspapers from the lunch room as well and sat back at her desk. Absentmindedly she leafed through it whilst waiting for the disc from Senior Constable Harrison.

Lerlene froze! Then a big smile crept across her face. In the comic section of the Courier Mail was the popular daily cartoon character ... Colin the Cat! C-A-T.

'Naaaaaaaah can't be, surely ...' she muttered and burst out laughing.

She picked up a file and said to Tom the Cheap up on the notice board, 'We haven't got you, you naughty boy but there's no doubt about Colin Thistleton, this is a sign, Colin the Cat, he's definitely our man!'

After what Fitzy termed a well-earned smoke, he decided to speak with Senior Constable Steve Brookes who was down the corridor, to catch up on details of the first two orchid thefts. He was in the unclaimed property storeroom with his feet on another chair eating a pie. A police radio control system buzzed and crackled in the next room.

'Oh, bardon if I don't fand and falute, fir,' he said through a mouthful of obviously molten pie. His body looked like a sock of porridge balanced on a chair.

'Don't be cheeky, Brooksie.'

They were mates who had been on several training courses together and also out drinking as well on many occasions. Steve Brookes was a competent, loyal, fun-loving practical joker in the police station. His fun-loving attitude did, however, step in the way of promotion. He could easily have been a sergeant and often acted in that designation, but he was content just turning up for work.

'No fir, I mean yeff fir,' he replied, swallowing and wiping tomato sauce from his chin. 'Hell, this bloody pie is white hot. *Fuck!*

Laughing, Fitzy pulled up a chair. 'Serves you right for trying to gobble it so fast. Come to talk about the orchid thefts you attended.'

'Yup.' He stuffed the rest of the pie in his mouth, poking excess blobs in with his index finger.

Steve stood up, went to the counter, grabbed a tissue and wiped his face. He guzzled half a can of soft drink, turned and burped loudly.

'Yeah, alright, what can I do you for?' Brookes patted his ample girth and burped again, more sedately this time.

'Kappo told me to see if you could put forth any ideas or suggestions regarding the Orchid case.'

'No, not really, I jes took details and placed them in the report. I would have done more but we got tied up in the demonstrations down at the racetrack. Devo told us to sit tight on it and ...' he looked around as if spies were hiding behind things in the room.

'And what?'

'Well, Devo was of the opinion it was just random thefts of objects worth at best maybe a few hundred bucks *and* when there was theft and damage in other cases worth thousands upon tens of thousands of buckaroonies he said to sit on it and pretend we were investigating it.'

'Gee, it's not like Devo to not do anything, is it?' mocked Fitzy.

'To be fair, nothing happened for another month and even then, still such a piddling amount, you know.' Brookes slumped down, the chair protested with a creak and a ping.

'So how come Kappo got thrown the next nine cases?'

'Devo moved me into traffic because they are short at the moment - I'm only here for me lunch break — been workin' me guts out. Gawwwd, that pie, burnt the roof of me mouth, well I shouldn'a et two, anyrate, s'pose. Been busy here, Stevenson had an accident on his bike, Rudy Voss got a bad call from the doctor, you know bloke stuff, prostrate I think, and Taggers Tagliatelli went on maternity or paternity leave, or whatever it's called. I'd be on stress leave if it was me, I tell ya, anyrate his missus is having twins and he's already got six bambinos. He should learn to keep it in his ...'

Fitzy burst out laughing.

Brookes continued, 'Anyrate, back to the story, Kappo was next in line. As far as I know she was told to concentrate on the other crimes involving more money. She wanted to actually be the investigating officer but there were more important things to do, weren't there? Anyway, the case would probably be in archives by now but for …'

'Is this a game, Brooksie? But for what?'

'But Old TC's missus, who is an orchid fanatic, started making his life uncomfortable and then Jacko's bride started making Jacko's life unliveable, because she's in some fuck'n orchid association as well, so that's why Dipstick caught the case and, guess what?'

'I'm not big on this game, Brooksie but I guess the guess what is, I've caught the case.'

'Right the first time, Fitzy, couldn't happen to a nicer bloke, me old son.'

'I've got a good mind to give you a clip in the ear and then report you for disrespecting a senior officer but it wouldn't be in the interests of smooth running of police procedures.'

'You're all heart, Fitzy. Tell you what though, you'd be doing Devo's job now, and you'd be doing a damn sight better job than him, if it wasn't for, you know, the little *incident* with that piece of animal shit Bagshaw, eh?'

'Thanks for reminding me. So, anyway let's get back to it; you didn't interview the victims other than on the day, correct?'

Brookes nodded and stifled a burp.

'That means I've got so close to fuck-all here it doesn't matter?'

'I'd say you are bang on there, mate. Gawd, I think I've got a touch of the old indigo suggestion as well as first degree burns to me mouth.'

On the way back to his office Fitzy slapped the wall when he thought no one could see him. He almost collided with Constable Gavin Wilson in the doorway.

'Nice little CD for youse to watch. Bloody horrible stuff, Christ there are some disgusting cretins in the world.'

He held out the CD to Fitzy as Lerlene joined them.

'Thanks, Weed,' said Fitzy grabbing it.

Chapter 24

Colin sat, almost reeling, on a stool at the bench in the shed, very drunk. Every day he noticed how much his hands shook until he downed a weighty slug of Vodka. As always, the alcohol spread over him like the tentacles of an octopus, bringing on a defused calm, but the warmth only lasted for a short time before the reality of his miserable life reared its ugliness. His only other pleasure was the magazines. He pulled out his favourite, an old one called Bountiful Beautiful Babes and it always fell open to the centrefold, a big, beautiful blond girl with dark hair ... down there in the nether region. His mind quickly returned to the case. *Those bloody cops.* Why did they pinch his computer? It was clean, he knew it was. *It was new for God's sake! At least that will clear me once and for all. The running gear of computer was new! Fucking bastards.*

Just then he experienced a flash and a then a blur of colour zipped by the old, colonial, cobwebbed window. By the time Colin realised it was a surf shirt and who it belonged to, he felt the presence of the arrogant, big nosed cop making his way through the maze. In seconds the cop was standing alongside looking down at the open magazine on the bench. The policeman winked at him. It was then Colin noticed the chunky female cop framed in the doorway.

Silence reigned for what could have been a full minute. Police Officer Diplock moved forward with a fixed stare on Colin and said, as if disgusted, 'Mr Thistleton, please stand up. I'm arresting you for possession of explicit child pornography.' She read him his rights. 'Come on, up sport! And turn around.'

She stepped quickly and spun him around, pushed him against the bench with a rigid upper thigh and then a nudge of her shoulder rendered Colin helpless. She roughly, but expertly, secured handcuffs.

Colin's eyes almost rolled back inside his head. The level of shock was apparent, and he was unable to speak.

Colin recovered enough to say, 'What? What child pornography? These magazines are … the girls aren't childr…?'

'Stop crapping on, we found the files on your computer, you didn't do a very good job of wiping them, did you *Mister* Thistleton,' snapped Lerlene. 'Also your school computer.'

Colin just shook his head in disbelief; resignation, defeat and bewilderment hovered heavily as he was led away. He blinked and continued to shake his head as if in a trance.

Fitzy stood at the bench while the others looked around. He was not very confident about much to do with the case. Maybe the child porn charge, maybe, he still was not convinced. But, who put the porn on his computer? Regarding the attempted abduction his nose told him Colin really was not the type. There were two key things he thought gave the investigation, what he termed, jelly legs. One - unreliable witnesses almost all, and two – plenty of soft circumstantial evidence but nothing solid. He conceded, the arrows pointed at Colin but deep down he felt they needed at least one solid piece of the jigsaw to nail Colin for good, if in fact he was their man.

Fitzy wore a forced smile and he figured it was just as well, Lerlene was the senior officer; it was her decision, not his. He was uncertain, and he did try to make a point with her, doing his best not to preach, if he had been in charge, he would have wanted something more, in fact a lot more solid evidence before arresting anyone.

Fitzy made a conscious effort of inclining his head and looking at her just before the arrest. He made his gaze harden towards her. She was his partner. Yes, he was mindful she was now in charge of a case he was quite capable of running himself. It was important to him to make sure *she* made the decision. *Are you sure about this?* She definitely gave an affirmative nod.

Fitzy couldn't shake it, he scrolled the information again through his thought process; Colin was a wreck of a human being, a depressed alcoholic with many problems, but a paedophile? Maybe, maybe not, but the computer? Did someone else have access to it? Who? Surely not Gretel? No, no way. What about visitors? Was he working with anyone else? And his daughter, no she was only a child herself. But the hard drive was supposed to be new. He sat in the back with Colin reviewing the information in his head.

The sour, wet dog smell of fear emanated from Colin who looked straight ahead in a trance state. He hoped they could extract a confession out of him in the interrogation room, which would tidy it all up. Deep down though, Sergeant FitzMichael was not thoroughly satisfied.

They took Colin back to the Lutwyche Police Station, booked him and placed him in a holding cell.

Chapter 25

Fitzy went for a smoke and a chat with Warren McTavish outside, overlooking the carpark, leaving Lerlene at her desk with a coffee and a pile of paperwork. She reflected on the scene at the Thistleton residence when they departed. They left Gretel standing in the driveway waving her arms, yelling and swearing.

Senior Sergeant Diplock had heard some women swear in her time as a police officer, and she knew she could go right off on the odd occasion herself, but this woman took some beating. Lerlene was astute enough to realise the woman was unstable and she decided to get one of the Liaison Officers to see if they could calm her down or make an assessment of the situation and offer some support. Twenty minutes later she poked her head outside.

'Right, gentlemen let's go. Time to gain some glory, eh?'

They discussed a few tactical points on the way to the interview room, but they agreed on no definite plan other than to pepper the suspect with questions. Being the senior officer, Lerlene Diplock would lead the interview, Fitzy to play bad cop and fire the odd question and McTavish to intimidate by his presence, standing at the door with arms folded.

The officers were trained to exploit the psychology behind the layout and condition of the room, as the rooms were much the same at each station. The interview rooms were grubby, almost airless and whatever air was left seemed to be saturated with fear, depression and the stink of sweat accumulated over many years. The cramped spaces were cold or hot, depending on the time of year and painted in a dull green or grey, and the chairs, at least the ones for the interviewee and legal counsel or guardian, were hard and straight backed. Some of those chairs were bolted to the floor for obvious reasons. Most police stations had slightly more comfortable chairs for the police and in some cases, swivel office chairs, sometimes an inch or two higher than the prisoner's chair. The rooms were designed by circumstance, as much as careful planning, to make the person interviewed feel as uncomfortable as possible. It was a way to use up old office furniture. Some rooms were almost sound proof but most were not and in some cases the police would leave the door open or slightly ajar so the prisoner could hear voices, sometimes angry and loud, doors banging, and other intermittent disturbances designed to upset the normal thought pattern. The tables were always solid and mostly screwed to the floor and provision made at certain locations for prisoners to be chained or cuffed, to the floor, chair or table, hands or feet, or both. Hard core prisoners sometimes become violent and there was provision to use a strait jacket system in exceptional circumstances.

They knew Colin Thistleton was certainly not a violent or troublesome person, in fact quite the opposite. He sat slumped, eyes fixed on the stainless steel table; head down with hands hanging either side almost as if he was trying to hold his body and soul together. His hair appeared as if it had taken on a shade of grey in the last few hours. Alongside him was his legal counsel, Barry Webster, known around the traps as the *Rash* because of his habit of standing close to whoever he was talking to. He was a slightly overweight man in a dark pinstripe suit, white shirt and a tie decorated with a history of TV dinners.

Senior Constable McTavish stood in the clichéd position, arms folded, just inside the door in full view of the accused. Lerlene introduced herself and the others in the room and repeated the charge for the benefit of the recording of the interview.

Fitzy glanced up at the new age video surveillance camera and scowled. He felt like giving it the finger.

She asked Colin Thistleton to acknowledge and confirm their presence. There was no response for a long moment until the lawyer nudged the prisoner. Colin lifted his head, glanced quickly around the room as if finally realising where he was. The reply took a second or two and was barely audible.

'What?'

The question was repeated and the lawyer, Barry Webster acknowledged them stating Colin was overwrought and if there was any badgering, he would call the interview off. He added, due to the prisoner's apparent condition, a doctor may have to be called.

Colin slowly, and with shaking hands, removed his wire rimmed glasses and stared through glassy eyes at a fixed spot on the wall between Fitzy and Lerlene.

'Mr Webster, I'm in charge of this interview, alright? You won't call anything off without my say so.' Before the lawyer could respond Lerlene continued. 'Now, Mr. Thistleton, tell us why you lied to us about all those photos on your computer?'

He began to gently sway in the seat, as if listening to classical music, a baby elephant swaying in depression and captivity. The expression on his face was as neutral as anyone could be. The lawyer nudged him.

'What?'

The question was repeated. Colin slowly looked around and the question again was repeated.

'I … they are not my photos, I didn't know they were there.'

Fitzy's stare bored into Colin's eyes. 'That's not good enough, Colin.'

'I …'

'Senior Sergeant, I think Mr Thistleton is trying to tell us they belong to his wife,' commented Fitzy sarcastically, still not breaking his stare.

Colin rubbed his eyes with the heels of his hands and then shook his head slowly. He appeared to be in a state of mild shock, not really understanding what was going on. Neither Fitzy nor Lerlene were prepared to acknowledge any psychological problems at this point but they were both aware things could go oblong if they ignored a prisoner's medical needs, especially with Barry Webster, the lawyer, who had a reputation for milking diminished responsibility cases.

'Well? You are going to have to talk to us sooner or later,' said Lerlene. She still looked at him with disdain, confident that he was guilty.

After a couple of strained minutes in semi-silence punctuated by noises down the corridor; a slamming door, a victimised cry and the clunk of metal, Colin appeared to gather his thoughts and the two police officers returned to some routine questions. The tactic was to try to put the accused at ease with some good cop, bad cop routine for a short while before going in hard again.

Lerlene's demeanour softened and Fitzy leaned back. She began with a series of questions about mundane things, family and school and Colin Thistleton relaxed a little. When they returned to the subject of the computer, he shook his head constantly and denied he was aware of any pornographic material.

Colin sighed and seemed to struggle for a second or two. 'Er ...the computer is new ... um the hard drive is ... and other components, not part of the memory, have been reconditioned or replaced, like a rebuild,' he said, 'er ... what more can I say?'

From then on his lawyer, Barry Webster, being the politically correct young lawyer he was, began interrupting and stating Colin was answering the questions to the best of his ability and was just repeating the truth. Further fruitful answers began to dry up.

Colin, with the backing of his lawyer, continued to deny any wrongdoing. The material on his computer was not his and he had no idea how the material came to be on the hard drive because it was a new hard drive. He claimed he never used the executive school computer system and did not even have a password to use that system. As far as the police knew this was most likely true because the school principal had confirmed that only the management team had access to the intranet password where the photos of children had appeared and only select staff had security clearance – which did not include Colin.

The person C whose digital initial appeared on the photos was cleared of any crime because they were of his own children. He was reprimanded for using the secure intranet school computer but that was irrelevant anyway to the investigation. The general school computer system, not the restricted executive system, access was available to all staff but there was no record of Colin using it anyway. Colin's home computer was clearly being used to store child pornography images and he had no explanation for this, only repeated denial.

As far as the police were concerned the key things from the interview were that Colin categorically denied trying to abduct or molest a child at the primary school and denied having put the child pornography images onto his hard drive.

~

'That went well,' said Fitzy pulling out a cigarette and putting it in his mouth.

Lerlene's look dared him to light up. He gave a wicked smile and put the cigarette in his top pocket.

She said, 'The little bastard seems to be pushing the sickness angle, pretending he's not with it. At least so far, the Rash has been co-operative. I did expect him to intervene and insist on Colin needing to be medically examined to determine fitness to be questioned and all the delaying tactics et-cet-er-ah. It would be a drag for us if he swung that argument. Either way Colin still has to answer our questions. We can let him stew for a while on the charge of pornographic material, I still feel very confident he's our man. He is the one who attempted to abduct Timothy Leak, but we might hold back on it because I'd like more evidence. I'm hopeful Thistleton will actually admit both crimes. Any thoughts?'

'Mmmm.'

He pulled the cigarette out and tapped the filter on the desk.

'Do you *really* want to know?'

'Yes, I wouldn't ask if I didn't.'

'I don't reckon he's the one. I just don't. It's a feeling, it's my nose.'

He tapped his nose. 'Fair enough, there is some weak circumstantial evidence, but it isn't solid enough. We know the hard drive is new, we have the packaging, it was supposedly vacuum sealed and seemingly only opened by the repairer. Gretel, is the only other person who could have fiddled with it, although there is the daughter – gets less likely as you go on, and aside from the fact Gretel's as mad as a hat-full of bum-holes, I'm certain she didn't add anything to the computer when they got it. Hazza checked with the supplier who gave him the packages the bits came in. All they do is receive parts sealed from the manufacturer, check to make sure they work and install them, like all spare parts places they order from overseas. Old hard drives are smashed with a hammer and recycled so we can't get hold of Colin's old one which could show incriminating evidence – if we had it which we don't. So, the evidence points to our Colzie-babe, no doubt, but it is not proof that he was involved in the abduction.'

'But he looks like a slimy little pedo, everything about him.'

'Looks can be deceiving, I mean those other high profile pedos, Captain Bubblebath, he was six foot or more, big gym-junky body, had a good straight job, all that, no-one ever suspected anything. And what about Fairy-foot Rogerson? He was a big bloke also, handsome, well dressed, sheilas threw themselves at him, but he was a kiddie bother…'

'*Stop* it, Fitzy. I take your point. Anyway, what about Colin attempting to grab Timothy?'

'What about it? Yes, Colin *is* in the firing line, I have to go along with that. If he is a pedo, meaning the stuff on his computer is his then he has motive and plenty of opportunity with all those children around – all ages but it just seems too neat. We haven't been able to come up with much information to prove anything; I mean we haven't proven the pen belongs to him for instance, we don't even know if the pen with CAT on it is relevant in anyway at all.'

He opened his hands and shrugged in a questioning manner.

'His wife didn't recognise it and I am certain she would have if it was his. Granted, it's pretty hard to convincingly deny a mountain of kiddie filth on your own computer though, but once again … he has glossy mags of nude women, and nude men associated with nude women for that matter, but nothing with children in any of the magazines we've found, at least so far. All the mags he's got are on the counter for over eighteen-year olds throughout our wonderful, liberal land … it does not prove he is a kiddie tamperer …'

'That'll do thanks Fitzy.'

She continued, trying to push her case. 'The time lapses could have given him time to carry out the crime, I mean he could have had more time than we think.'

'Well, yeah maybe but what was his plan if it was him? The car park is like a fish bowl, in full view of the admin block and from what I've seen, always someone going in or out. We haven't been able to establish there was a vehicle parked in the cul de sac – it is hard to prove either way cos a car could have been parked there and no one would notice. Then he would have to go missing from work, although granted it could have been longer than we think … but then he would have had to bundle the child into the car, or the boot, and drive away and the child, as far as we know, did not go willingly. So whoever it was would also have to deal with a protesting child. There is always the possibility Colin had an accomplice, but I don't buy it, there is no evidence whatsoever to indicate that. I mean we've spoken to his neighbours, his few friends – he's very much a loner – a brother as well, and nothing indicates paedophile tendencies. Except what's on his computer and as I said, it just seems too neat.'

Lerlene sighed. 'I'm getting a coffee, want one? That doesn't mean it will become a regular thing.'

'Yes, thank you. I'll be back in a mo.' A cigarette was already in his mouth.

~

'Okay Fitzy, change of tack, what's the drum on the Orchid case?'

'Seems as if none of the two investigating officers, er Brookes and Kaplan, did anything more than fill out a crime report for each and speak briefly to the victims. I've spoken to both of them, meaning Brookes and Kaplan and it seems I'll have to start at the beginning. So, I might check the orchid lovers and see if any pattern emerges. What are you smiling at? Did I say something funny?'

'No, not really.' She smiled again.

'Hey what is this?'

'So, it is true, eh?'

'Is what true?' he replied quickly, perhaps a little more sharply than he intended. Fitzy was not good at the games some people played.

'Story has it you and Kappo are, you know, sort of …'

'What? You have got to be kidding!'

Fitzy went as red as the watermelons on his print shirt.

She smiled even more. 'You're not much of a detective, Fitzy; you just gave yourself away, matey boy.'

'We just … it was a business meeting, I just happened to … you know bump into her at the pub and we had to talk business, that's all.'

'Yeah sure, Fitzy.'

She turned back to her paperwork. Silence reined for a moment and then she burst out laughing.

'Fuck' he said and walked out feeling like he wanted to kick a door.

'Arseholes,' he whispered, close to a spit.

There were no secrets at Lutwyche Police Station. Who was the mongrel who dobbed him in? And he was not even doing anything anyway and he may never get the chance. Hell, what if she started it? Oh no, and what if Kappo thought it was him? He really did feel like clouting someone just to release the tension. Maybe it was time to go to Basher's Gym again and have a go at Fridge.

Chapter 26

'Mrs Winston, did anyone know you were going on holidays?' Fitzy took a sip of tea from a delicate china cup with roses on it, and flipped open his notebook. Silently, in his head he struggled to pronounce the name of the orchid, Bulbophyllum Longisepelum. He decided to not bother in case he looked like a goose.

She patted her greying hair which was immaculately set. 'Well, my family knew, and my husband of course, my next-door neighbours, they collect the mail when we are away. You don't think …?'

'Are any of them orchid enthusiasts?'

'No, I've been trying for years to get both Belle and Joy and their husbands to get into it but, no. As far as I know there is no one else in the street I know of either.'

'It says here the value in the retail market is about one hundred dollars?'

'Yes, give or take but on its own it would be difficult to sell and doubtful if you would get a good price. But, sold in a collection of similar valued orchids, well it could be an awful lot of money, I mean if the collection was extensive, I mean. Collections are always saleable, especially to beginners. Biscuit? Scotch Fingers, my favourite.'

Fitzy took one and they continued to chat. She was a talker but very informative as well, rather than just a person who loved to talk for the sake of it. He needed to understand as much as possible about the finer points of orchid collecting. When to prune, potting mixes, weather tolerance and more. He figured he may as well be comfortable and load up the background. At least he gleaned the fact orchids should not be overwatered and there were some varieties that were difficult to propagate.

~

The interviews of the first seven thefts expanded in a similar fashion. One thing was clear; these orchid collectors were single-mindedly enthusiastic to the point of almost fanaticism. He still struggled to find a pattern although he kept in mind the thefts seemed regular, roughly once a month so far, the victims had probably been in an orchid society or group or association, they all seemed respectable and almost crazy about the hobby. He had seen their faces light up. Most were in their sixties or seventies and the orchids stolen were reasonably valuable but hardly worth the investigation the police had been forced to conduct. The type of orchids stolen from each place was of a different species which at least indicated to Fitzy whoever was stealing them was more than likely putting a collection together.

He wanted to speak with Pauline Kaplan about the case but was apprehensive, given the rumour mill grinding away at Lutwyche Police Station. He decided to go back and practice some Googling again and try to find out more information on orchids, orchid societies, prices and associated things. So far it was not driving him mad but he could see the case had the potential to do that.

When confronted with an unusual case Fitzy liked to work through whatever information was available and try to pick out a pattern, amass the information, compile the facts. He wondered about the regularity of the thefts and tried to structure it all into some sort of sequence. The thefts had probably been from someone in an orchid club but he should investigate to be sure this was the case. He was convinced it was by the one person but that was speculation. Two orchid organisations existed north of the Brisbane River, not all within his police area but in three police districts. He was not sure why but orders from high up requested the Lutwyche police handle it. Maybe the brass figured it was best for one department to deal with it for ease of centralising the information. Possibly the other police districts did not want to know about it because the case was undoubtedly minor. He figured that because two high ranking officers' wives were orchid lovers, the case was thrown in their direction. Fitzy was still of the opinion they, the police, should put the matter on hold until such time as something substantial happened.

As he sat in the car he rifled through the file and after a moment or two lit up a cigarette and looked along the street at the old, timber Queenslander buildings lined up in parade-ground order, wooden steps going up to ornate lattice front door alcoves, all similar, neat but not exactly the same. *Fitzy, old mate, there's a pattern there. What was the pattern with the orchids? Maybe there was not one.*

When he arrived back at the office there was a message on his desk. *Urgent - Please ring Kappo*, in Lerlene's writing.

'Bugger,' he mumbled, 'this better not be a setup.'

Just then Lerlene walked in.

'What's this?' he said holding up the note. 'Why didn't she ring me on my mobile?'

'Search me. Maybe she didn't have your number. I don't think they have been issued with new mobile phones yet and, anyway, I don't know.'

Fitzy was still wary, thinking of the rumour mill and the possibility it might be a trap.

'What was it about?'

'Well, she said there has been another orchid theft …'

Fitzy did not hear the rest, all he could say was, 'Has to be a pattern …'

'Pattern?' replied Lerlene dropping heavily into her office chair.

'Yeah, orchids being stolen regularly, once a month or thereabouts. Ah, maybe not. Just thinking out loud.'

He picked up his mobile, looked at Lerlene and walked out the back, lighting a smoke on the way. If there was going to be a trick with the phone call, he wanted to be in control.

'Ah, Fitzy, hey, did you mouth off about us being an item?' Right to the point. He could feel slight tension through the connection.

'In a word, no.'

'Well someone did. We are not an item.'

He had the distinct impression she wanted him to wear it even though he'd denied it.

'Pauline, I did not say anything, alright? But I can tell you when

I find out the joker who started the rumour, I'm going to knock his block off.'

'Are you sure you …?'

He butted in with a sarcastic edge, 'Okay, okay, I told everyone in the staff room and then I wrote it up on the white board to make sure everyone knew.' He took a quick drag. *We are not an item.*

'Are you angry with me?' Sounded like she almost pouted, a quick change of attitude. He could picture her lips near the mouthpiece. 'Why would I be angry with you, you just more or less accused me of spreading a rumour, something I didn't bloody well do,' he quipped sharply.

'Oh. I didn't …'

He took a deep breath and softened slightly, time to change the subject.

'Forget it. Right, so there has been another heist, eh?'

'Yeah, but this one is out of our area too, Greenslopes, south of the city.'

'Okay then we'd better go and speak to the victim; if we can call her a victim.'

'Well it isn't a her, it's a he, but yes. I've been seconded to assist where necessary. I spoke to the bloke, a …' He heard the rustle of papers, 'a Mr Tony Vanero about an hour ago so we should go now. Fitzy, I … I didn't mean it to come out the way it did, you know … someone saw us and made an assumption.'

'I wonder who that someone was,' he said without emotion. 'When I find the bastard I'll …'

Chapter 27

Fitzy slumped into the passenger seat of the police issue Commodore and glanced at Constable Kaplin. She looked completely different in uniform; most of her red hair was crammed inside her peaked cap with a substantial ponytail plaited through the back. She sported no jewellery other than tiny gold sleeper rings through each ear. Her almost Roy Orbison, black rimmed glasses made her look studious and straight.

He felt ready for a strangeness to exist between them, at least initially.

'Right, constable, let's hit the tarmac,' he said buckling up. 'What do you know about this theft?'

'Mr Vanero said he and his wife were away for a few days down the Gold Coast and arrived back yesterday. He went to adjust the irrigation because it has been dry lately, as you would know, and that's when he noticed the orchid was missing. Anyway, we can talk him through it. By the way, Fitzy, why did you look up at the building before you got in?'

'Look up? Did I?'

He smiled, noting she wore little makeup, a smear of eye shadow, maybe a wipe of pale lipstick.

'Well my friend, someone cranked up the rumour about us and I just wanted to make sure everyone in admin weren't sharing binoculars checking us out.'

'Er ... what do you mean?' she said looking over the top of her glasses.

'Let's just say I don't want to be the centre of entertainment for some dickheads who think it's funny to start a rumour. Anyway, what do you know about it?'

'Nothing. June Mayall, she's a new trainee, whispered it to me when I arrived at work first thing. I asked who told her and she just smiled.'

'What did she say?'

'Just that someone saw us drinking together at a table. I told her it was business, which was the end of it ... until ...' They slowed for road works. 'Later in the day Zubrenyck made some snide remark and a few people had a laugh ... bastards, anyway that's when I rang you. Sorry Fitzy, I didn't mean to accuse you of starting a ...'

Sure you didn't. 'Yeah, alright. Back to the case, constable. Was the stolen orchid of similar value?'

She seemed relieved. 'Yep, although this one is a fraction more expensive, or so the book of values says, and definitely rarer.'

When they stopped at traffic lights in the Valley, she flipped open a manila folder on the seat between them. He could see by the way she twisted her lips, pronouncing the botanical name was an effort.

'A Phalaenopsis Violacea, a real collectors' piece, so Mr Vanero said.'

Any animosity from earlier quickly dissipated and Fitzy wanted to put his hand on her leg. He remembered her bare legs from the other night that were now shrouded in police issue trousers.

'Have you any thoughts about who is doing this? I mean stealing orchids,' she added.

They crossed the Story Bridge over the muddy Brisbane River, winding its way in either direction. Fitzy brought his mind back to the job.

'Yes and no. It seems the thefts are happening approximately once a month, give or take. When I say give or take, I mean a week longer between two which means, in reality, it aint that regular but still I see it as a slight pattern in the absence of anything else. It involves two orchid organisations, approximately half the victims belong to each group but three other members belong to both groups. I'm going to check out the members one by one but focus on the punters holding dual membership first up. I have a couple of other things I may try if nothing sticks out soon.'

'What have you got in mind?'

'I've got a mate in Brizo in the Special Thefts Division; they handle artworks, antiques and valuable, collectable stuff that goes missing. Problem is, so far these orchid thefts amount to bugger all when you consider antiques and things of that nature are worth tens of thousands of bucks if not millions.'

She pursed her lips. 'Mmm, I see.' He looked sideways at her; she clearly felt his gaze. 'What?'

They pulled up at a neat old Queenslander with two bangalow palms either side of the gate and well-manicured tropical garden surrounds. An elaborate latticework entranceway fought off a prolific orange trumpet vine.

'Nothing. Let's get cracking.'

~

Tony Vanero was explaining, 'Phalaenopsis Violacea, a beautiful specimen, originates in Indonesia, Sumatra to be more specific. They range from purple, similar to those wisteria flowers on your snazzy shirt *and* those almost translucent looking violets, sergeant, through mauve right through to almost white with a delicate ...'

Fitzy was looking at Pauline and he was sure she was rolling her eyes behind her black rimmed glasses as Tony – he insisted they call him Tony, *everyone does, you know* – continued to do his heritage justice by speaking with his hands. The man was in his late sixties, short and wide with muscle gone to lumpy folds, with a great mop of grey, tumbling curls flopping around as he gesticulated. The top two buttons were undone on a pastel blue, short sleeved shirt and a light weight silver cross played hide and seek amongst the grey and black chest hair.

'Thanks Tony, that's great. I see you have security but are you certain it was switched on, sometimes people forget to ...' Fitzy performed some hand rolling to join in.

The interview continued and they would not have stayed but Tony insisted his special coffee was worth hanging around for because he was a trained barista. It seemed to Fitzy that Tony was more interested in keeping them there because he laid on the charm every time he looked at Pauline. Seemed he was more interested in her presence than his. Tony gave them a special lesson in coffee making and then showed them through his extensive nursery housing almost a hundred different bromeliads, as well as his enormous collection of orchids. Fitzy was glad of the Cooks Tour because it gave him a greater insight into the industry.

On the way back to the station both police officers agreed not much had evolved out of the discussion. It seemed the same pattern as before, people away for some reason or other and on return, discovering a semi-valuable orchid missing. Fitzy was hopeful something would come out of the names on the membership lists. They both agreed on the fact that people being absent and being part of an orchid society was indeed a loose pattern but so what?

Fitzy watched her as she drove. 'You drive well, constable.'

He wondered what it would be like to touch her slender neck.

She turned and gave him a sardonic smile. 'That's bullshit, Fitzy. How come I can tell you are leading up to something?'

'Ease up, I was just trying to be polite. Anyway, seeing as you asked, how about coming out for a drink and dinner with me tonight and really give those arseholes something to talk about, eh?'

She did not respond for a moment and Fitzy almost thought he had pushed things too far. He placed a cigarette in his mouth.

She burst into a chuckle. 'Don't give up, do you? Look, Fitzy, we are not an item, alright?'

He recovered. 'We don't have to be setting a wedding date and putting a deposit on a block of land. A drink then, not dinner, just a drink that's all.'

'Look, I'm sort of in the middle, well not the middle but in a ...'

'I see, you are involved with someone, right, why didn't you say so?'

He went to light up. Her earlier comment *we are not an item* sat up front in his mind.

'You're not supposed to smoke in the car, Fitzy.'

'Oh, sorry I spoke. Come on, Kappo, one drink, we strictly discuss the case – business - and you can go home to your floosy, okay? Done.'

'Not done at all, I didn't agree. It's complicated, alright? I'm trying to sort out things, you know. And he's not a floosy, we've been together for a while and well, hang on, why am I telling you all this?'

Fitzy leaned in. 'Beats me. Hey, how about this? Okay, okay we'll go to a pub I know, have a drink where no one will see us, how does that sound?' He added, 'and I'll forget you accused me of ...'

She glared at him and seemed to tense up. Silence hung for a few minutes.

She exhaled and gave a weak smile. 'Look, Fitzy, I'll say yes but it's strictly business and only one drink.'

Fitzy could not believe it. 'Very decisive, constable, you'll go places in the Queensland Police Service.' He went to pat her on the thigh but erred on the side of caution.

She sighed, 'Let's be clear, one drink and we are not an item, understood?'

'Clear as, clear as. And remember, not a bloody word to anyone.'

'Whatever you say, Fitzy, and I say the same to you. And, please put your cigarette away, if a member of the public sees you, they are sure to complain. I'm in uniform, you're not, alright?'

Chapter 28

'Gawd, that was fun,' proclaimed Acting Senior Sergeant Diplock dumping an armful of files on her desk.

'Say what?' Fitzy looked up and stretched.

'Just came from a meeting with Old TC, Super Jackson, our wonderful mate, in-bloody-spector Devious Devo Deaver and this stuck up whacker, a representative from the East Coast Orchid Society, *Mister* David Edgar.'

'Yeah, I can feel the joy emanating from you already.'

'I thought it was going to be a one on one, me and Old TC, for me to brief him on the Thistleton case.'

She sat down heavily and leaned back in her chair. Fitzy was about to make a crack about the one on one when Lerlene put up her index finger.

'Shut up, Fitzy. Anyway, I walk in and the three of them seem as if they are ready for me, I felt like a goat – a scapegoat was what I felt like, walking into a cage of bull terriers, all ready to tear me to shreds. Old TC starts nice enough by asking me about the progress on the Orchid case. I tell him what I know, stretch it out a bit and say we are working at it. Then bloody Devo says, beat this, "So you're saying you haven't made any headway in this matter? I gave you enough background to almost wind the case up." Old TC lets Devo take me down, says how he gave us a head start with good info and all the rest, and as professional officers, meaning you and me, we should have at least a few suspects in sight. And this *Mister* David Edgar who's some business big-wig and president of the East Coast Orchid Society starts going on about how the police are not taking the matter seriously. And I gathered Old TC and Jacko's wives have been cranking up the pressure on them so bloody Devo decides to transfer the blame on to me. Bugger.' She shook her head.

'I told you he was a cu....'

'Stop it Fitzy, you know I don't like that sort of language ... but ... yeah he is something bad ... worse than a bastard.' She gave a weak resigned smile and almost whispered in a faltered voice, 'You don't know what it was like for me in there. Devo didn't stick up for me.'

She turned away but not before Fitzy thought he saw the diamond glint of a tear in her eye. He let silence reign for a moment as she fiddled with papers on her desk, embarrassed by the show of what he knew she considered to be weakness.

All he could think of saying was, 'I'll fix the bastard.'

He was as embarrassed as her because a crying female was something he was unable to deal with.

She steeled up quickly. 'Please don't do anything, Fitzy, we just have to soldier on and after all, there's no room for my personal ... er weaknesses. We have a job to do. If I can't handle crud like that then I shouldn't be doing this job, right?'

He nodded. 'If you say so but as far as I'm concerned Devo is in my sights. Don't worry, when it happens, he won't know where it came from. I'm going out for a smoke and to show what a decent bloke I am, I'll bring you a lovely cup of mud from the café bar. Do you want sand and white death with that, boss?'

'Yep, milk and sugar, please, and um, thanks Fitzy.'

'I'm all heart, you know.'

When he returned she was all business.

'Okay, Fitzy, bombard me with rock hard facts about your adventure today. I hope you have a trailer load of information that will all but seal this damn Orchid case. We can talk about Thistleton later.'

'First, what we *have* got?' He outlined what was in the file so far, collating papers as he went. 'At least we have a substantial file, ha-bloody-ha.'

She asked, with a straight face if he had found out anything worthwhile from Constable Kaplan. Fitzy's mood changed and he stared at her, not sure if she was stirring him up.

She put up her hands like stop signs. 'Just asking, just asking, keep your shirt on.'

'Well, yes, I did as a matter of fact but there won't be any need for her to be on our payroll, at least at the moment, right?' He had already thought it through so as not to give the gossip mongers fuel.

'Will you be keeping her posted if anything comes up?'

He thought he saw a slight flickering at the edges of her mouth.

'Listen here, *Dippy*, cut the smart-arsing around, orright? Kappo and I are not a bloody item, get it?' His brow tightened.

'Just asking, as the senior officer and a friend, that's all and just because you're cheesed off, there is no need to call me Dippy. Remember what I said, I won't hesitate to report …'

'Have you found out who started the frigging rumour?'

'I haven't got time to chase up unimportant stuff like that, besides you never asked me to. Anyway, please tell me what you did today.'

Fitzy related the meeting with Tony Vanero and as he talked, made notes in the file.

They both agreed they were at a standstill but because the Thistleton case was, in Lerlene's words, all but sorted out, Fitzy was to work on the Orchid case and try to come up with something to report to the brass. They bantered ideas and suggestions and then moved on to the status of the Thistleton case.

Lerlene said, 'I've decided not to charge him with attempted abduction of a minor as yet, hoping when we speak to him again, he will admit to that particular crime.'

She made the point that as far as she was concerned, Colin could deny whatever he liked, the evidence was strong enough in relation to the pornographic material on his computer. Pornography of that degree and paedophilic material was clearly illegal and no lawyer would be able to argue otherwise. They both knew, of course, you got the law, not justice in most cases. Slick lawyers could put convincing arguments to judge and jury to secure pathetically insufficient punishment in the modern court. They drifted into whingeing to each other, the way frustrated police sometimes do, about how regularly the really bad criminals with the best lawyers managed to get off lightly in many cases.

'Anyway, are you sure about it?' said Fitzy, returning to her question about Thistleton admitting to the crime.

'There is no doubt in my mind at all. Why?'

'I feel it is my duty to say, in my humble opinion, Colzee-babe doesn't seem to fit the molester profile and the porn on his computer, hell, I don't know.' He paused. 'I have my doubts.'

'Don't worry your head about it, Fitzy, I'm the senior officer and as such, important decisions have to be made, you know that.' She winked at him.

'You're the boss, boss.' He turned and went on with his work.

Lerlene figured Fitzy might have been a little put out because he was not the one to make those decisions, not now anyway because she was, *indeed*, the senior officer.

She mused over the current situation. The decision to charge Colin Thistleton with the child pornography was a win for her because it added, and crossed off at the same time, one more paedophile from her Q-PED investigation. Although very happy with the results she was slightly depressed because now she was hardly in the Chief Superintendent's good books.

It was further disappointing that Old TC had been breathing down her neck in recent months summoning her to meaningless one on one meetings. She was keen on promotion but was not struck on his advances. Her policy was to keep well away from any relationship with anyone in the force. She once again fretted over the fact the all-male contingent in the Chief Superintendent's office dumped all the bricks in her lap. Further disappointment threatened to envelop her as Old TC let Inspector Deaver drop her like a sinker. She needed to harden up if she was going to survive in this job. She sighed, a heavy-duty sigh, full of frustration and tiredness.

'Fitzy? I'm going home; I've had a guts full of this place. Tomorrow I will try to get a one on one meeting with Old TC so I can bring him up to date with the Thistleton case.'

He turned to make a wise crack but decided on valour instead, or more truthfully, because she could have sunk the boot in about Kappo.

'I'm on my way, too.'

They walked out to the car park together.

Chapter 29

Pauline would not agree to be picked up, so Fitzy was forced to accept the fact that she was continuing with the playing hard to get strategy. He figured there was a good chance he could engineer their meeting beyond the one drink. As far as he was concerned, a little bit of alcohol helped people to relax.

Fitzy decided on the Breakfast Creek Hotel because it was not known as a police hang out and he was certain he would not bump into anyone he knew.

Fitzy arrived early so he would have a chance to watch her when she walked towards him. It was as much a police tactic as a male tactic, but it said much about him as it enabled him to check out the surrounds and people in it. He ordered a beer and wandered over in the direction of the pseudo plush seating arrangement in the lounge. To his surprise Pauline was sitting on a lounge chair, leaning back scanning a sheet of paper, but clearly looking past it in his direction. She was a cop, too. She wore a low-cut pink top, and one leg was crossed over the other with a red high heel dangling off the foot. Bright red lipstick complimented her hair and contrasted with her tight, light, skirt. By his male eye, she looked stunning and it took a moment to regain some composure.

'I'll be ...' he said to get past the time lapse before he could continue. 'Um ... there was no need to dress up; we're not going to a ball.'

'Ha-ha. Don't get too excited. I didn't dress up for you; I had to go to a Toastmasters meeting and give a speech - as if I was at a wedding.

I was a bridesmaid; how do I look?' She tilted her head to one side and pretended to shape her hair which was wound up with a plait on top.

'Well,' said Fitzy, 'you certainly don't look like a cop.'

Mild disappointment passed over him as he realised she did not dress up just for him. He thought he would voice it anyway.

She laughed. 'My speech went okay, in case you're asking.'

He smiled, 'Yes I was just about to enquire.'

She emptied her glass and held it out. 'Now, a drink, one only, Fitzy, I'll have a gin and tonic this time, thank you very much.'

Fitzy went to the bar, wondering if she was for real or just stirring him up. When he arrived back, she placed the sheet of paper into a file and closed it.

'Hey, where are your glasses?'

'Very perceptive, sergeant. I wear contact lenses when I'm not on duty, most of the time. I wear glasses when working in case some cretin throws something in my face or spits at me, you know. Right, my business is now out of the way – it's just some stuff I'm working on.' She indicated the file.

He placed the drink in front of her. She leant forward and he held her gaze. He fumbled out his cigarettes.

'I hope I haven't let you down, Kappo. I'm somewhat underdressed.'

He pointed to his neatly pressed surf shirt, jeans and Docs.

'Never mind, I didn't know I had to dress up until just before I left home. My friend who was picking me up sprung it on me, so I had to jump to it. Don't worry Fitzy, no one can see us and I'll be leaving soon anyway.'

He tried to suppress his disappointment at the thought she was leaving by looking around at the décor.

'Take your time with the drink. Er, do you come here often?' He reasoned she probably did not bring her car.

She laughed. 'Nice try and that's a bad cliché. No, do you? Right, come on, back to business. The Orchid case, right?'

'Suppose so.' He offered her a cigarette which she took.

They chewed over a few facts of the case but his heart was not in it. To his surprise she stood and suggested another drink which she insisted she paid for. They drifted off discussing the case and then had another drink. He wanted things to move forward, keep her there.

'Hey, I've got an idea. Why don't we go and have dinner at a Thai place I know in the Valley?'

'Gee, Fitzy, that's a great idea,' she said playfully but with a slight sarcastic edge, 'but I can't make it, I've got, you know, things to do.'

'You have to eat or you'll die,' he said as a last attempt, trying to wrestle back control of the situation.

She seemed to consider things for a moment.

'Okay, but just to eat and then we go our own ways, right?'

'Wouldn't have it any other way,' nodded Fitzy, holding her gaze which was easier because she was not wearing glasses. He stood up and stepped over to grab her hand and help her up. She allowed the gesture.

They drove in his car to the Wat Pak Thai restaurant in New Farm. When they arrived, he opened her door and tried to take her arm but she resisted for a moment, smiled, reconsidered and then slipped her arm into his as they walked the short distance to the restaurant. Her heels clicked on the concrete footpath.

Throughout dinner they chatted over the courses, several gin and tonics and a bottle of wine. When it was time to pay the bill, she insisted on going halves. Fitzy went along with it because it was clear she was not going to take no for an answer.

Walking back to the car he put his arm around her and she leant into him.

'My place?' he said. *Worth a try.* 'Er one drink?'

She took a few moments to answer. 'Righto, just one.'

He smiled at her.

~

Back at Fitzy's home unit they never made it to the bedroom. As soon as he opened the door, yanked the key out and elbowed it closed, she kicked off her red high heels, undid the buttons on her blouse and released the clips on the front of her bra. She turned. Her breasts hung freely almost in his face.

'What are you waiting for, Fitzy?'

She grabbed his belt and worried it undone, fly down and jeans on the floor in quick time with a certain amount of help from him but he was also busy clawing for her panties. There was no time for talk as far as either of them was concerned when he noticed she did not have any on.

In the meantime, their mouths and tongues searched frantically, nipping and sucking and devouring and it was fortunate there was a small antique vestry table in the hallway and even more fortunate there was no priceless vase displayed. Fitzy wrenched her dress up around her waist and his hands gripped her buttocks as they lost balance and slammed into the wall, with her almost sitting on the table. Instead of the antique vase, a turned, mango wood, fruit bowl about the size of a football toppled and hit the floor throwing all sorts of household odds and ends, including dried flowers and a banister brush, in every direction. It was doubtful either of them noticed anyway as, like a pair of animals, they pawed, grunted, gasped and panted, him urging, her almost screaming. They ended on the polished wood floor amongst the jumble of clothes and various household items, as well as a picture which had fallen off the wall.

Fitzy tried to be funny. 'Is *that* all there is?' He said, panting, barely able to talk.

She shrieked with laughter and said, 'Just as well we're not an item.'

Someone from next door thumped the wall. 'Hey, cut it out unless ya gunna invite me to join yas, eh?' Female laughter followed.

They looked at each other in the dim light from the street, flooding through the lounge window, and both burst out laughing. Then they went to bed. He only had red wine, whiskey and some Coca-Cola in the house so they made do and spent the rest of the night drinking and having sex. As the night wore on into early hours, the sex became less frantic.

She sat on the edge of the bed, dishevelled and looking very sexy, as far as Fitzy was concerned.

'Okay, Fitzy, I have to go. I can't wake up here and then go home, have to go now.'

'You mean *now* now?'

'Oh, well, in a minute then.'

Twenty minutes later she said again, 'I have to go, now, alright? Now as in right now.'

'I understand, officer, I'd hate to get arrested for disobeying the law. I'll get a taxi,' he said grabbing his phone, fully understanding their situation. She needed to go home to change anyway.

He drifted off to sleep, cocooned in her scent, dreaming and wondering if she had removed her panties earlier in the night. Just as well he was not aware of it at the restaurant or he would have had great difficulty eating his food.

Chapter 30

The next day, nursing a slight hangover, extremely sore and tired but well and truly on a high, Fitzy checked in with Acting Senior Sergeant Lerlene Diplock. No new information had been added to either case overnight.

'I wonder what you are smiling at, Fitzy. Good night last night?'

The smile left his face. His first thought was to wonder if someone had seen him and Constable Kaplin.

'Just asking after your welfare … as a friend, of course.'

'Why do you want to know?'

'No reason, it's just that you seem happy for a change. Usually in the morning it takes a while for you to, you know, warm up.'

'Well it just so happens I had a quiet night. Any other questions?'

'No, I guess not. I'm off to see some computer geeks and then an appointment with Old TC, to update him on all the Thistleton info. After all, I'm responsible to him and he, in actual fact, has the final say as to whether I charge Colin or not – for either charge. You're at the helm in this office now,' she said cheerily. 'Ooroo and wish me luck.'

'Good luck, sir lady dame.'

She poked her head back around the door jamb.

'Watch the smart-arse comments, Fitzy.'

~

Some people had hunches; when Fitzy had a hunch, his cop nose tweaked. He downloaded a list of libraries in the metropolitan area from the internet, proud of himself for developing the skills necessary to use what he still classified as an intimidating device. During the last 12 months he had attended half a dozen computer classes, because the police department insisted all staff understood how to use them, so he had a basic knowledge.

Harrison had conducted courses at various times to help those who experienced difficulty understanding the new way of doing things. The earlier computer models of the seventies and eighties were cumbersome but now in the late nineties computers were much more user friendly. In the initial stages, police officers often made statements like, *no way in the world am I ever going to use those bloody things.* It was the same mantra with mobile phones, but they at least were now being used more widely and most officers had been issued with one or were in the process.

All the orchid thefts occurred within a certain radius and only three libraries covered the area. He decided to include New Farm as well which was only just over the river. Sunnybank was the odd one out and there was a library at Sunnybank Hills.

He rang Pauline Kaplan's office on the off chance she would be able wrestle some time from her boss to devote to the Orchid case, but he was told she was working on a case on her way in. Fitzy thought he heard someone laugh in the background. He bet Pauline was sleeping off the rubble from the previous night as she had drunk more than him.

He booked out a vehicle, called into a bakery, grabbed a pie and take away coffee and went to the closest local library, which was at Hamilton. The young female librarian, called Cristina, impressed Fitzy. She had a radiant smile and told him it was no trouble to go and retrieve the books he requested. Unfortunately, there were 16 books on orchids, so he found a quiet table to sit and examine them. Exactly what he hoped to find, he was not sure, but his nose told him this was as good a place to start as any. He made bullet point notes and compared orchid names with the open police file.

After forty minutes nothing really stood out to him except the fact that only one book specialised in rare orchids. He returned to the counter and asked the friendly young librarian if he could have a look at the names of the people who borrowed the books. She fidgeted and could not meet his eye, clearly not wishing to refuse.

'Sorry to have to pull rank,' said Fitzy with a smile, trying to lighten the moment. He discretely held up his identification. 'Police,' he added. 'This is part of an investigation.'

'Mm, sorry, we are not allowed to hand out that sort of information …' He continued to stare at her.

'Maybe I could speak to your supervisor? I'm sure she will understand the circumstances.'

'Yeeesss, of course.'

Fitzy watched her walk away. He needed a smoke, his head felt heavy and it reminded him he should not mix beer with gin and tonic, and whiskey and red wine, for that matter.

'Yes, can I help you?' The strong, efficient stereotypical voice of a middle-aged librarian wrenched him out of blissful thoughts.

'Ah, yes, my name is …' and he discretely held up his identification and continued to explain his mission to the efficient looking woman.

She looked over the top of her wire-rimmed glasses. 'This is most unusual; we really need to get three signatures from responsible people before we can even proceed, you see, we have to be assured this information is not misused – confidentiality and so on – not suggesting you … anyway if you get my meaning.' She tilted her head to one side and her short straight grey hair hung vertically.

'I do understand but the easy way to do this is to allow me to look at the names, and I can assure you the information will be used confidentially if at all, or I will have to obtain a warrant, which will change the whole equation.' Fitzy raised his eyebrows, using all his charm.

'In what way?' Her reply was not rude or aggressive, just inquiring.

'Well,' said Fitzy leaning forward in a conspiratory fashion. 'If we go that way, it's a lot of mucking about, time spent organising it and some time before we get back here, several officers involved, results have to be assured, then you will have uniformed police crawling all over the place, doors locked, the public not admitted and probably staff asked to go home.'

She managed the smallest of smiles. 'One moment, please.'

She disappeared for about five minutes and returned with the record cards. 'We are transferring all our records to a digital form and in a couple of weeks I could have run you off a copy from the list. But, if you wish, provided you sign for it, I can put these cards on the photocopier and give you copies of the names.'

'That will do very nicely thank you.' Fitzy added, 'I will need to get names and addresses of these people.'

Her brow tightened. 'That is a different matter; there are hundreds of names ...'

'It's okay; I only need the names of people who have borrowed the books within the last year.' He leaned across the counter and pointed. 'See, with the first one only four people have taken the book out going 12 months back.'

She mused for a moment. 'It will take a while to ...'

'No worries,' said Fitzy, 'I can come back later today.'

~

Back at the station Fitzy scrolled his rolodex. 'G'day Bleary, Fitzy here.'

'Well I'll be stuffed. What the hell do you want? You must want something cos you wouldn't be ringing just to say g'day, now would ya?'

'I did say g'day if you paid attention, you dickhead. How're things?'

Sergeant Ted Bisleri from the Special Theft Division in Brisbane laughed uproariously. Fitzy held the phone away from his ear. They knew each other from training courses they attended as well as numerous nights on the town. He became known as Ted *Bleary* Bisleri because he often came into work looking worse for wear from a night out. Bisleri had an interest in antiques and paintings and his hobbies worked well for him as far as the force was concerned. After a short time in uniform he was seconded to the Special Thefts Division in a relief position and when a vacancy came up they grabbed him and made him a sergeant.

'Bloody hell Fitzy, you haven't improved your manners, eh. What can I do you for, you old bastard?'

Fitzy briefly outlined the Orchid case.

'No wuzzas, mate, I'll check it out and see if we can find anything that leaps out.'

Fitzy promised to send a list of names as soon as he could compile a mini-file.

'We must get together and have a few drinks, eh mate?' said Fitzy.

'Yeah, we must, maybe the weekend?'

'Yep, I'll give you a ring.' It then occurred to him he would rather be spending time with Kappo than downing schooners with Bleary. Better still, maybe he could do both.

~

When he returned to the library, Cristina made a bee line for him when he walked up to the counter. 'Here we are Inspector, copies as requested. I'll have to get you to sign here.'

'Thank you, Cristina. Sorry to disappoint you but I am a lowly sergeant, however I am flattered.' Fitzy was thinking ahead as he signed the form. 'Do you have a card in case I have to contact you at a later time?'

'Of course.' She leaned along the counter and pulled a card out of a display rack. 'There.'

'Thanks,' he said and gave her his best look.

'Sergeant, did you know you look just like, what's his name? Aha, that's it, Bryan Brown, a younger version though, you know, I mean, you look younger.'

'Yeah every now and again someone says that. Right, thanks for all your help. See you.'

He gave her a gentle salute with her card, an almost wink and walked out, shoulders squared inside his neatly pressed surf shirt.

Chapter 31

Fitzy laid out, on one side of his desk, the names from the library and on the other, the list of members' names from the orchid societies. Lerlene walked in.

'Before I get into all this,' he said pointing, 'how did you go with Old TC?'

'Phew. I should take up smoking again. I used my charm and he was happy enough about a result, or at least, half a result regarding the Thistleton case but he became a bit snappy about lack of progress in the Orchid case. He's clearly getting agro from his wife. Without showing my outrage about Devo's transfer of blame tactics, I tried to make my point. Either way, we need to get some mileage on the Orchid case. I have put in a request for more staff to assist both cases. I'm really up to here with all this Q-PED stuff that I am supposed to prioritise. Now, Sergeant Rodney FitzMichael, please tell me your, hopefully, good news.'

'Sit back and relax, I don't really have much but the car salesman in me tells me we are this far from something significant.' He indicated with thumb and forefinger and went on to explain.

'It sounds very much like typical car salesman talk, if you ask me.'

Fitzy made a point of saying he did not know if anything would come of it but he was hopeful a name might jump out. He intended to phone other libraries within coo-ee to see if they had any books on rare orchids.

'Long shot alright,' said Lerlene. 'If I was thieving orchids I would go on-line, but still, many wouldn't. Don't forget we can use Hazza to research any computer leads, also I have spoken to Meredith and she can help if we keep it under our hats about what she is actually doing for us. Anyhow, I'll leave you to it. I'm still putting evidence together for the Thistleton case as well. His lawyer is kicking tyres as expected. I'm going to schedule another interview with him. Are you in?'

'Yep, should be okay for it.'

'Righto, so plenty to do. Good hunting.' She picked up a heap of files and walked out.

~

Fitzy returned from the lunchroom with a coffee just as the desk phone rattled.

'G'day Fitzy, getting anywhere with the Orchid case?'

'Well, Devo, in three words, yes and no. Yes, I'm doing a lot of farting around trying to dig up something meaningful, and no, I really don't have any leads to speak of. How does that grab you, eh?'

'Bugger. The president of the East Coast Orchid Society was just on the phone. He's mouthing off about how we don't seem to be giving the case any priority. He also piddled in Old TC's ear as well and we're under the hammer to get a result.'

Fitzy noticed the *we* and thought he'd slot it in to use to his advantage later. 'I've got something to say to you, you cunt. If there is a repeat of what happened in the chief's office with you not standing up for Dippy and I find out you are shovelling blame onto her, or me, in the future, you will regret it. Get the picture, you bastard?'

Fitzy could feel Deaver's instant surprise and anger.

'Well fuck you, Fitzy, you have no right to speak to a senior officer in that fashion …'

'Well, you dickhead, I just fucking well did, you command zero respect from anyone in this station because you are a selfish, self-serving mongrel.'

Fitzy held the phone away from his face. He did not want the other man to hear him breathing heavily, nor did he want the other man to twig he was battling to hold his temper.

'Now listen here …'

'No, you listen here, let's cut the bullshit, Devo, I have virtually nothing to lose, I'm already in the bad books, but you? Well old mate you better watch your back.' He was about to say, 'Accidents happen'. Fitzy was glad no one else was nearby because he knew his face was almost crimson.

Silence reined for a long, boiling moment.

Fitzy took a deep breath. 'Now, *sir*, let's get back to the job we are paid to do and let's try to work together. Right, *sir*, we are understaffed to buggery here, aside from the attempted abduction case which threw up child pornography, Dippy is up to her you know what in the Q-PED backlog and all we can muster is skeleton help from two other officers, and it takes more time to fill out the frigging paperwork for their hours than it's worth, and they were not allowed to be used on this Orchid case. So far Kappo's boss has only allowed her to accompany me once to the most recent theft. She has her own work to do, as well as helping someone else who's short staffed.' Fitzy was calm enough now to not add that he had been working with her after hours, no overtime.

'Hey, *FitzMichael*, I heard you and Kappo are, you know ...'

Fitzy's temperature rose again and he waited a second before responding. 'Watch it Devo. No, we are not. Who told you?'

'Oh, it's like a grass fire around the place.'

'Christ. Anyway Devo, *sir*, if you want to get some mileage on this case you will have to give me an officer for at least half a day right now for starters and then ongoing.'

'It's going to be difficult but I'll see what I can do, alright and in the meantime, I want you to go and speak to this upper-class dickhead in the orchid society.' He recited some details over the phone.

'Just to recap, Devo, remember what I said about back-stabbing Dippy, or me, right? And if hear one peep of the Kappo rumour I'll come after you. Are we clear?'

'Ease up, Fitzy. One, I know fuck all about any rumour, two, I'm standing up for you guys, not back-stabbing youse, and, three, you stop talking to me like that or I'll have your nuts. I'll let this one go through to the keeper, just this once.'

Fitzy grunted, 'Get *fucked*, Devo,' emphasis on the middle word and slammed the phone down, ending the discussion. He went to the Gents, splashed water over his face and pressed his head against the cool of the mirror.

~

Later, Fitzy rang the number given and a woman who answered, 'Robinson's Global', introduced herself as Mr Edgar's personal secretary. She said he was busy right now but she would pass the message on. Fitzy hung up and clamped his hands around his ears and sighed.

'Hey, that looks like me, I do that,' said Acting Senior Sergeant Lerlene Diplock walking in, 'you look like how I feel about my work load at the moment. What's up?' She dumped what seemed like more files than she left with onto her desk.

He explained the heat coming from the brass up top to make some progress on the Orchid case. She groaned but picked up a bit when he said Deaver was trying to arrange for some help to come their way to assist with the ground work. He made no mention of his discussion with the inspector.

'Devo has given me the task of dealing with the president of the East Coast Orchid Society. I just rang his number, seems like he's some big shot in a multinational company. Probably the orchid society is a part time ego gig.'

~

Fitzy looked up from a rap on the door.

'Fitzy? It's me; I'm here to give yas some of my valuable assistance. Note, I get to wear civilian clothes, no uniform.'

'Brooksie? I suppose any help is better than nothing. You certainly look like a detective, that's for sure,' said Fitzy sarcastically, pointing to the other desk which was covered with files, piles of paper and the shared desktop computer.

At least Senior Constable Steve Brookes had as much information about the case as anyone and could be a help.

'Oi, Brooksie? No eating in here. The pie smells a bit like … never mind,' said Lerlene. 'You might break the chair. Be careful when you sit.'

Steve poked the rest of the pie into his mouth and made a big issue of sitting gently. The wooden chair creaked.

'Right, son, this is what I want you to do.' Fitzy explained where they were with the case and asked him to flick through the stuff on the desk and take the relevant files and find a quiet spot. There's a spare piece of desk next door and there is a phone point so grab a phone from Meredith and I want you to ring the other libraries and find out if they have any books on orchids, and then you and I will have a chat, work out a strategy and maybe then, if you are good boy, you can go on an outing.'

Brookes gave him the middle finger. 'If you say so, sir.'

~

By the end of the day Mr Edgar had not responded. Fitzy decided to push things along. He was not going to sit and wait for some big-shot to condescend to ring him when he felt like it.

'Ms Personal Secretary, it's Sergeant FitzMichael here again. I haven't heard from Mr Edgar.'

'Well, I gave him the message.'

'Well, how about buzzing him again, now, eh?' He was about to add, "I haven't got all day".

'Mr Edgar is a very busy man.'

'Well so am I,' quipped Fitzy. 'Would you please remind him that *he* rang us in the first place and requested some feedback regarding the orchid thefts? I need a complete list of the members of his organisation. It is extremely important. The list I have is not complete. So, I would appreciate some cooperation, thank you.'

'Yes, I will pass on the request, again.'

Fitzy thought the again part of the sentence was delivered with mild venom that he felt was often used when people were being recalcitrant.

He hung up. 'Dickheads,' he said.

Lerlene smiled at his colourful language as she walked out. 'I'm with Meredith if you want me. Q-PED responsibilities call again.'

Chapter 32

Fitzy decided to catch up on some of his other paperwork, mindful of the fact a larger percentage of his job was being taken up with mindless unnecessary forms and reports seemingly every week. Timesheets, legal reports, prisoner information – who's back in the jug, who's coming up for release from jail, revision of procedures updates and other probably necessary documents but tiresome just the same – *make sure all cups are washed after use with detergent to remove the chance of infections, tea towels to be used only once* – and so on. An hour later he went outside for a smoke before checking in with Steve Brookes.

Of the remaining three libraries, only two had books on rare orchids so Fitzy sent Steve Brookes to do his best to obtain the membership lists of the orchid societies and lists of the people who borrowed the books from the libraries. They both knew it was probably a waste of time, but he had to start somewhere. Lerlene's point about the use of the internet was hard to ignore. He asked Senior Constable Harrison if there was any way he could find out the names of people who hit the only website which gave a list of prices of the more valuable orchids. Harrison explained it was actually possible to do it, and if so, the result could just be email addresses or other site providers. Harrison explained that even if the provider was forced to give the details of the people who checked the site, there would be other legal hurdles to jump over for a myriad of reasons. Then to narrow down the time to do it all could easily takes weeks or months.

Harrison mentioned various devious ways to sneak confidential information but the conclusion they arrived at was to keep things as legal as possible for the moment. He suggested if they started the search from the other end, meaning, an email address or the hard drive of that computer, then there might be ways to circumvent the accepted protocol.

Fitzy was going to obtain whatever email details he could glean from members of orchid associations, and library borrowers, but he had learnt people often kept several email addresses. Clearly the police did not have the manpower to go confronting website and email provider companies.

'Well, Fitzy, there is a way. This website has a contact email address and we could find out the details of anyone who requested information over, say, the last six months. It wouldn't be too hard, but we'd need a subpoena.'

'How long would it take to do it?'

'First part, hours. Scrolling the net, not sure but a day, a couple of days. Second question re subpoena? You could use Devo's clout or even Old TC; they are the ones who are putting the pressure on you. I'd be glad to help, no one need know because I'm only approved to assist Lerlene with Q-PED and the Thistleton case in relation to computers. No cost either, I mean not even a carton, although ...'

Fitzy chuckled into the phone and his estimation of Harry Harrison went up several notches.

Harry went on. 'Then of course we have to use our powers to trace the email addresses to find a street address or phone number. Long shot at best but worth a go, I reckon. Hey, might it be possible to short circuit some of this by going through Investigative Priority Branch?'

'Yeah, sounds like an idea, I'll get right onto Devo and wise him up ready to get a subpoena or warrant, whatever is needed. Maybe you could start the ball rolling and put pressure on the website company who sell the expensive orchids.'

'Will do, Fitzy. Hey by the way, are you and Kappo, you know ... kind of ... you know ... sort of ...?'

'What? Where did you hear that?'

'A bit of rumour going around, that's all.'

'Fuck. Well, there is no truth in it and when I find the bastard who started it I'll belt the shit out of him, or her for that matter. Get it? And you can pass that around as more than a rumour, too.'

'Sorry, Fitzy, didn't mean to you know ...'

'Get back to the Orchid case, please, officer.' Fitzy hung up and swore. He rang Pauline's new mobile but it rang out.

Later, Fitzy and Steve Brookes commandeered the large table in the conference room and laid out all the lists. Brookes explained that from his contacts he'd had difficulties obtaining a full list from the East Coast Orchid Society because the president was loathe to include senior members and committee members.

It seemed almost all the members of the organisations had borrowed one of the books at one time or another. Tedious though it was, they made a new list with names in alphabetical order and the corresponding email addresses. Fitzy decided to focus on a dozen names, those who had borrowed all the books from one or another of the libraries and whose names had appeared more regularly than others for the moment.

Senior Constable Steve Brookes muffled through a mouthful of the remains of a slice of cheesecake. 'Be fhoub pfhep poo fee if ebby ob beese punpers bar ...'

'Why don't you stick more food in your cake hole?' He poked Brookes in his spongy gut with a ruler. 'Hell, you're a pig. Don't have a heart attack when you swallow now, will you? Gawd.' Fitzy shook his head and pretended to wipe spit from his face. 'Now what in the hell did you say?'

'Can't you understand the Queen's English?' said Brookes swallowing, 'what I said was, we should check to see if any of these punters are ... and I didn't get to finish 'cos you interrupted, but check to see if any of these are on the committees of the two orchid organisations.'

'Well, well,' said Fitzy, 'you are an extreme smart-arse. It was what I was about to do but, and there is a but, we still haven't got a complete list for the East Coast Orchid Society, see? That stuck up prick Mister bloody Edgar was supposed to ring me back.'

Fitzy's head hurt, a hangover was creeping in and lack of sleep had almost caught up, it was about knock off time so, time to go home. Still no answer on Pauline's phone.

Chapter 33

Next morning a bright-eyed Fitzy reviewed their minor cases and then went on to the Thistleton and the Orchid cases. When the hour seemed decent, he rang Edgar's number again. The personal secretary told him the great man was not in. Fitzy restated the importance of obtaining the list of senior and committee members and went so far as to tell her it was holding up his investigation. She said she had spoken to Mr Edgar the previous evening and the man was of the opinion the list in question was of a confidential nature and he was reluctant to release it to the police.

Fitzy grumbled a measured, 'I understand, even if it seems as if I don't,' and hung up.

Lerlene breezed in and picked up a pile of papers from her desk.

'What's up?'

He explained the situation with their case load and the lack of cooperation from Mr David Edgar. Before departing she suggested he contact Inspector Deaver to show they were doing their best on the case, but their resources were limited. Fitzy rang and informed Deaver of the lack of co-operation from Mr Edgar and the fact the man had not rang back after three requests. Fitzy took a quick trip to the lunch room, and with a cup of coffee in front of him, checked the details again of the nine names. A couple of minutes later his phone rang.

'What the hell are you playing at, FitzMichael?'

Fitzy knew the voice. He could almost see Old TC's chins wobbling with anger. He suspected what the call was about and had been expecting it but not for another couple of hours.

'Sir, I'm not sure I understand. What …?'

'Don't fuck me about, FitzMichael. I just received a call from a very angry prominent member of the public, David Edgar, who just happens to be a Justice of the Peace for MPs and who also happens to be the husband of a friend of my wife's.'

Fitzy also knew he was a member of the same service club as the Chief Superintendent.

'What is the problem, sir? I've tried to ring this person, three times as it happens, and he has not returned the calls.'

'He's extremely cross about the fact you keep pestering him for the names of some of the senior members of the society. What in the hell do you need those names for?'

Fitzy took a breath. 'Well sir, I'm trying to narrow down the names of people who have an interest in rare orchids …'

'Damn you, FitzMichael, these people are eminent pillars of society.'

In the limited space, Fitzy continued, '… and I need to know who is on the committees of the orchid associations to see who would have access to names and addresses of other members who have rare orchids.' He wanted to add it was basic police procedure. 'I'm sorry if I have upset anyone, sir but I need to get the list.'

Just then Brookes walked in carrying a paper bag in one hand and a sausage roll in-the-action of being crammed into his mouth with the other.

Fitzy made a wanking gesture with his hand as he pointed to his phone.

'Yes sir,' continued Fitzy as Brookes slumped down in Lerlene's seat. 'Yes, it would be much appreciated, thank you, sir, yes, I will sir.'

He replaced the receiver. 'Fuck, Old TC, he was just going crook at me for aggravating Mister-bloody-Egghead when all I was doing was trying to speak to the bastard. And I told the silly old prick that Edgar would not ring me back.'

Lerlene walked in. 'Hey, Brooksie, no eating in here and outa my seat, right? And Fitzy, language?'

'Sausage roll?' said Steve Brookes, 'I haven't taken a bite or anythink. There's two, just thinking of me mates. I et mine.'

'Oh, what the hell,' said Lerlene with mock horror.

Fitzy added, 'Ta mate, nice of you to think of your old mate *and* our commanding officer.'

'I'm a worthwhile addition to this almost famous unit. Anyway, let's get on with the show. Need I remind youse that I am a very busy man. I haven't been sitting on my hands; I managed to get them names, email and phone details of the committee members of ECOS, East Coast Orchid Society.'

'Well I'll be rooted; how did you swing that?'

'Well I got chatting to the president of the other group and he said, *yeah no worries, gottem all right here.* Couldn't believe it. So Fitzy, me old supervisory officer and long-time mate, let's do some checking and fuck Old TC and Edgar-egghead up the Khyber Pass in the process. Give us a hug, eh?'

'If you didn't stink so bad, I'd … no I wouldn't. Right have a look at this.' Fitzy turned and brought Lerlene up to date with the altercation with Old TC.

She said, 'Don't worry about him, I'll deal with it.'

She winked at Fitzy. He rolled his eyes and thought better of making some wise crack about her relationship with the Chief Superintendent.

~

Over the next hour Fitzy and Brookes collated information. Debate ensued as they narrowed down lists focussing on committee members, with the idea that at one time or another, those on the lists would have access to members' addresses. Now they had eight committee members who topped the list. Just as Brookes expressed the suggestion to buy something to eat from the canteen, Harrison rang.

'Fitzy, I have a mob of email addresses for you and it'd take forever to check them out. But I ran all of them through using sophisticated programmes and with help from a mate in Federals, AFP in Canberra, and our very own Investigative Priority Branch. I just picked out the email addresses on the lists you gave me. We just have to be a bit careful sharing some of this stuff, so it'd be best to route it through me if you send anything to anyone – send to me and I'll hide it deep, muddy the source and resend it, just to be sure. Seems like most of the email addresses showed up as inquiring about rare orchids but only two checked alongside the stolen orchids' names. I'll send it over.'

'Thanks, Hazza, you're management material, we'll talk soon.'

Chapter 34

Fitzy and Senior Constable Steve Brookes visited the top four people who were committee members and whose names appeared on Harrison's list. They were lucky, because being committee members of the orchid societies they all had addresses within greater Brisbane. Other possibilities included Gold and Sunshine Coasts, and Toowoomba.

Unfortunately, nothing of any significance led them to being any closer to finding the person or persons responsible for the thefts in question. Fitzy was beginning to feel somehow the whole investigation was steaming towards a dead end. He hoped to discover something, a word, a clue, an idea, an inconsistency, a name, anything that would help them. Fingerprints did not count, nor did witness statements because so far no one had seen anything, mainly because the thefts took place within a relatively long time frame, all the owners having been away for a length of time. He was still puzzled by the fact that the total value of the orchids was inconsequential in the scheme of things.

~

Early the next day Lerlene and Fitzy met with Colin Thistleton and his legal representative in an interview room. Colin's stay in remand had clearly not been kind to him. He had a prisoner's pallor and he looked thinner than the last meeting. He had been lucky, if it could be called that, by being held in isolation because of the child sex charge. It had been reported that he was unwell and an appointment with a medical professional had been scheduled for later in the day, which was why Lerlene wanted to get to him before the medical exam because she feared access to him later could be problematic.

His lawyer objected and pushed to delay the interview but Lerlene was insistent and it went ahead.

As it turned out, Colin answered questions put to him, but mainly with, no comment and even with a bit of Fitzy bullying about how child sex offenders were treated in jail and how they may be able to arrange a lighter sentence with protection, the interview was a waste of time.

Back at the office Fitzy spun around in his chair facing Senior Sergeant Diplock.

'Boss, I can't help thinking we've got the wrong man. Okay maybe for the stuff on his computer and that is a big maybe, but the attempted abduction of Timmy I just can't see. Are you still going to hold him?'

'Yep. We checked out the company who supplied the new hard drive and all the stuff they get comes in brand new, sealed in plastic.'

Fitzy rubbed his chin. 'Have our legal people looked at your, our case?'

She nodded.

'What was their take?'

'They reckon we've got a very good, not just good, chance of a conviction on the possession of child porn material.'

'Right then, so be it, I've got a few calls to make,' and Fitzy ambled out to fossick through lists.

Fitzy's level of frustration was reflected by the number of cigarettes he was smoking. He was finally able to contact Constable Kaplan and he sensed there was interest in getting together later in the week. She seemed to be guarded in the way she communicated but maybe that was because there were other people in the office around her. He would have liked to see her sooner, memories of their night together being the only thing keeping him from punching a wall. He knew he needed a few rounds swinging his boxing gloves after work.

~

Later in the day Lerlene ambled in to the spare room next door, coffee cup in hand. Everything had been pushed aside which gave them a desk top, and room for one chair only. Temporary only.

Fitzy said, 'It probably means very little but I put the words orchids and paedophilia together into the Q-PED search engine and got an interesting hit. Not sure if it's any value to us for our case but I've slotted it in. A bloke by the name of Godfrey Dalton Hughes was busted about five years ago in Sydney. He was a big orchid collector - as well as a collector of little boys and girls it appears. He jumped off the cliffs into Sydney Harbour on the day he managed to get bail; how he got bail is anyone's guess but he must have had friends in high places. There's very little factual stuff because he managed to destroy most records pertaining to what the police wanted to know. Might be handy extra info on your Q-PED records but I thought it worth mentioning. I'll email the details for your files.' Fitzy looked at her. 'Makes one wonder about friends in high places, doesn't it?'

'Certainly does,' she replied with a scrunched up face. 'Maybe some of those friends in high places helped him jump off the cliffs, never know.'

~

Later Fitzy returned from a smoke break when the phone rang.

'Fitzy, you might be interested in this,' said Harrison. 'There is an email address that seems to be identified as a regular for enquiries from an overseas company specialising in rare flowers and plants, not necessarily orchids. It just came up flagged when I used the program the Investigative Priority Branch boys let me use. The email address enquired about all the orchids, the names I mean, that were stolen, along with a few others, sure, but still, it could be worth a look. The programme is supposed to be confidential, so I have to be careful; the boys let me use the facilities with strict rules, nudge and a wink if you get my drift?'

'I'm all innocent and haven't heard a thing you've said.'

'Right, I'll email it to you straight away. I have a name and an address.'

~

'Hey Brooksie, have a gander at this. Hazza sent over this email address. Now, the email address doesn't ring a bell, but the street address does, *but* the resident's name doesn't. The name we have from what we dug up from the library and orchid associations' list is different.

'Listen to this, according to us we have a Mrs Betty Holdsworthy, she's the secretary and membership officer for ECOS, the East Coast Orchid Society, remember we already talked to her; she was the youngest person we met, not sure if it means anything. According to Hazza the email address he found is different and the owner of that address is Mr Gregory Hitchens.'

Brookes held up a sheet of paper and looked at it as if he was wearing bifocals.

'Maybe we should go and pay these people a visit? Her husband's name is Gregory ... er Holdsworthy, he's a member, too.'

Steve rubbed his chest, then burped. 'Ooops, 'scuse me, I'm not normally like th...'

Fitzy rubbed his nose. 'You're always like this, God Almighty, maybe you need to eat less. Now, I need to think about the best way to handle this. She showed us her greenhouse; she didn't seem concerned we might see something we shouldn't. Brooksie, run both their names through everything we have, right? Now git. I've got some stuff to do with the Thistleton case. Let's meet back here in a couple of hours.'

~

Fitzy was standing up stretching when the phone rang. It was Sergeant Ted Bisleri.

'G'day Bleary, what exciting stuff have you got for your old mate?'

'Not sure if this helps but I've come up with the name of someone who was convicted some twenty years ago for theft of some paintings, valuable ones. There was a Drysdale, several Stretton's and a Margaret Preston. Now, interestingly when they raided the place they were watching, his known city address, they found nothing suspicious there. But they discovered he owned another property near Toowoomba where they found a cache of rare plants, some orchids but bonsai mainly.'

'Name?'

'Gregory Goldsworth.'

Fitzy wrote down the address. 'Got to be him. I really do owe you a beer, Bleary. I'm pretty sure we might actually be getting somewhere with this Orchid case. I'm going to give Fridge a belting at the gym tonight after work but how do you feel about a few beers at the Brunswick later?'

'See you at the Brunzo, Fitzy, you're buying the first three rounds, right?'

'Ha-ha, piss off, Bleary.' He hung up.

Brookes walked in. 'Gregory Goldsworthy, that's his real n….'

Fitzy held up the sheet he had written the same name on. 'Gold lotto mate, bingo.'

'He's got a history of theft from day one. I checked through Deed Poll records with more than a little help from our central registry section, discovered he changed his name from Goldsworthy to Hitchens. He's used several aliases, including Goldsworth and it seems he could be our man, Holdsworthy. Lands and Property said he has a holding under an ambiguous company name at Esk, just up from the Sunshine Coast.'

'Great stuff, Brooksie. Seems as if we know where the info and addresses are coming from, the secretary of ECOS, Mrs Holdsworthy telling her husband, Mr Holdsworthy slash Goldsworthy, slash Goldsworth slash Hitchins all the details he needs to build up a lovely little collection. He's got a history of theft and hiding away in the country. We've got enough suspicious goings on to warrant a bit of a look around. Guess we're going for a drive tomorrow mate, right?'

'Sounds good to me, you'll have to clear it with my boss, though,' said Steve Brookes.

'Will do.'

~

Fitzy briefed Lerlene Diplock about the Orchid case. She was enthusiastic about the progress. They moved on to the Thistleton case and she informed him she had thought about it and was considering charging Colin the next day with the attempted abduction of the minor, Timothy Leak. In her opinion, the evidence was strong enough to defend in court and besides, she was absolutely convinced he was the person responsible.

'What do you reckon, Fitzy?'

'I told you what I thought. Have you got any more evidence?'

'Um, no, but I'm sure of this.'

'Look, Lerlene, you might think I'm opposing you because, you know, because you are the senior officer and you think I'm jealously dragging my boots because I didn't solve the case and I want to big note myself so I can be a senior sergeant again. The first part of that is not true but, yes, I do want my old rank back. Just the same, in my opinion the case has not been solved. If it were me I'd hold off a bit. Put the poor bloke out of his misery, stick with the possession of child porn charge if you have to, although you or we should investigate further. Get someone to try to find the old hard drive and interview the company who did the work on their computer, or something more. I was about to do that but the Esk thing cropped up. If you can't get someone to give them a visit I'll do it when I get back. I know it's unlikely to be them, they get the gear sealed, but, you never know. But we need to look further into that, I reckon. Actually, I'd release him under strict bail conditions until you are dead sure, he's not going anywhere, I mean look at him?'

'Well I *am* sure and I'm going to charge him with the abduction as well,' she said almost defiantly.

'Sorry to hear it but you have to go on your instincts, I know that.'

She continued to look at him.

He replied almost testily, 'What? Yes, alright I will back your decision, you do know that but I'm uneasy about it, okay. Anyway, you should try to get Old TC to actually make the decision, after all, he is your commanding officer. If things go jelly, best if he is the ringmaster. Would you at least consider that?'

'Yeah, okay, I get it. Thanks Fitzy.'

'Another thing to consider, we could do a line up, get the child to examine some faces, make a choice if he can, even though from what we are told he didn't actually get a good look at the perp. Can we deal with those things when I get back from Esk?'

She nodded. 'The kid would probably pick Brooksie again out of the line-up.'

He smiled.

She added, 'Anyway, his mother would object to a line up. How long will you be away?'

'Might just be one day but could be a couple of days. You've already got him nailed with possession of child pornography so a couple more days won't make any difference. Never know, something else could turn up. Although I still reckon you should let him go under strict conditions.'

'Yeah, yeah, got it. Pigs might fly, too. Old TC wants a result soon. Righto, good luck with your outing, looks like a good chance to, at the very least, get closer to the culprit in this Orchid case, if not actually nail the bastard. I'll sort out the warrant, keep me in the loop and tell Devo as little as possible so he doesn't ride up on his steed and claim glorious victory.'

'Understood,' said Fitzy smiling. Not long after he left for the gym.

Chapter 35

Early next morning Fitzy and Brookes wound their way through the lush, picturesque Brisbane Valley, recently gifted with good rains, up past Lake Wivenhoe towards the town of Esk.

Fitzy recalled thoughts of last evening, in the ring with Ron Bleeker. Fridge was not quite on his game and according to the strapper, Fitzy got the better of him on points. It made him feel buoyant as the last few days had been laced with negativity because of little or no progress on the Orchid case. A certain number of unnecessary requests by the lawyers on both sides of the Thistleton case had not helped.

Lerlene had been testy at times because the powers that be up the ladder had cranked up the pressure for more speed and results on setting up the Q-PED database to be user friendly. Some of the pressure was political as the government was keen to go to the coming election with the promise that much was being done to combat that dark part of humanity that seemed to be oozing into the modern world.

She was exhausted because of the volume of material involved with compiling usable data on paedophiles, not just in Queensland but Australia and worldwide. Setting it up was a new thing and lack of extra staff made it harder. The staff she had, with the exception of Harry Harrison, had limited computer skills, which did not help either. Meredith was handy but not an expert and she was only used intermittently.

After the satisfying boxing bout last night, Fitzy had been all set for a few drinks at the Hotel Brunswick. He rang Pauline Kaplan's number on an off chance of a get together, but it rang out.

Bisleri was already there, holding up the front bar, when he arrived and it was good because Fitzy did not want a late night, especially a long night on the drink. They had a few and then a counter meal and Fitzy begged off, explaining the case. His mate, although good naturedly mocking him, understood and Fitzy was in bed by 11pm wishing Pauline was in there with him.

~

The quaint little town of Esk loomed ahead and Steve Brookes said he was starving because he had only consumed two toasted cheese, ham and tomato sandwiches they picked up at a roadhouse on the outskirts of Brisbane. He insisted they stop at the Esk bakery because he'd heard they sold award winning pies. He went on to explain how the bakery won hands down for their chunky steak pies at the Kenilworth Show the year before. They were both dressed casually with loose fitting long sleeved shirts, Fitzy's being the loudest. The idea of the long sleeves was so they could hold their extendable tactical batons hidden up their sleeves if need be. Senior Constable Brookes was out of uniform so as not to arouse any suspicion. Unbeknown to them, two neatly dressed young men, with short haircuts, wearing aviator sunglasses, one of them decidedly tubby, sitting at an outside table, with a clean late model Commodore parked nearby, would scream, *cops* to every local who walked past.

They were blessed with an azure blue sky; sword stroke clouds decorated the horizon; perfect winter weather. They had coffee, pies and a cigarette and discussed tactics before going to the local police station. Fitzy had no way of knowing if Hitchens would be at home and if, in fact, the farm even belonged to him, and a good chance that they may find nothing. He knew there were always plenty of unknowns but as a police officer he had to always consider all options and punt for the worst.

Half an hour later they were sitting in the one-man police station and exchanging information. Fitzy knew the local officer, Senior Constable Adrian Halloran, known as "Wombat" Halloran because of his interest in rescuing wildlife hit by vehicles or from dog attack, and abused pets, horses and ponies. He was an imposing specimen, nearly two metres tall with wide shoulders and a trim waist and was very active at the local rugby league club. Halloran was known as an *old style* policeman, able to talk offenders down rather than jail them. He had been unpopular in suburban police stations because he was uncomfortable booking people for minor traffic infringements, preferring to give warnings and in some cases, most probably, a clip under the ear to young offenders. He was never able to satisfy his quota of traffic violations and, more than likely, it was the reason he was still a senior constable in a country location, not a senior sergeant or an inspector in the city. The result, being banished to a country station, seemed to sit comfortably with him.

The previous afternoon Fitzy briefed Halloran on the phone and arrangements were made to provide assistance if the need arose. Halloran was also a glider enthusiast and had badgered a friend to take him up for a spin in his Cessna just before dark that evening.

'There is an interesting structure south west of the house, about five hundred metres away. Two sides rusty tin, other two sides clear shade cloth or plastic corrugated, sort of translucent roof. Looks like a really old shed with the roof stoved in in places but on a swoop we figured it could easily be more. Could be legit, who knows, could be marra-joo-wahna too.' The big man chuckled.

'Still not enough for a warrant,' said Fitzy, 'but we're all set. We need more and I hope we can find something when we front up and snoop around.'

'Still wearin' them same surfy fella shirts, Fitzy? Didn't know they made long sleeve versions.'

Fitzy smiled and said, 'Well, old mate, ya learn something new each day, doncha?'

They all laughed. Fitzy went on to explain they did not expect trouble, but Halloran said he would be on standby in the office all morning ready to run and the police vehicle was equipped with riot gear in the boot. He had also organised two Motorcycle Traffic Division officers from the Sunshine Coast to rip up the range for a ride. They had already reported in and were on a patrol ride to Ravensbourne towards Toowoomba and on their way back.

~

With Fitzy behind the wheel, and Senior Constable Steve Brookes eating a sticky bun, they headed out of town on the Gatton - Esk Road to the address of their suspect, Gregory Hitchens. Green rolling hills indicated rich farming land and on most hillsides, clumps of trees sheltered cattle and the occasional horse. Occasionally a farm shed or dairy could be seen among a clump of gum trees.

About a kilometre out they pulled into an old quarry hidden from the road and surrounded by old Blackbutt gum trees. They checked handcuffs, prepared and holstered their Glocks and laid the batons on the seat for a quick grab. They both clipped their silver badges in their top pockets facing inwards so they would be easily accessible but would not drop out.

Steve Brookes leaned against the Commodore, arms folded.

'Did you ever find out who dobbed us in about the surveillance film in the interview room?'

Fitzy stopped what he was doing and stared. 'Nup. Why did you bring it up now? It pisses me off just thinking of it.'

Brookes was clearly talking about *the incident* when Fitzy was caught on surveillance camera smacking Roscoe across the back of the head.

'It pisses me off, too. It can only be one person I know of.'

'Who have you got in mind?' said Fitzy, eyes narrowing.

Steve Brookes opened the boot, loaded the shotgun, clicked the safety and wrapped it in a raincoat. 'I'd rather not say because …'

'Arr come on Brooksie, you wouldn't have brought it up if you didn't want to name the cunt. Who?'

'Who do *you* reckon?' He placed the shotgun on to the front floor.

'Not again, mate? Do we have to play 20 questions?' Fitzy's face became pink as his blood pressure rose.

'Well, it's really two bastards who are in the frame. Zubrenyck and devious Inspector-fucking-Deaver.'

'How so?' said Fitzy lighting up a cigarette, trying to contain his annoyance, not at Brookes but at the mention of the *incident*. He offered his packet to Brookes.

The Lutwyche Police Station was one of the workplaces selected to trial more modern technology in interview rooms and at key locations around the station. Some stations already had video equipment but the new cameras were higher tech with greater coverage and more sensitive audio facilities built in as well. The red light only came on when the camera sensed movement and it was common practice to stick a piece of Blu Tack over the light so the interviewee would not be aware it was on. They were to be installed in the interview rooms as well as front and rear entrance doors, carpark and other places where the public frequented. Interview rooms were previously equipped with audio tape recorders only.

'Well, mate, I found out both of them bastards were on duty in the surveillance room the morning we got busted so they musta seen what happened.'

Brookes explained. Senior Constable Warren McTavish, immediately after Fitzy left the interview room leaving Bagshaw with a sore head, realised the video camera had not been switched off. He immediately deleted the sequence and as far as he was concerned there was no evidence. He rang Steve Brookes, who at that stage was the relief desk sergeant in the main entrance area and told him. He then zipped down to the control room where an officer sat twenty four hours a day. No one was in the room so he quickly deleted the footage and left thinking that was it.

Meanwhile, acting Sergeant Brookes had five monitor screens on the desk nearby where he glanced from time to time. He had not seen the footage because he was at the counter dealing with a member of the public, so he immediately deleted it after McTavish rang.

Fitzy rubbed his chin. 'Is that fucking-well so? You sure? I was told no one was in the room at the time.'

'Yeah, that's what I was told, too. Wowzer went down there straight after the incident with Baggy and the control room was empty. He deleted it from what he thought was the master but obviously someone had already *taken* a copy. But, get this, bloody yesterday just before knock off I was given this fucked up office jockey job of counting all the waste paper bins, shredders, desks and office shit for the inventory. Beat that, talk about give a bloke a shitty job. Anyrate, I happened to be talking to one of the cleaners and ...'

'For fuck's sake, Brooksie get on with it!'

'Yeah, right anyrate, in general conversation it comes up, we're just, you know, bumping gums and he says he replaced the bins that day – and he knows it was that day – Thursday and he heard Devo and

Zubrenyck talking about it. It was almost 12 o'clock, I knew it was 12 also because I was just about to go to lunch – so was he. The cleaner kept his mouth shut, he's only a new bloke and didn't really …'

'I'll be rooted,' growled Fitzy and he kicked the front tyre, perhaps a bit too hard. 'Fuck!'

He remembered McTavish reportedly claimed, in his interview about *the incident* with Old TC, there was glitch in the tape. The Chief Superintendent reportedly laughed and said, *nice try, son*. McTavish received a reprimand with no record against his name. Brookes' claim fell on even deafer ears and he received a similar reprimand, but he was also told the chances of his step up the ladder to sergeant might be steeper than before. He didn't care anyway.

Fitzy perpetrated the crime. Fitzy knew he had to pay the price. He valued his mates for jeopardising their careers and closing ranks to get him off the hook.

Fitzy tried to be the voice of reason. 'Well, mate, we don't know for sure, but one thing is for certain, I'll find out one way or the other.'

Brookes looked hard at him. 'Don't do anythink silly, old mate, orright? At least not for the moment, eh?'

Fitzy managed a tight smile. 'You know me, mate, everything by the book. Now let's get on with the job in hand so Devo can take credit for our work, right?'

As they drove off, Fitzy reminded Steve to focus; the visit was a reconnaissance mission but firearms were involved and there was always a danger of things going wobbly, so they needed to stick to training procedure. Their mission was to speak to Mr Hitchens/Holdsworth to see if he could give them some background information on rare orchids. Fitzy had a series of questions and if satisfied they had something he would detain the man until Lerlene arrived with the warrant. The warrant could be pre-timed, meaning issued at 7.30 that morning rather than the actual time they found something.

Chapter 36

The non-descript, rusty farm gate displayed a sign, ***Greenfields Dairy - Trespassers will be prosecuted. Guard dogs patrol this area.*** A phone number followed, requesting visitors to ring and await instructions. Fortunately, the gate was not locked, otherwise they would have needed to cut the fencing wire and repair it on the way out and claim the gate was open when they arrived. Fitzy did not hesitate to employ white lies occasionally in the art of policing because they did not have enough evidence at this point to obtain a warrant. Private property was exactly that but if a gate was open, well …

'We aint scared a no dogs,' said Brookes in a battler's voice as he tapped his Glock.

They drove through the gate and Fitzy texted Lerlene, copied to Halloran. He did not want the warrant until he was sure, but he needed the infrastructure in place well beforehand. It was always possible there would be no evidence of stolen plants or other misdemeanours. Brookes had a new mobile as well and the contact numbers were ready on speed dial, in case …

In the distance was a dense patch of approximately an acre of trees with a few sheds and, Fitzy guessed, the farm house. They drove slowly over a pot-holed track, past dairy cows with big udders. Some looked up and fixed them with trusting eyes and no more than passing interest, chewing on their cuds, others continued to gnaw away at the green pasture.

When they turned a corner, the homestead complex became visible. Typical rusty farm machinery lay dying in waist high grass along the track but a selection of relatively new, obviously well maintained, machinery was parked in front of two large farm sheds. A person holding a mask and welding straddled a trailer draw bar at the furthest shed about 50 metres away. A block building with weeds growing high around it, obviously the dairy, became more visible the closer they drove.

'Dairy looks unused, I reckon,' said Steve, pointing, 'cows we saw probably belong to a neighbour.'

A smaller, double lock up garage with a roller door and the old, sprawling timber house made up the picture. The Queenslander looked as if it was in the process of being re-painted because tower scaffolding was constructed down one side and across the back.

'Can't see the shade house.' Fitzy sighed.

Steve looked over and pointed as the whole valley came into view. 'Hey, see down by the dam, d'rectly to the right, I reckon there's a chance.' A rusty old shed peeked through the camphor laurels. 'See, a clear corrugated roof. I think the sign about them dogs was frog shit, eh.'

Fitzy edged slowly, but with gentle purpose and engine at low revs, right up to the front steps of the house. A standard police method to make an unobtrusive presence. They pulled up alongside a utility with *Cooper's Painting* written on the door, and paint drums and other painting paraphernalia in the tray. Because their vehicle was quiet, it was only when they jumped out, four blue heeler dogs came flying out from under the house, barking furiously.

'Shit!' said Fitzy as one of the dogs came close and snapped at him.

Steve made a brave chuckling sound. 'Just ignore em,' mate', as he cooed to the other dog, 'Good boy, good boy.' The dog continued to bark and became more aggressive and two more joined in harassing the officer. 'There's a good b…'

'That worked well. We can't just shoot the bastards, can we?' said Fitzy, and with a calmness he did not feel, picked up a rock and pretended to throw it. He allowed his baton to slip into his other hand.

At that moment someone came out the front door and yelled, 'Shut up, dogs, *now!*'

Fitzy stepped forward, Steve Brookes stood just in front of the passenger door, baton dangling freely to show the person who spoke he was ready to bash the nearest dog.

'What can I do for you guys? This is private property, you know,' said the man, who looked to be in his early fifties, dressed in work shorts and a long sleeved, drill shirt covered in paint. The request was a balance between firmness and aggression. He couldn't have mistaken the two men confronting him to be anything other than police officers – almost obvious holstered firearms under their shirts and baton sticks dangling at their sides.

Fitzy nodded to Steve and they showed their badges.

'Queensland Police, sir. I'm Sergeant FitzMichael and this is Senior Constable Brookes.' Before he could continue the man interrupted.

'Well, like I said, what can I do for you?'

It was clear someone else or others were working inside the house. By then the dogs had retreated a few feet and Fitzy mounted the steps. One dog made a lunge. Fitzy took a swing at it with his baton.

'Piss off, Cobalt,' the man yelled. The dog backed off.

'Your name, sir?'

'Who wants to know? Alright, alright.' He held up his hands. 'Hitchens, Gregory Hitchens. What do you want?'

'We think you might be able to help us with something. It would be appreciated if you would chain your dogs up.' Fitzy lifted his shirt just enough to reveal the butt of his service firearm, Glock 22.

'Yeah, righto,' the man replied roughly. He picked up on the implications if he did not comply with the request. Sweat became obvious on his brow.

Fitzy nodded in the direction of Brookes, winked and said, 'The shed down there.'

The man turned to go under the house.

'No, sir take them to that shed down there. We don't want the dogs causing any problems for us, do we?' said Brookes, obviously on to the idea that they could check it out.

Brookes turned to follow the man who clicked the yelping dogs onto leads.

'No need for you to come,' said Hitchens, clearly uncomfortable about the police officer accompanying him.

'No problem, sir,' retorted Brookes.

They headed in the direction of the sheds.

Fitzy waited for about one minute; he knew the man was going to turn and check him out. Hitchens stopped, turned and stared, and then stormed off, yelling and waving his arms in the direction of the man with the welder. Fitzy locked the car, mindful of a loaded shotgun on the front floor. Then he went up the stairs, hand on holstered Glock, and walked into the house.

Renovation work was in progress and he could hear hammer noises towards the back. Drop-sheets and paint tins lined the passageway and a commercial radio fractured the air. Fitzy peered into the rooms as he walked down the passage, finding nothing but dust, paint fumes and pieces of timber with nails protruding.

In the kitchen, the last room along the passageway, a young man up a ladder with *Cooper's Painting* written on his tee shirt, turned.

'G'day, mate, you here to measure up?'

Fitzy held up his badge. 'No, police.'

The painter climbed down, placing the hammer on the floor but still holding a duster brush. 'Oh. What's … what's the problem? I'm just a lowly painter, mate, sorry I mean, sir.' He smiled and rolled his hands out as if to say, *see all this painting work I'm doing*, would prove he was a gentle, wonderful bloke.

'Maybe nothing. We'll start with your name?'

'Er … yeah … um Barry Cooper.'

Fitzy fired a few standard questions and when he asked about shade houses it seemed as if the person did not really know much about the place other than the painting job. Fitzy was convinced he was just working there. Just then, footsteps thudded along the passage towards him.

'Right, detective whoever you are, what's going on? Why are you here?' Hitchens stood, hands on hips and stared. A definite provocative gesture.

'Mr Hitchens, or do we call you Gregory Goldsworth, Goldsworthy, Holdsworth or how about Gregory Holdsworthy, which one is it?'

Fitzy saw Brookes hovering in the background, on the phone.

Hitchens blinked, sweat covered his face and continent maps stained under his armpits, more than likely not just from the exertion of walking down to the shed.

'What? Go back to work, Cooper,' he directed towards the painter. Obvious to Fitzy it was said to give him time to think.

'You heard me,' repeated Fitzy.

'It's not illegal to change your name. I did it by Deed Poll.'

'You changed from Goldsworthy to Hitchens legally but what about Holdsworthy and the others?'

'Umm, that's my partner's name, it aint illegal … it's just easier to …'

Fitzy kept up the stare; Hitchens broke it and looked around, for the first time, nervously. Fitzy did not care too much about the aliases, he figured it would sort itself out later, if need be.

Brookes, behind and out of view of Hitchens, made texting signs with his fingers and pointed down towards the outbuildings.

'Mr Hitchens, would you please step outside?'

Fitzy braced himself in case the man was going to do a runner but the presence of Brookes in the doorway negated that. They walked through to the back of the house.

'Is anyone else workin' here other than the bloke doin' the welding, and the painter in there?' enquired Brookes, leaning his weight against the wall and hitching up his trousers.

'What the fuck is this? You guys just can't come waltzing in here and start pushing people around.'

Brookes stepped forward in an intimidating way. Even though he was overweight, there was a fair bit of muscle there too.

'No, no-one else … I mean yes, they are the only ones here.'

Fitzy pointed towards a squatter's chair. 'Grab a seat and stay there.'

'Hey, look you can't just … have you got a warrant?'

'Sit.'

Fitzy and Brookes walked down to the corner of the verandah. Brooks leant in; Fitzy could smell stewy pie and tobacco on his breath.

'While he was chainin' the bloody dogs up I zips around the back of the small tool shed which opens into that there bigger shed and sticks me head into the lean-to. He called to me to keep me away from there but I was back at the front again before he knew it. I had my Glock unclipped and ready to draw because them dogs were still carrying on. He was having a time settling them down. Thought I mighta had to shoot one of the bastards. I don't think he knows if I actually saw anythink because of the dogs givin' him agro. Anyway mate, irrespective of what he's up to, we have probable cause. I caught a glimpse of about a dozen dope plants hangin' up in the corner and I'd bet there was more in the next section of shed; me eyes weren't used to the dark but it looked like hundreds hanging up, the smell of marijuana resin was pretty strong even though there was an exhaust fan in the roof.

'I took the initiative, *sir*,' he added, 'to ring Lerles and text the Wombat. Even if we find nothing else someone is gone for marijuana – more than personal use and even that is a fine if not jail.'

Fitzy smiled. Normally he would have been annoyed at someone taking the initiative but in this instance, he was glad because the warrant would be in the pipeline and Halloran would be almost on site.

'Well done, Brooksie, you might get a medal.'

'Ha-ha. And I got her to do a check on them vehicle regos and Cooperzie the painter as well. Now, I think we should keep ol' mate right there and one of us can have a wander …'

'I give the orders here, senior constable. Okay, we should keep ol' mate right there and one of us can have a wander around the place.'

'Smart arse. Just wait 'till I'm an inspector, Fitzy.'

Fitzy smiled. 'Did you notice any evidence of anyone else on the property other than Cooper and the welder?'

'Naaah. The welder probably didn't see us, we was hidden from his view most of the time and if he did there was no indication he gave a root.'

'I don't think Cooper's involved with anything, but we have his ute out the front and we'll formally question him later. How about you keep an eye on old mate here; don't say much to him, we'll keep the questions for when we get the warrant because legally we have to be careful snooping around. Right, I will scout around, okay?'

Chapter 37

Fitzy went out through the front door, telling Cooper to not leave the premises until further notice. The young man asked what was going on, but Fitzy declined any information. He seemed more worried about not getting paid rather than any criminal charges. The day was clear, and even though early winter, was moving towards hot and Fitzy grabbed a peaked cap from the car. The man, who was welding earlier, was in the big shed, most of his torso hidden under the gearbox of a backhoe.

Fitzy gently tapped the man's boot with his own. 'Hey mate? Got a minute?'

'Yep, what can I do you for?'

The welder was well rounded with a number one haircut and dressed in dirty drill overalls with no shirt underneath. Fitzy thought he looked like Curly from The Three Stooges.

'Police.' Fitzy pointed to his badge.

Curly glanced in all directions. 'Er ... umm what can I ...?'

Fitzy felt no aggression from the man, only nervousness. It was always best to let the nervous ones hang themselves.

'Do you know anything about illegal activities around here?' said Fitzy, staring straight at Curly who kept glancing everywhere else. A silence kept vigil for a long moment. 'Well?'

'Aah fuck! I told him not to involve me, I didn't have anything to do with it, and he jess said he'd give me some money jess to not see anything ...'

Fitzy smiled inwardly as Curly told him Hitchens had a huge greenhouse down by the creek with hundreds of marijuana plants and also a drying set-up in one of the smaller sheds.

He said in a wavering voice, 'I seen it by accident when I was cutting down two straight saplings to beef up the gantry here … to use to swing the motor out of that tractor there … heavy … see?' He pointed to a frame with a block and tackle hanging from the centre. 'The boss went crackers but eventually calmed down when he realised it was an accident I seen 'em. I mean I don't even smoke the stuff.'

Fitzy did not mention orchids; he wanted the warrant in his hands before he did a search that any politically correct lawyer worth his legal aid fee could deem as illegal.

Fitzy recorded Curly's driving licence number and other personal details and after assuring him the police would go easy on him for his cooperation, told him to keep busy and not to leave the property.

Formalities continued from there, Fitzy took a quick look through the door of the shed where the marijuana was stored but he did not enter. Once his eyes became used to the dark, he could see at least a dozen large marijuana plants hanging upside down. The wet, sticky, tarry smell of marijuana resin, hung like malt in a brewery in the confined space. He went back to the house just as Halloran arrived with two constables.

Fitzy found out Brookes had arranged for Halloran to bring a box of ham and cheese buns and coffee for everyone.

'Who's going to pay for this?'

'You, sir, but they are for everyone,' replied Brookes, stuffing his face with food.

'Might be an idea then to leave some for everyone, you guts.'

Five minutes later the two motorcycle police arrived, and they stood around talking and familiarising themselves with the situation.

Steve Brookes grabbed another bun and stood at the top of the steps in an intimidatory fashion, occasionally glancing at the owner who smoked continuously.

~

Half hour later Acting Senior Sergeant Lerlene Diplock, Senior Constable Warren McTavish and two more uniformed constables arrived armed with a warrant and in the vehicle behind was Sergeant Brian Bilton from the drug squad.

Bilton was a quiet, bordering on surly man, not over happy with Fitzy leading the investigation but with direction from Lerlene, conceded line of command. He made the point that because it was a drugs bust he should have been informed beforehand. Fitzy stressed that they were investigating the theft of orchids and drugs were not on their radar until a few hours ago, when indeed Bilton had previously been informed through Deaver. Although Fitzy and Brookes knew him they had not worked together and were aware he was a by the book police officer, and what was commonly referred to as a brown-noser – an obsequious person. Fitzy knew something was not right and realised he needed to be careful because Sergeant Bilton said he had received direction from Inspector Deaver to make a report directly back to him. Anything to do with Deaver had a reek to it as far as Fitzy was concerned. Fitzy's brain clicked into overdrive, wondering how the Inspector had managed to wangle a confidential report from a Drug Squad officer which should normally go directly to superintendent or higher. He further mused the point as to why he and Lerlene had been left out of the loop.

Lerlene's driver opened the boot of their vehicle and handed out Walkie-talkies. Fitzy told everyone to work in pairs, to report back to him, not Bilton and to not touch or remove anything until they had an overall appreciation of things. He also said that if any money was found it should be reported straight away, videotaped, and counted by three officers, one being a senior.

This little speech was for the benefit of everyone, but particularly Bilton because, although the Fitzgerald corruption enquiry had been and gone more than a decade earlier, police had to be careful to document details of money and drugs with accuracy. In years gone by, a certain amount, usually a large amount of marijuana would have disappeared and found its way back on to the street and, if a large amount of money had been discovered, most of it would have been trousered by officers all the way to the top.

Bilton wandered back to his car to change into overalls and boots. The others exchanged pleasantries which included wise cracks about Fitzy and Brookes' sightseeing trip and what dream jobs they had while others had to do real work.

They were sent to specific areas to comb. Fitzy, in private, quizzed Lerlene about Bilton and the report. She was not aware of the direction and was clearly annoyed. She had squared things with Old TC before speaking to Deaver and thought everything was sweet. Fitzy decided not to say anything more about it, but he called Bilton over to be witness to all procedures so they went up the steps and confronted the owner, Mr Hitchens.

Fitzy issued him with the warrant which included the correct date on it but no time. They were to charge him later when it was known the extent of his misdemeanours. The man just looked at it and sneered but leaned back in his cane chair and lit up another cigarette. It was obvious to Hitchens he had been caught with his hand in the safe and there did not seem much he could do about it. At least there and then. Fitzy figured the man would have access to a white shoe brigade legal representative, a slick lawyer.

The three senior officers then inspected the shade house which someone had obviously put a lot of work into aging everything and making it blend in with the surroundings to look like an innocent old tumbledown shed and their expectations were more than satisfied. Grass had been planted on part of the roof and camouflaged shade cloth had been draped cleverly around the place. Three hundred and sixteen almost mature marijuana plants, lined up like Afro soldiers on guard duty. In a separate section, with fans and climate control, a display of hundreds of orchids, which would amaze the most diligent of gardeners, lined the walls and hung from the roof. It was high tech with watering equipment, grow lights for dark days and a sophisticated ventilation and extraction system.

~

The exercise at the farm took time to sort out. Cooper and Curley were allowed to go after being interviewed. Both of their vehicle's plates had been run and the cars were systematically searched; nothing incriminating was found. Mr Gregory Hitchens was arrested, charged and escorted back to the Esk Police Station to be held in a cell until the following day when he would be taken to the Brisbane Watch House. Lerlene and Fitzy directed others to do the usual crime scene things;

photos were taken, measurements were made and details documented. They also checked stolen property manifests in case some items turned up. Overall, Fitzy was very happy with the result.

Sergeant Bilton sleeked around the place like a wet rat, took a few photos and then walked up to them. 'Will you send me a copy of your Form 19-Section A, plus the file?'

Fitzy's ego stepped in before Lerlene could speak. 'Yeah, Bilko, I suppose we could but how's about you give us a copy of your report first?'

Bilton looked at both of them and rubbed his chin. 'Sorry, mate, can't do it. This report is for Inspector Deaver, his eyes only, you know …,' said Bilton with hands splayed as if it was no big deal.

'No Bilko, *I don't know*, we are responsible to Old TC, not Devious Devo.'

'Look, Fitzy, you have to play the game. The orders are from up top, you know how it is …'

Lerlene Diplock was moving her head from side to side as if watching a tennis match. She was happy to let the boys widdle in the corners of the sand pit for a while.

Fitzy leaned in towards Bilko. 'No, old mate, I don't know *how it is* … alright?'

Acting Senior Sergeant Diplock noticed Fitzy had pinked up and a vein pulsed at his temple. She metaphorically stepped in.

'Righto, gentlemen, whether you like it or not, I'm the senior officer here.' She held up an index finger. 'Sergeant Bilton, this investigation is responsible directly to the Chief Super, like it or not. However, in the interests of harmony between areas of responsibility, I'd be happy to send you a copy of Form19-Section A but it has to be cleared by Old TC, okay? And, as far as the file is concerned, there is a lot of photocopying and it is not complete either – Meredith will be digitising it soon and would, I'm sure, make it available to you. In the meantime, you'll find Inspector Deaver has most of the documents contained in his paperwork anyway.'

Sergeant Bilton smiled in the way a rat would smile if it could be seen. 'I understand.' He tucked his clipboard under his arm and said, 'Right, I'll be off,' and he spun around and walked purposefully to his car, like a Gestapo officer.

Fitzy mumbled to Lerlene, 'We are going to hear more about this, I just know it.'

'No doubt about that but whatever way it goes we, or I, am directly responsible to Old TC and he has to back me on everything that went on here today – and with this investigation.'

'Well, Ms Diplock, I wouldn't count on it. How come Devo gets to direct the Drug Squad and can demand reports to go to him for his eyes only?'

'It could be all bullshit, I mean Bilko could just have been trying it on so he could cut and paste our report and ...'

'... and tell Old TC we copied his report? Yep, I can believe that, no worries, but I smell a nest of rodents and fucking Devo is King Rat.'

An hour later Fitzy was seeing off Lerlene. He leaned on the passenger's side windowsill of the Commodore.

'See, I told you if you stuck with me you'd be a hero, you might even be a senior sergeant without the acting bit, that is of course, if we clear up the Thistleton case.'

'Yes, well I might get a bouquet. You will get credit for all this, much as I hate to admit it. Anyway, there is still a bit to go before any of us get medals. Far as Thistleton goes, I'm still working on him. I've got to go back to the station and discuss all this with Old TC, much as I would like to celebrate with you jokers.'

He saw her off in the carpark, with a uniformed female constable driving, as clouds of green marijuana smoke drifted across the valley.

'Don't breathe too deeply, Fitzy,' she yelled out the window, laughing as she put her phone to her ear.

The department had recently decided to burn crops rather than hold them for evidence because marijuana went mouldy in plastic bags. On many previous occasions, police stations had reeked of cannabis resin to be followed later by the smell of rotting compost. Also, there were other problems, volume and security and then the job of lugging it to court. At least the latter had ceased years ago; photos and videos were sufficient as evidence these days. After all, large amounts of marijuana in evidence bags went missing. In South Australia the plant could be grown for personal use and a few plants were allowed and in other states small amounts were tolerated by the police but remained illegal. In Queensland, because of the hangover from the heady days of the notorious Licensing Branch, and the predominantly Christian National Party, marijuana was still considered to be a dangerous drug. The Goss Labour government had promised to decriminalise the drug for personal use but so far nothing had transpired.

Like many members of the public, some police secretly smoked the drug for recreational purposes and Fitzy knew of one or two. Therefore, prime, bulging, resin soaked heads were always a temptation for any person who used the drug. Fitzy did not use any drugs other than cigarettes, alcohol and coffee. He also didn't have a position on other officers partaking, he only cared about how the law was interpreted so he could police it, or do his best to. Weighing quantities, photographs and video evidence taken on site, and the incineration of the crop was now the accepted practice.

~

'Hey Fitzy, get a load of this.' Brookes grabbed the remote and turned up the television set above the bar where Inspector Eric Deaver's handsome, shiny face, and his well-groomed nine-hundred-dollar-suit and two-hundred-dollar tie - managed to make it seem like he did everything associated with solving the thefts of orchids as well as the massive drug bust.

'Arsehole,' chorused the two constables who had stayed behind to rotate shifts with two other officers keeping vigil at the property. A couple of locals whooped as well, enjoying the frivolity even though they had no idea what it was about. Inspector Deaver was unpopular among most officers who worked at the station.

The day had been exhausting and Brookes and Fitzy, after a few quiet drinks, went to bed early. The other two police officers rotated shifts at the property. They lit a fire to keep warm and sat in a couple of camp chairs to while away the night.

~

The next morning, they took more photos and tidied up the site where the plants had been burnt and generally made the place look as if nothing had happened. Everybody was most unhappy about Inspector

Deaver's apparent claiming of accolades, but they also realised it was par for the course in being a police officer, especially lower down the ranks. The people at the coalface did all the lugging and the brass creamed all the glory and won all the medals.

The rest of the police went back to Brisbane and Fitzy, Halloran and Brookes wound up the job over a cuppa and some custard tarts - most of which Brookes scoffed - swapping details and writing reports in the Esk Police Station.

Fitzy was well pleased with everyone and figured it could put him back on the path to senior sergeant again. There were plans to have a few at the Gordon Arms Hotel the following Saturday night as a celebration for work well done.

Chapter 38

Next day, back in the office at the Lutwyche Police Station, Fitzy was in early for a planned catch up with Lerlene. They squared up the reports and evidence for the Orchid case and the big marijuana bust, to present to Old TC at 9.30am.

~

'Seems like a job well done,' said the Chief Superintendent, 'you're lucky to have Inspector Deaver's input with the case. He had a hunch there would be drugs involved somewhere. 'Now,' said the big man, chins wobbling as he leaned forward, 'it has come to my attention you were not cooperative with the Drug Squad; have you anything to say about that?'

Lerlene silently cleared her throat and explained the matter as it had transpired. Fitzy noticed she omitted saying anything about the Form19-Section A and copies of the file to be handed on.

Old TC leaned back in his executive office chair. 'Sergeant Bilton, although junior to you, informed you a copy of your report and the file was to be given to him …'

Fitzy had taken about as much as he could stomach. 'With all due respect, Sir, Lerlene is responsible to you, I mean we were not given any advice we were to hand on, or give copies of, anything to anyone without your approval, also the file was still open, and Devo already has copies of most of the paperwork in the Orchid case anyway.'

'That will do, FitzMichael, it is *Inspector* Deaver to you.' Old TC glared. They were both aware there was a battle of wills going on and Fitzy decided he should back down in the interests of Lerlene and the section.

'I'm … er sorry sir, but … if *Inspector* Deaver had a hunch that there would be marijuana growing there, well then, why weren't we informed?' He went on, '*Deaver* seems to be taking all the credit for …'

'*That's enough!*' Those two words were only a couple of notches down from a shout. Almost a minute passed, Fitzy could feel Lerlene stirring. He was about to make an issue of why Deaver needed the report but decided it did not really matter in the overall scheme of things.

Old TC seemed to rein in his anger, sighed and continued. 'Fitzy, on another matter I need to remind you that you managed to upset Mr Edgar, you don't deal with people like him by pushing them around … He's on the panel that controls our extra funding as well as being our JP who signs off official documents.' His chins wobbled again, indicating impending anger.

Fitzy went red and leaned forward in his seat. '*Pushing them around?* We tried to obtain the list from him, and *you* as well sir, and as it turns out, his secretary, the secretary at his place of employment, did her level best to mess me around, under his explicit direction, in fact *hinder* the investig … never mind, anyway the secretary of the orchid society that *he* is president of, that secretary, Mrs Goldsworthy who was handing on confidential information to her husband, Mr Goldsworthy, read Hitchens, were responsible for the thefts.'

Old TC's eyebrows formed a grey-black railway line and his face was as rosy red as Fitzy's. The old man was just about to interject but Fitzy was committed to soldier on; it was not clear whether he knew he'd gone too far or he did not care, his anger carried him forward like a tidal wave.

'*The* thefts of the orchids that *Mister* David Edgar kept harassing us to investigate. *The* secretary and *her* partner, Sir, of the organisation that *he* is president of.'

Fitzy now knew he had gone too far. He could feel heat from Lerlene whose eyes were bulging and who he guessed was trying to stop herself from reprimanding him. Old TC locked Fitzy in another iron stare.

Fitzy's breathing moderated and he took a deep breath which indicated, *here goes.*

'Incidentally, Sir, *Inspector* Deaver was supposed to have used his influence to get that list as well, and you can guess the result there, zilch, so we reverted to other creative means and were able to come at it from another angle. I feel as if we have been disadvantaged by ...'

'*FitzMichael*, do you want to be washing police cars and getting the lunches in Charleville?' Old TC was leaning forward, too. 'You are an insolent bastard. *Christ Almighty.*'

Fitzy thought about making a crack about the Chief Superintendent's precious pillar-of-society mate, Mr fucking Edgar who could not organise the chops for a barby, in Fitzy's opinion, let alone a society with less than 50 members. He decided to shut up, in the interests of ... he was not sure what. He looked across at Lerlene who was staring at him and he was not sure if it was admiration for sticking it up the establishment, sticking up for her or placing her further in trouble, or concern for the future of both of them in the Queensland Police Service.

Old TC placed his hands on the desk, splayed fingers. He took several measured, deep breaths and exhaled loudly through his nose. His stare had the power to lock Fitzy in his seat. Then surprisingly he seemed to relax.

'Did we find out why this Hitchens character set up an almost worthless orchid stash at the same location as a marijuana crop?'

Lerlene nodded towards Fitzy, indicating he should take the question.

'Yeah, I was wondering why he was very defensive and bad tempered from the first minute we spoke to him at the farm. Later when I interviewed his partner, Mrs Goldsworthy, the secretary of ECOS, it became clear he was almost more cheesed off at being wrong and her being right than actually getting busted. She told him it was a bad idea at the start to have the orchids at the same place as the marijuana crop and it would bring them down. If they were caught with one crime they'd be done for both.'

'Did either of them say what his or their plan was for the orchids, I mean what was the motivation for collecting orchids that were not of high significant value?'

Fitzy rubbed his chin. 'She was more talkative than him when she realised what trouble she was in. She did her best trying to convince us it was all his idea etcetera. She said it was more of a passion of his rather than a money making venture at this point although she said they had intended to add to the collection, as we thought, by purchasing some extremely rare orchids once some money came in from the sale of marijuana. Also, the long range plan at a later time was to get some orchids that were difficult to propagate and secure, maybe steal, rare and expensive orchids. The idea was to set up a big state of the art orchid farm, propagation and distribution outlet down at the Gold Coast selling orchids on a world scale, you know, via online selling, all legal. It wouldn't surprise me if they had international contacts at the moment too, so we handed that info on to Customs and the Federal Police.' Fitzy rolled his hands. 'They were thinking big but ... early stages.' He splayed his hands.

'Right. Well done, you and Lerlene did a good job... and Fitzy? Don't spoil it, and just try to keep your nose clean, right? Now buzz off and Lerlene and I will go over the report and we can get it all finalised.'

'Umm, yes sir.' Fitzy glanced at Lerlene as he turned and walked out of the room.

An hour later, Lerlene arrived back at the office. The note on her desk said, *Gone to Basher's Gym to belt the shit out of Bleeker. Back at noon, Fitzy.* For a moment, she feared for the safety of his old mate and mentor, Fridge.

~

'Welcome home, Fitzy,' said Lerlene, stacking up the files in a neat pile. 'Did you hammer Fridge into the ground?'

'Ha ha. Yeah, had him on the ropes early but he managed to get a few lucky ones in to make it a draw.' He pointed to his left cheek which was pink and slightly swollen. They both laughed. Fitzy continued, 'How did it end up in the lion's den?'

'Well surprisingly Old TC calmed down a bit. You really got his blood pressure up though, eh?'

'Yeah, well I wasn't going to hang around and listen to him crapping on, especially about golden boy, *Inspector* fucking Devious. Look, Lerlene, I feel as if I don't have a great deal to lose. I don't give a fuck anymore.'

'Oh come on, Fitzy, that's not true, things will work out, just try to pull your head in a bit. The Deavers of the world come and go, you know that, soon he will be Chief Constable of Scotland Yard if he keeps at it. We know they promote the idiots and incompetents sideways or upwards, don't we?'

Lerlene ran through the details of her hour with the boss.

~

First up, they really did not have much evidence against Colin Thistleton and Old TC said they may have to let him go soon because the lawyer was kicking up a fuss about the lack of real evidence. Lerlene had two or three more days at most to get something solid. She tabled Fitzy's suggestion that they bail Colin but the Chief Super disagreed.

The Q-PED investigation data base was increasingly seen to be essential for the future. Old TC was in the process of prioritising the formation of the unit under the present name Q-PED. The positions would be advertised soon and he told her she was a shoe-in for heading the unit. He said the government was under constant pressure by the public and media to be seen to be doing something to negate the spread of online pornography, specifically child pornography. He explained to her, chins wobbling as he laughed sarcastically, the government knew there were votes to be had for caring or pretending to care about child protection. She was as aware as him the police were keen to take advantage of the extra funding because it was clear that computer crimes were the thing of the future. Just as she was wondering where Fitzy fitted in, he explained that Fitzy was still going to mark time with the Q-PED unit but at a later time would move on. At the moment *the incident* still hung over Fitzy.

She outlined to the Chief Superintendent several cases she had investigated, how dumb some people were, not properly deleting files, making no provision to wipe hard drives, boasting out there in the e-world about their disgusting exploits and often using their real details or pseudonyms that were easy to trace. They were both astute enough to realise the main paedophiles were always going to be hard to catch and as is the case with all the major criminals, the big shots almost always seemed to get away.

They returned to details of the Orchid case. Old TC again made a point of telling her how lucky she was to have Inspector Deaver oversighting the Orchid case. She rolled her eyes, looking up at the ceiling from time to time, as the big man mused. He stated further the good inspector would overview some of her more difficult cases in relation to Q-PED in the future. Lerlene tried to say, as diplomatically as possible, Inspector Deaver had very little to do with the Orchid case and even less in solving it. She also wanted to say her unit was better off without the opportunistic Inspector. More than that, she was wondering what Fitzy would say if Deaver was to poke his nose into the running of her new proposed unit. She knew Old TC would not be receptive for her to raise those points. She decided to not say too much more for the moment, remembering how the men ganged up on her before.

Fitzy's earlier good mood had flagged with the talk about the Inspector.

'Bugger me, it's been bad enough having to listen to Deaver's interviews with the media over the last two days about how he conquered the world, *without* getting a toe up the ginger from Old TC about offending his arrogant, lodge friend, Mister fucking Egghead Edgar. Bloody Devo's straight into it, the bastard didn't take long to claim credit for the big drug bust and recovery of the orchids. The shithead would have got a fucking knighthood under Joe Bjelke. Mongrel hasn't even rung me yet! Prick, fuck-wit.'

He threw a file at the wall.

Lerlene tried to be the moderator with a weak joke. 'Well Fitzy, when you become inspector, you can take credit for everything, eh, how does that sound?' She was not game to chastise him for his bad language. 'However, matey boy, not too many police officers would have got away with the way you spoke to the Old Man. You probably don't believe me but I think he likes your style.'

Fitzy's face was becoming pink, blood pressure on the rise, but his demeanour was black. 'Well, I might be an arsehole at times, but I always look after my mates. Fuck *me*!'

Just then his mobile rang which probably saved everything. Fitzy hoped it was Deaver so he could give him an earful.

'FitzMichael,' he grunted.

'Day, Fitzy, I hear you are a super hero.'

He knew the voice and a smile broke out over his face, much to the relief of Lerlene who then went about her business in the welcome calm.

He did not say her name until he was outside. 'Kappo, what took you so long, I've been trying to get you for nearly a week.'

'I've been busy. Great to hear you had a win with the orchids, we must talk about it sometime.' The voice had Hollywood female honey in it.

Fitzy's heartrate went up. He knew he was obliged to invite her to the Gordon Arms on Saturday night but was afraid of the gossip. She seemed to read the play.

'I hear you are having a few at the Gordon on Saturday night? Relax; I can't go, believe it or not, we've been seconded to be on duty for the Premier's do at Parliament House. Wayne Goss has some presentation awards-thing going, head office wants a good police presence, more female officers. Sexist bastards. Gossy's not as popular as he was; good chance Rob Borbidge will romp in at the next election. At least there will be more money for overtime for the first six months. The Nationals like that, more police, more prisons.' She laughed dryly. 'Want to get together later Saturday night?'

His heart had been down for a second, then up and then down again. 'Um, why not tonight?'

'Sorry, we are on call to look after VIPs until after Saturday.'

It seemed as if she sensed his disappointment. 'Don't worry, we'll make up for it later, *hun.*'

He could almost feel her sweet tongue in his ear. 'Hard to refuse,' he murmured and ended the call.

Chapter 39

When he returned, Lerlene, who had seen the immediate change in his demeanour, asked, 'Who was it on the phone?'

He replied, 'Ah, no one really.'

She knew. To cover her smile, she told him she was summoned yet again to see Old TC the next morning to try to get some resolution on the Thistleton case.

Fitzy said, 'I suppose I'm not invited?'

'Spot on there, matey boy. I'm still keen to have a future,' and she went on to talk about the official formation of the unit he was now part of.

'How long do you think I'm going to be part of the new unit?'

'We didn't go into that but remember what he said, keep your nose clean.'

'I wonder how long we have to put up with that mongrel Devo hovering over us?'

Lerlene chose not to answer, just nodded non-committedly.

He continued, 'Everyone on the case knew the mongrel did fuck all to help; bastard just took credit for everything. I think after we sort out the Thistleton case I might just apply for a transfer.'

She had heard it all before. 'Don't worry Fitzy, Old TC will hear the truth sooner or later and you will be back in a senior role.'

Lerlene explained she wanted to keep Fitzy in the team to investigate paedophiles and help with the data base. She told him the Chief Superintendent reminded her that Fitzy had not been overlooked and the intention was to move him back to the murder squad in time, but he felt it was best to keep him under wraps for the present until the hierarchy forgot about *the incident* in the interview room, because he was still considered a loose cannon.

Fitzy bristled again at being reminded of the *incident* and he was clearly not too keen to be chained to a desk investigating paedophiles, but it appeared as if she convinced him it was worthwhile for the present because Deaver was attached to Homicide and if he went there, well ...

'Bugger,' he said, pulling out a cigarette.

She was aware Fitzy much preferred to be out there in the world chasing what he called hard-core crooks, murderers and thieves. Both knew if he was transferred elsewhere, things would be a lot tougher for him because it was made clear after his demotion, it would be some time before he gained his stripes again. However, Lerlene was mindful he was a very competent police officer and, in her opinion, it would not be long before he made a comeback because he had kept his record clean since then. She was not aware of Fitzy's altercation with Inspector Deaver only days ago.

'Well, boss,' he said in a resigned voice, 'if I have to work with someone it may as well be you.'

He did not appear to be buoyed at Lerlene being in charge. Reluctantly he acknowledged it was best for him at the moment to be part of the new Q-PED investigation section. Anyway, it was not a choice. One thing was apparent to her, getting Fitzy to do anything he did not want to do was very difficult and he had the potential to be a hindrance if he so chose. Lerlene, however, was astute enough to read the play because if he became cranky, she knew how to handle him better than most.

'Right, I've got a few things to do,' he said and walked out.

Chapter 40

Later he appeared at the office door. Lerlene noted he was smiling when previously he had whinged about all the paperwork they had been lumped with. She had been wondering what had occupied him for the last few hours.

His job was to coordinate all the material they possessed which included floppy and the new fashioned CD discs, and copies of hundreds of documents. It was obvious he did not like that sort of work much, but, being a professional, he got on with it. He was wise enough to see that computers were the thing of the future and it did not hurt to be conversant with the medium. Fitzy was a good investigator and had a keen eye for details other people quite often missed. He had a certain tenacity, never leaving anything unfinished as many a criminal around south-east Queensland would verify. He was as keen as anybody to finalise the Thistleton case.

The cleaner, Kelvin Hargraves, was not exactly happy but Fitzy managed to get his room which was across the passage and one down. Fitzy realised that they needed more space and the cleaner's room was much larger with a window, sink and potential to find a spot for a kettle. They were old school friends and often worked out at the gym together. Kel told him it would cost a counter lunch for the shifting operation and four schooners for taking his office. Fitzy had told him that he would report him for smoking in the building.

Kel had said, "But mate, I don't even smoke."

Fitzy replied, "Yep, but they don't know that so how about we drop the counter lunch and I buy the first round?"

"One day you'll go out to your car and all your tyres will be flat and you won't have any idea who did it," said Kel throwing a wet rag in Fitzy's direction.

Fitzy was able to score another location for Hargraves on the ground floor.

~

'Listen, Acting Senior Sergeant Diplock, I reckon I've stumbled on something that might be worthwhile. Follow me.'

He pointed at the sign *Cleaning Supplies.* 'This is ours now.'

They had lost their previous room on the other side but it was too small anyway and the general office staff needed it for an extra person and storage.

She yawned. 'How did you manage to get this room? On second thought, don't tell me.'

The room was the same two-tone pea soupy green on the walls, darker at the bottom separated by a narrow groove from the lighter colour on the top.

Sparse broken furniture, damaged chairs and two broken tables were covered with boxes, mops, mop buckets, brooms and the like.

'Yeah, I know, looks like your desk ...'

She opened her mouth to protest because her desk was always neat and tidy and he knew it.

'Kidding, anyway all this shit is going and I got Hazza to give us another computer terminal, phone connection and a new thing called a scanner, anyway that's not all, have a gander at this.' He picked up a sheaf of papers. 'Now, there's a computer company called Computer Quality Solutions, CQS, their name has surfaced a few times in the paperwork you and Hazza have given me, here, see? Now this info is from the Q-PED investigation side of it, *not* Thistleton's side, orright? It's hard be sure about anything but there could be a link ...'

She lifted an eyebrow, clearly interested. 'Link?'

'Okay, when we do a search, and the *we* being more Hazza than I, we keep coming up with *access denied* but there are some interesting cross overs, all seemingly passive, normal, unremarkable but they keep cropping up. By accident Hazza found GEEKS who are a company who sell new computers, but they started off doing repair work ... and they still continue to do some repair work.'

Overloaded with information she gave a measured, 'Yes?'

'Well,' Fitzy's eyes glistened, 'Thistleton's computer was originally purchased from GEEKS Computer Services. So, I got Hazza to run some checks and comparisons, using those security systems and things he's got, on Colin Thistleton's computer and guess what?'

'Is this Bob Dyer's Pick a Box or are you trying to be Brooksie? You tell me.' She leaned forward.

'We find out they have a subsidiary company, based in Hong Kong called ... called, wait for it,'

She rolled her eyes, waiting.

'Computer Quality Solutions. CQS! Now, it's a long shot at best.'

His eyebrows formed a straight line and he stroked his chin with a pincer movement, deep in thought. Lerlene was on the verge of saying, 'Get on with it,' when he continued.

'Now, you probably remember Mark Hammer from Homicide, who left just after you got here, anyway, he's a private investigator these days and we see each other at Bashers' occasionally. He is at present investigating a certain Scott Sumich for misappropriating trust funds ... work Mark is doing for a bank, another matter, totally unrelated but his computer guys found a heap of kiddie porn in the process, hidden deep in one of Sumich's computer files they managed to hack. So, he hand balled the info to me, just a couple of hours ago thinking we may have an interest with the paedophile angle – of course being illegal it's a police matter.'

She looked at him. 'Mmm, took a while but think I get it.'

Fitzy put up a big right hand in a stop sign. 'Remember, I suggested we check out the people who repaired Colin's computer? Well now is the time. There's a lot of stuff there but wait, there's more, I know it's speculation, but remember Hazza was saying he was slightly puzzled because Colin's hard drive was a new unit and there was something about that hard drive, couldn't quite put his finger on it then. But now he can confirm the serial number suggests a hard drive of the same model that doesn't match up with the paperwork that's on the sales docket. So, my question is, what if the GEEKS mob did put a second hand hard drive in the computer even though it was a guarantee job and it should have been a new hard drive? Those sorts of things go on all the time according to Hazza because most people who get repair work done aren't computer wizards and wouldn't have a clue if internal repair components were new or not. Now what if the hard drive was contaminated and was put in Thistelton's computer?'

He leant on the side of the table and crossed his arms. His head tilted to the right and he opened his eyes wide.

Lerlene wiped her hand over her face in a tired gesture. 'Mmm, I see, well ... er it means what, Fitzy?'

'It may mean absolutely bugger all and not be the case which means Colin is still our man. But this does put a new dimension on this sorry tale. You have to admit though, pretty well everything we have on Colin is weak. I mean, yes, it is his computer, or at least when we confiscated it, it was. But the rest of it, the pen, him going missing from the staff room for only a few minutes ... unreliable witnesses at best as well. Then when we showed Timothy the handful of photos, he picked Brooksie first.' Fitzy stifled a laugh. 'Admittedly the kid did say he wasn't sure. I guess with a mother like Deidre Leak, no wonder the poor little bloke isn't sure about anything.'

'Ease up, Fitzy.' She did not smile as it seemed her head was full of thoughts.

He continued. 'I asked the doctor, the one we got to look at Colin just before we locked him up, if he could give an opinion as to whether Colin is one of those pieces of crud, a pedo. The doc, like all professional types, said officially he could not comment, but he reckoned Colin babbled to him nonstop and he was of the opinion Colin was not a rock spider. Of course, it probably does not mean much and is certainly not worth a crumpet in court. Also, for what it is worth, you would have thought there'd be some sort of pattern or evidence or a sniff of something indicating previous subversive behaviour in Colin's history. You know, him being a teacher, with kids, a complaint here or there. No such thing. Squeaky clean. There are a lot of loose ends everywhere but now, I reckon we may be on to something. Now, this may not mean we can prove

Colin's supposed new hard drive was used by the GEEKS crowd but it certainly puts things in a new light. Lerles, can we get a warrant to raid the GEEKS warehouse?'

She clicked back on track. It took her a minute to process everything as Fitzy stood looking at her. She stroked her chin. It was clear things were moving quickly for her.

'Mmmmmmmm. Alright, yep, no worries, I'll make the call in a minute. No point in going now and it will take until tomorrow morning to get the warrant anyway and a situation of this nature won't change overnight. Gives me time to chew it over and get specific info from Mark Hammer so we can zero in on what we need to do.'

'Already done it, sir.'

'Stop the bullshit.' She yawned saying, 'Nice work anyway, Fitzy,' as she walked out.

Chapter 41

The next morning, they waited for a call from an unmarked police vehicle to say that two people had gone into the GEEKS warehouse office.

Acting Senior Sergeant Diplock slipped a gun into the holster and clipped it onto her leather belt. 'Let's go Fitzy.'

As she drove, Fitzy contacted, with his new mobile, Brookes, Harrison and McTavish to organize back up, not that any trouble was expected but things were delicately poised and he figured a bit of manpower would not go astray. They found the warehouse nestled in an old rundown factory parallel to the Brisbane River at West End. Over a bank of worn wooden doors with upper glass panels was a grubby sign, ***Galaxy Extra Experience Komputer Services – please enter.*** It was difficult to see because several layers of transfers and labels of all kinds had been stuck haphazardly everywhere. Just as they approached the doors another unmarked police car eased into the parking area. It was Warren McTavish, Harry Harrison, Steve Brookes and one other police officer.

Fitzy did not wait for any go ahead from Acting Senior Sergeant Diplock; he just barged through the doors and took the three steps to the front counter. Computer components and boxes were stacked on every available surface, a radio hammered out advertising on a commercial station. In the small gap between two piles was a customer bell. He hit the bell with the palm of his hand, probably harder than necessary, and was just about to do it again when a tired looking young woman wearing jeans and a grubby T-shirt saying, *I survived Expo*, appeared from behind a worn door jamb. She had tiny pupils and was rubbing her nose.

She clearly had trouble stringing the two words together. 'You ... er ... um ... orright?'

Fitzy snapped loudly, 'No, I'm not alright. Does it look like I am alright? We are police officers!'

He flipped open the wallet, displaying his identification and slipped around behind the counter.

'We have a warrant to search this place, see? Now, we want to speak to whoever is in charge here, right?'

She rubbed her nose again. 'Er ... um, that's Scott Sumich ... he's ... I'm not sure if he's in ...'

Fitzy butted in. 'Take us to his office!'

He quickly handed Lerlene the warrant which freed up his right hand to flip open the stud on his leather holster.

'You can't just ...'

'Just what?'

Lerlene Diplock cringed at Fitzy's brash behaviour but she knew there was no one better than him at handling these situations. Also, she appeared dazed by the speed at which events had been unfolding in the last few hours. She was more than happy allowing Fitzy to assume command.

'Let's go!' commanded Fitzy, 'Just take us there, right?'

Just then Senior Constables McTavish and Harrison walked in. Any doubt about the seriousness of the situation was expelled by the presence of the police uniforms. The young woman in the Expo T-shirt put her hand to her mouth and turned quickly, now realising the implication of what could follow. They followed her, threading their way between pallets of boxes and stacks of computers and components. At the back of the warehouse was a row of offices and store rooms with a male and female toilet at each end. No one else seemed to be present.

'There,' she pointed with a shaking hand at a door marked, Managing Director.

Fitzy pushed past her, drew his firearm, holding it behind him and threw the door open with the other hand.

A pale-skinned young man with a blonde crew cut looked up from a computer. The glow from the screen reflected a green deep-sea wash in his glasses.

'Hey! Who in the fuck do you think you are? You just can't go barging into my off…'

'Shut ya face, mate!' Fitzy held up his identification.

Acting Detective Senior Sergeant Diplock introduced herself and at the same time held up a sheet of official looking paper with government letterhead.

She said firmly, 'This is a search warrant. Please place your hands where we can see them. Sir, your name is?'

'Wwwhat …warrant? Look, what the hell is this?'

Fitzy put his hands flat on the desk and leaned his upper torso, so his nose was only inches from the other man's face. His powerful arms strained the stitching of his pineapple and pina colada surf shirt.

'Name, dickhead!'

'Umm … er … Scott Sumich. What … what is this warrant thing about? Yeah, what's with this warrant bullshit, man?' There was a hint of insolence, perhaps even bravado on the last part of the question.

Like a flash, Fitzy was behind the desk and grabbed him in a vice-like grip by the upper arm. He was also quick enough to note Sumich had pulled the power cord out of the wall with his foot just a split second before he moved. The screen was blank.

Sumich tried again. 'Look, what is this? You've got no right to …'

Fitzy increased the pressure.

The other man winced. 'Hey, man, you're hurting me!'

Lerlene stepped in. 'Is this your business, Mr. Sumich?'

He nodded, 'Yes.'

'We have a warrant to search your premises and confiscate your personal computers.'

'What? Computers?' The pale, little man blinked a bead of sweat that had started on his forehead and trickled into his eye.

Fitzy smiled, 'Right, you, up! Quick! Now this police officer is a computer expert and he is going to sit in your seat for a moment or two and just have a squiz at what you were watching when we walked in.'

Fitzy almost physically lifted Sumich out of his seat by increasing the hold. It looked almost like a levitation act.

Lerlene eyed Fitzy. Her look said, 'Remember why you were demoted?'

He noted her glance and relaxed a little although mindful of the need to show aggression to remain in control. He then sneered and released the hold completely.

'Right, *sir*, please stand right here.'

Constable Harrison plugged the computer in again and flopped down in the seat.

'Aha, have a look at this.' It only took a few seconds to retrieve what Sumich had been watching. 'Well, well, well.' There were explicit images of naked children. Harry just shook his head, 'Bloody hell, bloody hell …' He looked down and opened a desk drawer. 'God Almighty, Fitzy have a goosey-gander at these!'

Fitzy had been looking at the screen and then shook his head in disgust as Harry held up some photographs of children, most in compromising positions with adults whose faces were blanked out. He turned and said firmly. 'You're in strife, mate.'

'I … I didn't know it was on there … this is … er … a computer I'm fixing, it's not … not mine and those photos, anyone could have put them there …'

'Save it, you dirty little prick,' snarled Fitzy, showing pink anger.

Lerlene could read the signs.

'Take him away,' she said quickly and nodded towards McTavish who stepped forward and grabbed Sumich by the other arm and led him outside where he was officially charged.

Fitzy took a couple of deep breaths and directed the others to search the area and confiscate the office computers, and as far as he was concerned, they had all they needed for the immediate charge. The benches out in the warehouse were piled with computers in various stages of repair and Senior Constable Harrison had already requested officers from Central Electronic Surveillance to come and check it all. He considered it easier than taking everything to the police station.

Although there was no proof at this stage the pornographic material on Colin's computer was installed or used by Sumich, it was clear it originated from the warehouse, as the receipts for Colin's new computer indicated. They would check fingerprints on Colin's hard drive also. Lerlene agreed with Fitzy that it was highly likely Colin had been set up, more than likely by chance rather than intentionally.

'What are we going to do about Thistleton, Fitzy?'

'We? We, Acting Senior Sergeant?' he said almost playfully.

She frowned.

'Just kidding. Truth is, I don't know. I think *we*, that is you, should order his release, set the wheels in motion at least. I'd check with Old TC first though, doesn't hurt to cover your bum. I don't think he's your man for the attempted abduction either so I'd let him go. But, we need to have a stern chat to this weasel Sumich because he needs to admit the hard drive he put into Colin's computer was not new and did have kiddie porn on it.'

He winked at Lerlene. 'Give me five minutes with him boss and he'll confess to the Belangalo killings.'

'Take it easy, Fitzy. I don't want to see you as a trainee Constable in Blackwater Police Station for the rest of your career. You've got to step back, Fitzy. Understand? We will question him by the book. Right?'

'All right, all right,' he mumbled and pulled out a cigarette. 'I'd better give Mark Hammer a buzz; his client will now want to press charges for misappropriation of funds, so we want to get in first. Sumich's in deeper sewerage than he thinks. Right, Lerlene, let's leave the boys here and go do some interviews, eh?'

Chapter 42

Back at the station they interviewed Sumich but he was not prepared to concede anything as his lawyer kept insisting his client had no comment. Fitzy was prepared to let them stew for a while and then try to frighten Sumich with stories about what happens to paedophiles in jail. As far as the police were concerned, they caught him actually looking at, and in possession of child pornography so there was no problem getting a conviction on those charges. But what they wanted, and Lerlene was prepared to offer, was some sort of leniency if he would come clean on the hard drive that was put in Thistleton's computer. Leniency meant a certain amount of protection in jail. In normal circumstances, paedophiles are kept separate from the general prison population anyway. Sumich probably did not know that so they could pretend to offer protection inside even though it was what happened anyway.

Fitzy said to Lerlene, 'I don't give a root what happens to that slimy little shit, Sumich, in jail, in fact I hope some bastard bashes him to death. I just want him to admit to the contaminated hard drive so Thistleton can be cleared.' Fitzy's attitude to paedophiles was well known.

'Where are you off to?' queried Lerlene.

'I have a feeling we have missed something. Don't know what it is but you know … Anyway, I spoke to Meredith this morning and got her to follow up again the info we requested from the NT and ACT – about paedophiles released from prison and public institutions.

We hadn't heard back from them so I wanted to at least exhaust that avenue. We've only got Colin for the attempted abduction and …'

Lerlene just grunted and nodded.

Ten minutes later, Fitzy came storming back. 'Bingo,' he yelped, 'there's this joker, a rock spider by the name of Henry James Thompson, released from jail in the ACT. His release address given was, let me see.' Fitzy ran his finger over the map of greater Brisbane. 'Eight Garron Street, there, one street away from, you guessed it, from the Gordon Park Primary School. Meredith is in the process of putting his name in the system, Queensland first but if nothing comes up we will go Australia wide.'

~

'Well I'll be,' said Fitzy, 'you won't believe this, it gets better by the minute. This Thompson character is in the holding cells at Gold Coast North Police Station as of right now. Not sure what for but I'll give 'em a ring.'

Lerlene sat with her hands squeezing the sides of her head. Things were happening fast and there was a lot to digest.

Fitzy finished his call. 'Just spoke to Sergeant Lex Clayton and they arrested Thompson yesterday on an attempted abduction of a minor, a kid from a kindergarten in Southport. Hang on, his report is coming through to the station now, should be coming to your email as well.'

'Yep, got it,' said Lerlene. 'Mr Henry James Thompson a repeat offender, has a history of mental illness, drug addiction and paedophilia. I'll just cross reference …'

She gasped. 'Bloody hell, Thompson's name came up, as a reference flagged marker from Q-PED - in the investigation of Godfrey Dalton Hughes. That orchid and bromeliad collector bloke who jumped into Sydney Harbour we talked about earlier!'

Fitzy barked, 'What relationship did he …?'

'Well, only by association but Thompson worked as a labourer kitchen hand at one of the community groups that Hughes was patron of, the Hudson Street Shelter, Sydney. Says here the manager of that place, a Jonathon Boland, was convicted of child sex offences and is still in jail in NSW. Gawd, love a duck, Fitzy, this is getting so big my head is about to explode.'

'Right, well Lex Clayton at the Gold Coast said that Thompson failed to abduct the little girl in Southport yesterday because a tradie working on the roof saw what was going on and yelled at him. They caught Thompson by accident, literally speaking. Just after leaving the Southport Kindergarten in a panic he pulled straight out in front of a tip truck. The tradie had quickly come down from the roof, told a child care worker to call the cops and followed in his ute. He caught up with Thompson at the accident site and stood over him; he was shaken up but uninjured, then the police arrived. What a wonderful little story, eh?'

'Right,' said Lerlene.

Fitzy stood. 'Okay. We have to go and talk to him pronto. They have to keep him for a while because the recent crime occurred in their district, obviously, but he will be transferred to the Brisbane Watch House when they have finished with him. I told them not to worry, we will zip down there and interview him. Er, boss?'

'Yep?'

'I suggest we go now, it's only eleven, and we might be able to square this all up. This guy has to be a strong suspect for our abduction as well – it is certainly worth interviewing him. Seems like he can't help himself. We can put the screws on Sumich later for a confession re the hard drive and maybe let Colin Thistleton go later today?'

'Affirmative. Hey Fitzy?'

'Yeah?'

'I wish you were doing my job at the moment. Things are happening so fast I'm almost shitting myself.'

She covered her face with both hands and slowly dragged them back to squeeze the bun at the back of her head. As if that would ease the tension inside.

'Language, language, Lerlene, I understand but you're the senior officer here. It can be lonely at the top.'

His attempt at humour at least brought a softening of her facial features.

~

Sergeant Lex Clayton, of the Gold Coast North Police Station, gave them copies of the paperwork and he was briefed on the topic of Thompson's possible involvement in the alleged abduction of Timothy

Leak. Clayton and Fitzy had met on few occasions and they both shared a keen dislike of paedophiles. Fitzy explained that they did not want the interview recorded first up because the evidence related to their case was a little thin.

After his arrest Thompson had been put back on medication that he had stopped taking not long after being released in the ACT. Clayton led the way down the corridor to the interview room. He was a slim, very tall man with a slight stoop that some tall people tend to adopt out of learnt experiences from knocking their heads on door frames.

Lerlene whispered to Fitzy, 'We'd better take it easy on this Henry Thompson because, although he's a paedophile, he's also a fruitcake. We know he's back on medication, so he will probably come across as sane as anyone at the moment. We need to be careful because if he pushes the fact that he was not taking his medications at the time of either of the attempted abductions, he might get off a lot lighter.'

Fitzy nodded, 'Yeah, righto, I'm with you.'

Lex held the door open for them and Fitzy went over to the video camera which was hard wired to a bank of switches. He turned off the camera and the backup audio equipment and as an extra measure placed the plastic cap over the lens. Lerlene smiled at the action but narrowed her eyes at Fitzy as a warning that it was all to be by the book.

Thompson was a short dumpy man, balding, with a comb over which was a very bad attempt at creating the illusion of a crop of hair. His eyes were red rimmed and blue sacks hung under each. They knew he was 41 but he looked at least ten years older. There were only the three police officers and the accused in the room.

Thompson looked around like a startled rabbit and was about to say something when Fitzy put up his hand. He introduced the three police officers by name. 'Right Mr Thompson, mind if I call you Henry? Right, mate, this is only an interview, alright? You haven't been charged with anything other than the existing attempted abduction of a minor at Southport, okay?'

Thompson rubbed his pudgy face and said, 'Hey, don't I need me lawyer, I mean you probly gunna twist words around again to suit yer own …'

'Henry, this is only a quiet chat about another matter. The surveillance equipment has been turned off.'

Senior Sergeant Diplock said. 'We have evidence that you were identified abducting a child at the Gordon Park Primary School on, let me see …' She outlined the details, playing the soft, sensitive, understanding cop.

Thompson shifted uneasily. 'What? I admitted to yesterday at the kindergarten, you know, didn't take me meds, wouldna done it if I had, you know that but this other thing, naaah … don't know nuthin' about that.'

'Come on, Henry, you lived two streets away, we have witnesses, you were identified by the child, we have your footprints, we've got a DNA match.'

Lerlene was fishing but she knew they had to get him to admit to it or slip up.

'Nah, weren't me, I wasn't even in the area.'

Fitzy just sat dead still and glared. Lerlene looked at Sergeant Clayton and then back at Thompson. Silence reigned for a full minute.

Lerlene stated, 'So, this time at Gordon Park, a girl? You usually like little boys don't you?'

He looked perplexed. 'No it was a b… Oh, look, I'm confused, I didn't do nothin', anyway how can a kid identify anyone, he'd be too young, could be anyone done it… you're putting words in my mouth.'

Fitzy stood up quietly and walked behind Thompson and stood stock still, a highly intimidating action. He leant down and whispered. 'Now, mate, I'm going to lay it out for you, alright. Look at me.' Fitzy and banged his fist on the table.

Paperwork and pens scattered and Thompson almost jumped out of his chair. The reek of despair and intimidation hung heavily in the room.

Thompson stuttered, 'Bbbut …'

Fitzy put his huge hand on the seated man's shoulder.

'Look at me. Be quiet. Henry? You of all people have a pretty fucking good idea of what they will do to you in prison, eh? Those hard core cons will just love to make you pay for your sins. In Queensland we can recommend you be placed in the general populace, alright, not isolated and protected with your slimy little rock spider mates like before. Up here you will be out there with the big boys.'

Thompson was about to say something.

Fitzy barked, 'Shut up!'

Lerlene looked on in alarm, thinking Fitzy was going to assault Thompson but nothing happened. Sweat poured off Thompson's face as Fitzy returned to the other side of the table and sat down again.

'Now, sport, let's do this again. We know it was you who attempted to abduct the boy at Gordon Park, you know it was you. We can put in a good word for you so you can get special treatment inside, I mean you got caught in the act yesterday, one more aint going to matter. We can set up the charges so your sentences can be served concurrently. Alternatively, if we recommend otherwise you could easily spend the rest of your miserable days in prison, but you won't last long, we'll see to that, so think about it. You will need as much help as you can get inside. *Mate*. Now, I'm going to turn on the surveillance equipment and while I do it, I want you to think hard about what you are going to say, then we are going to do this properly, okay?'

Lerlene introduced the officers in the room and repeated her earlier outline of the charge. After some initial reluctance Thompson confessed to attempting to grab a child at the Gordon Park Primary School.

Half hour later everything was tied up neatly. During the interview many other finer points of evidence were ticked off. They asked about the pen, and the initials CAT and Thompson had no knowledge about this so they surmised that it had been stolen or the owner of the pen had simply dropped it. Either way it had no further bearing on the case.

Both Fitzy and Lerlene Diplock were exhausted and content with the courts sorting out the future of Thompson. At least as far as the police investigation, the sorry episode at the school had been finalised and the man was no longer able to abduct children, for the present anyway.

As they were walking out, Lex jokingly suggested that Fitzy should come down to the Gold Coast for a few interviews with crims to help them with their clean up rate.

On the way back to Brisbane Lerlene said, 'Are we going to do the paperwork to have his sentences served concurrently? And, what about putting a good word in for him?'

'Pig shit we will. I'm a man of my word, but not to paedophiles. I couldn't care two hoots if he gets bashed to death in remand.'

Chapter 43

Back at Lutwyche Police Station, Lerlene prepared herself to ring Mrs Leak whilst Fitzy was given the job to re-interview Sumich. They needed his admission that Thistleton's hard drive was either from one of their office computers or was used by them before they could let Colin go.

Fitzy promised to hold back his prejudices and behave himself but Lerlene made Senior Constable McTavish sit in with him just to make sure. She was to view the interview through the two way glass when she had finished with Mrs Leak.

There was not much the lawyer could do to stop Fitzy colouring up life in jail for a paedophile. Sumich's attitude had changed considerably from his arrogant stance at the first interview. He was visibly shaken, nervous glances shot everywhere and beads of sweat speckled his brow.

McTavish tapped his pen on the table and Fitzy moved his cigarette packet in a slow small circle. They continued to grill the charged man, with the standard police silent treatment, staring at him and saying nothing for minutes at a time. The young man could not hold any eye contact and after a short time just looked at the table in front of him. The atmosphere was as fragile as ice.

Fitzy broke the silence. 'You are in very deep Winnie the poo, Mr Sumich, you are gone for all money. We have located more explicit child pornography on two other computers in the GEEKS office ... so far.' He paused for a moment then added, with great restraint, almost gently, 'Now, here's how it's going to be.'

He explained how they might be able to go lighter on the other two computers with porn on them and maybe offer him some protection inside for the truth about Colin's hard drive. Sumich and his lawyer huddled and whispered as Fitzy stood up and walked behind them and stood, not making a sound. This intimidating tactic confused a prisoner into making quick decisions.

After a few minutes, Sumich admitted the Thistleton hard drive was out of one of their office computers and child pornography had been on it before it was supposed to be wiped clean.

'A bit careless there old son,' said Fitzy glaring at him.

The lawyer looked up at Fitzy and said, 'Please give my client the opportunity to explain his side of the story.'

Fitzy shrugged. 'Let's have it then, the whole lot because if we find you have been holding out on us you can guess the consequences.'

Sumich confessed that they often used second hand parts on warranty repairs. He gingerly told them two other people who worked as technicians were involved with child pornography but the girl on the front desk had no idea what was going on in his office. He stated there was an organisation called Playground Pyjama Party and he would be willing to give them information about that in exchange for a more lenient sentence.

McTavish spoke in a measured tone. 'We don't make deals like that, but we will see what we can do.' The lawyer rolled his eyes.

The interview went on for over an hour and everyone was exhausted when Fitzy called a halt with the idea of continuing the next day. In the meantime, he was going to instruct the police officers, who were still searching GEEK premises, to arrest the two other suspects.

~

Fitzy had just walked in when the phone rang and Harry Harrison excitedly informed them that from Sumich's computers they had uncovered a major paedophile ring called Playground Pyjama Party.

'Beat you to it,' said Fitzy, 'Sumich just told us a bit about it then but we can grill him tomorrow for more.'

Lerlene said it was a group the Q-PED investigation now knew about and she was trying to get hard evidence as some prominent people were involved.

Then she said, 'I'm going to have to release Colin Thistleton.'

Fitzy put his feet on the desk and leant back in the office chair.

'It is something you should authorise quick smart. I'm glad you said the word I, Acting Senior Sergeant, the poor, miserable little bastard has got the wrong end of the pineapple up his date and you'd better hope he doesn't decide to make a big deal about wrongful arrest.'

He pulled out a smoke and popped it in the corner of his mouth.

'Right, I'm out for a smoke to celebrate a string of successful outcomes.'

Fitzy swung his feet off the desk and ambled out, lighting up just outside the door. Ten minutes later he wandered back in with a handful of papers he had picked up from the main office down the passage. Lerlene had her head buried in her hands.

'What's wrong?'

She looked up, her face was red and her eyes glistened. He froze in his size eleven-and-a-halves. He was not used to seeing her like this.

'Colin Thistleton ...' there was silence for a terrible moment, 'he ... he just tried to hang himself in his cell.'

'Fuck,' said Fitzy and just stood there looking at her.

Fitzy was not much good at comforting anyone, least of all, women. He took a step towards her and gingerly placed a hand on her shoulder. Another couple of minutes ticked by. She was still looking at him with no expression.

'Is he okay?'

'Yes, just.'

'I'll ... er ... get the coffees,' he said quietly, to break the chilly silence and quickly walked out.

He knew he would have to talk to her but there was no way he could he deal with it at that moment. The sight of her and the look in her eyes really rocked him. Of all people, Fitzy knew what it was like to make a mistake. He was more than aware that rotten things happened in the police force and it either made you ... or broke you. He knew, with sinking heart, the issue was going to be difficult to discuss with Acting Senior Sergeant Lerlene Diplock. Probably more for him than her.

Chapter 44

The next few days were spent winding up both of the cases and Fitzy was put back on research for Q-PED and Lerlene took the rest of the week on sick leave. The brass was none too pleased a person had been wrongfully charged and worse still, an innocent man tried to hang himself. An enquiry was in progress, the dogs were out. It was a given that not much would happen to Lerlene, a temporary demotion was always possible but unlikely. Fitzy made a point of emphasising to her that Old TC was the one to make the decision. That being the case, the officer on duty at the lock up would more than likely be the sucker to wear the blame. It was established early on that Colin Thistleton was a *watch* prisoner and the officer who was supposed to be monitoring him was in much more trouble than Lerlene Diplock.

Wrongful arrests happen from time to time; police don't always get it right. However, if Thistleton had died, it would have been an entirely different matter. Fitzy, a tough campaigner, felt a pang of sorrow for Colin and Gretel Thistleton. As a police officer he often came across people who were born to make up the victim percentage of the population. People who, for whatever reason, maybe made bad decisions, were depressed, undervalued and every step in their miserable lives seemed to be backwards. Collateral damage.

Gretel was currently receiving psychiatric care in an institution and Colin was under medical watch in hospital. Fitzy wished he could go and apologise to them but he was worldly enough to know it would only make things worse.

Fitzy opened his bottom drawer and looked at the contents. The bottle of Vodka was still unopened in its paper bag. He grabbed a small box that was lying on a bench nearby and put the bottle in it. He wrote, For Constable Phil Linden – buck-show on the 21st of May" and signed, From Fitzy and Wowzer. He picked up the magazine, opened it, smiled and chucked it in the box as well; he placed the box on the desk in the main office where other gifts accumulated. Phil Linden was getting married and some of the blokes had organised a buck show for him. It did not make Fitzy feel any better, but he figured those confiscated items would go to some use.

Fitzy went home, tried Kaplan's number, left a message and had an early night. Sleep came very quickly for Sergeant Rodney FitzMichael but it was the sleep of exhaustion, not gentle restful slumber.

~

Friday morning, he arrived late with the view of tidying up whatever needed tidying up. Fitzy knew Constable Kaplan was at work, but he resisted the urge to see her. Later in the day, after he was satisfied the Orchid and Thistleton cases had been wound up he went back to the Q-PED file.

Just as he was closing down the computer and preparing to lock everything away, he again noticed a name that seemed to have popped up a couple of times during the afternoon. He tried his search engines and came up with a few more names he recognised. Fitzy's computer skills stopped about there, so he rang Harry Harrison, hoping. Harry was just pulling out of the carpark.

'What ya got, Fitzy?'

'Better get your arse up here, pronto! It'll be worth your while.'

They worked for the next couple of hours, Fitzy tried to raise Lerlene on the landline and mobile but both rang out. He did not blame her; he knew she was playing hard to get; he would have done the same. He left a support message each time and hung up.

Fitzy said to Harry as they left the building just before midnight, 'It can wait until Monday. Just keep it under your hat and we'll work out a strategy.'

Chapter 45

On Saturday night at the Gordon Arms drinks flowed and Fitzy drank mid-strength beer so he would not be too bombed when Kaplan came around later. He made the excuse he still had plenty to do on the case with all the reports and loose ends to be tidied up. Someone stirred him up about being pathetic and not leading by example, but it was not uncommon for officers at various times to lay off the drink when work needed to be done. Also there was always a danger there was a rat ready to dob someone in for drinking whilst on duty or in the middle of a case.

Lerlene popped in for a couple of drinks early on. Her colleagues gave supportive words and as far as Fitzy was concerned, she seemed to be handling the ordeal alright. He knew outward appearances could be deceiving but he knew she was tough enough.

When she finally got to Fitzy he whispered, 'Come over here, boss.'

They sat at a table; Fitzy leaned in so no one could hear.

'Yesterday I was sifting through Q-PED offenders' files and guess whose name came up by the chanciest of chances?'

She looked at him impassively. 'You win, who?'

'Mr-fucking-David Edgar, or more precisely, Mr Edgar Davids.'

'Whaaaaat? How did you …'

'Well, remember a few days ago, Hazza hacked into some of the pedo sites and he managed to get access to an email request site where punters can order CDs, mags and I guess, other stuff. From there we found another forum site where rockies can contact each other, pretty complex because they obviously use codes and aliases all the time. I mean if I was trying to be hard to find I'd do the same, cover the tracks. Hazza left me to it. Now, I just stumbled on Edgar's name; Edgar Davids, just rang a bell, you know, the Edgar bit and with all the practice we experienced with the Holdsworth/Holdsworthy/Goldsworth and so on play on names … somehow, I thought it worth looking at. The email address was not the same as his on the Orchid Society list, but I noticed another two names, male names, first name last name thing again and guess what? Two committee members of the East Coast Orchid Society. Their emails didn't check either, but I figured there was a good chance these spiders have several email accounts and we traced them to a link to one of GEEKS employees who we know is linked to the Playground Pyjama Party. So, anyrate, I brought in the artillery again, Hazza, and he managed to trace the email addresses through our friends in Investigative Priority Branch. They were far from stoked to have to work on a Friday night, but I stressed the importance of this and I mentioned the Chief Superintendent's name.'

'Bloody hell, Fitzy, you didn't. If anything comes back about it he'll go crackers.'

'Well, I figured, he was the one who dumped pressure on us, came on with all this Mister Edgar this and Mister Edgar that, impeccable character, pillar of society etcetera, all that frog-shit and he also held back the list we managed to obtain by foul deeds via our man, Brooksie.

'Don't worry, Lerles, she'll be sweet, besides it won't do either of us any harm in the long run. Old TC likes results because it looks good for him. At the end of the day, if it becomes a case of him or Edgar, he won't protect a mongrel like Edgar, particularly because too many people know about it and when we tell Old TC, he needs to know others are privy to the information as well from this investigation. It's not that I think he is corrupt but, you know, ex Licensing Branch *and still in the force*, a network of public associations mates, and a high flying exec who has plenty of clout he might be tempted to put a lid on it, or maybe exclude his mate from the list because someone owes someone a favour.

'Also, our mutual friend, that prick Deaver, hovers in the background and I wouldn't be surprised at anything he did. I'm pretty certain he is not involved in any of the paedophile investigations, but you can bet if there is any credit to be taken, he'll be right there.'

She appeared surprised at the severity of his verbal attack on Deaver.

He continued, 'Remember, someone has to be the es-cape goat. Not us, Lerles, not us. I mean, how do you pick a rock spider? It aint a joke because you can't. Imagine if there is a high court judge, or the bloke who mows your lawn, or a ... the premier even? See? Who bloody well knows? We just have to make sure these arseholes are charged.'

'How many people *do* know about it?'

'Only me, you and Hazza, but I've recorded the info so it cannot be wiped or tampered with, even if I disappear or die. Also there's a copy on a disc for you I slipped through the air vent of your locker.'

'So, we better get in early Monday morning, eh Fitzy?'

'Aha, back from sick leave, eh? Sure thing. By the way, that c... er bastard, Devo, still hasn't rung me. We make certain the prick doesn't have the opportunity to take credit for this latest development as well. In fact, I reckon I might add his name to the list of people to be investigated. There's another thing that came up, too.'

Her eyes widened for a second thinking Fitzy was serious about adding Deaver to the list.

'Um, something else?'

'Yep. Another interesting name came up in the circle.'

'Well, get on with it, you're as bad as Brooksie, I've got a dinner to go to.' She smiled.

'O'Neill. I have no idea if it is the good Father in question, but he is now in our sights until such time as we discover he isn't the O'Neill on the pedo list. And he's linked to ... wait for it, Godfrey Dalton Hughes, our Sydney swallow diver into the harbour.'

'Gawd, that's all we need. Old TC won't be happy with that; you know how much clout the church has with the police.' She massaged her temples.

'There are plenty of people named O'Neill so let's hope for, I don't know, everyone's sake, it has no bearing on the good Father. I mean, so far the Father has come up clean. And, the name Playground Pyjama

Party came up linking one of the members of ECOS whose emails I just mentioned. Anyway, it is important to keep you in the loop. I have it all documented, you know … Christ, we are going to need more staff I think, I mean this thing is so fucking big. Right, enough of that, now can I get you another drink?'

'No thanks, I've got to go because of a dinner engagement. Bloody good work Fitzy, just what you need at the moment, to be associated with a few successes. You could end up being the Commissioner out of this.'

He laughed and then turned serious. 'Hey … Lerlene, Lerles, I'm not very good at this sort of shit but, well, things happen and if you, you know, want to … er talk …'

'I do know and …er … thanks Fitzy, we have talked…you *are* really all heart. See you Monday; you are … a good friend. Thanks again.'

She winked, casually saluted and rubbed him on the shoulder on her way past. Fitzy watched her make her way through the drinkers. There were a few raunchy comments, but she laughed and said, 'I wish,' but then assured everyone it was her sister's birthday.

Fitzy played eight ball, but he was beaten in the second round. The noise level rose and even though Fitzy was enjoying the banter with mates and colleagues, he was keen for Kappo to wrap her legs around him. Only an hour and a bit to go.

~

Later in the night Inspector Deaver, dressed immaculately, waltzed in, followed by Sergeant Bilton.

'Hey everybody, congratulations, drinks are on me!'

Brookes leaned towards Fitzy. 'That'd be right, arriving jess before everyone goes and pretending to be generous buying drinks. Fucking parasite,' he slurred, downing the rest of his schooner. 'I'd rather buy me own. Anyone got any Ratsak?' he mumbled which raised subdued laughter nearby. 'One again Fitzy?'

'No, I'm right thanks, mate,' he replied, his crystallised glance bristling with anger towards Deaver.

Five minutes later Deaver sidled over.

'How're they hangin', Fitzy me old comrade in arms?'

Deaver placed a well-manicured hand on Fitzy's shoulder and breathed beery breath in his face.

'It might be a good idea to remove your hand off my shoulder, you selfish cunt.'

'Whaaat? What's up with you ... *mate?*' He drew back in mock alarm.

'Didn't take you long to claim credit for everything we've done, did it?'

'Aaaar come on, Fitzy, the right people know you guys were part of it ...'

'Part of it? You did fuck-all. Piss off. Devious Deaver, the name suits you. You're a fucking rat.'

Fitzy took a deep breath. He and Brookes made the decision not to say anything about Deaver or Zubrenyck dobbing them in for the Bagshaw incident until they were certain. That matter could wait.

'Don't be hard to get on with. Hey, Kappo not opening her legs wide enough for you, eh?'

Deaver braced himself slightly, aware he was pushing it. Brookes' eyes widened, feeling the heat coming off Fitzy.

Brookes took a couple of steps and nudged Fitzy, 'Hey, come on, mate, let's go over and talk to Hazza. Hey, look Wowzer jess came in, come on Fitzy ...'

Fitzy ignored Brookes and turned to face Deaver.

'What did you say, shit-for-brains?'

Temper Fitzy, temper. Deep breaths, make it work for you.

'Come on, Fitzy, just a joke, I mean you and Kappo, you know, doing it, word's all over the station ... hey maybe you and Dippy too. Dipping your wick? You dark horse, you,' he smirked, moving lightly on his toes.

They were about the same height but Deaver was heavier. The mistake Deaver made was to glance away, smirking, for a second. Fitzy's hand shot out, grabbed him by the tie and dragged him like a puppy, three steps and through the open lounge door into the beer garden. Almost one swift movement. Most people in the bar were occupied drinking and talking and did not register the disturbance. Those who happened to notice looked on in shock. Fitzy's move was like a flash. He jabbed Inspector Deaver in the mouth with a left and followed with a solid punch in the nose, a square on whack with his right. Deaver, off balance but trying to give the impression he was ready for it, clearly was not. Blood spurted out of his nose which was clearly broken.

The inspector put his hand on his face, took his hand away and looked in shock at the blood. It took a couple of seconds to register, then his eyes widened in rage as he mumbled something incoherently. He steadied and came at Fitzy.

Fitzy was a street fighter and had already registered the other man's intentions probably before Deaver really knew himself. He was already balanced in a slight crouched boxing stance that allowed him to sway out of reach as Deaver swung a heavy uncoordinated right which, had it connected, would have been a jaw breaker. Fitzy was fit and far too quick, and fuelled by anger jabbed Deaver four times in the face with his left and the inspector went down, backwards into an ashtray garden bed, almost unconscious.

Fitzy was on top of things enough to realise that if he used his right the other man would not have been be able to get up. The action was calculated, quick and savagely brutal. Practice with Fridge paid off.

By then Brookes and McTavish were in through the doors as others funnelled in behind. They grabbed Fitzy's shoulders, preventing him from doing anything else, not that Deaver was in any state to challenge again.

Deaver tried to sit up and from everyone else's point of view, it looked almost comical if not so serious, with his brilliant tie and expensive suit covered in blood and dirt from the garden bed.

He burbled a few incoherent words again through a mouthful of blood seeping through his fingers and dripping all over his once white shirt.

'Sorry, *sir*, but I was only defending myself. Your word against mine, *sir*,' said Fitzy struggling to control his breathing. 'You should not say nasty things about other officers in this department, particularly women in this day and age, matey-boy ... I mean, *sir*,' said Fitzy still trying to rein in his breathing.

It was only at this point Fitzy realised no other members of the public, just police, were out in the beer garden. *Maybe there is a God, Fitzy, eh?*

Just as Fitzy turned, Sergeant Bilton rushed past him to help Deaver to his feet. Bilton was wise enough to give Fitzy a wide berth.

Fitzy breathed deeply again, exhaled a few more times and walked through the gathering group, shaking his head and saying, 'Get back to the free drinks you good officers who helped make the Orchid case the success it was. You will all be remembered and thanked personally by Inspector Deaver. He loves to share the credit as well as buying the drinks. Take him at his word, he's buying!'

Fitzy walked out, heart beating fast. The smile on his face was not joyful but could be described as satisfying.

Chapter 46

Fitzy arrived at his unit half an hour later after a slow drive over the Story Bridge, around the Gabba, to a drive-through bottle shop and back. By then he had vented all his anger and was as relaxed as he could be. He knew there would be repercussions from the incident that night, but he was almost certain no one saw it all. Even though Deaver did not deliver the first punch, as far as Fitzy was concerned the man did by denigrating Constable Kaplan and Lerlene Diplock; that resulted in the first blow and Fitzy was defending himself from then on. Further, Brookes and Warren McTavish were the only two who could have suspected something, but he was sure they did not actually see the first punch. He knew they would not say anything because neither had any love or respect for Inspector Deaver.

Bilton was on the other side of the bar at the time and would not have witnessed the first punch. Deaver was not particularly well liked around the station anyway for giving the lousy hard slog work to others whilst taking the glory for himself. There was always the possibility that Deaver might jump him one day or night somewhere, sometime, but Fitzy thrived on altercations and being alert in equal measure. Deaver did have one or two followers, likely Bilton and Zubrenyck, but not really supporters and if anything came of this Fitzy felt strong enough to deal with it head on.

He poured himself a straight whisky, downed it, poured another and sat down. There was a knock on the front door.

'I thought I'd never get away,' said Pauline.

She pecked him on the cheek. She looked good in uniform and he would have loved to grab her and run his hands over her back and nuzzle her neck, but things were not as spontaneous as last time. Something was up.

'Come on in. Drink?'

'G and T if you remembered to get some tonic.'

'Coming up.'

She followed him into the kitchen, taking off her police issue peaked cap and shaking her red mane free.

He handed her the drink. She downed the lot, and then threw her arms around him. She pressed her lips against his, forcing his mouth slightly open and squeezed an ice cube into his mouth. The action happened quickly but the embracing lock lasted a minute. She stepped back.

'Time for a shower, Bryan Brown. Make sure you bring me a towel, won't you?'

He heard the shower going but she left the bathroom door ajar.

'Hey, Fitzy, would you come and soap my back?'

He walked through the door. The shower cubicle door was open and she stood unashamedly nude, a daring, provocative smile on her face, firm breasts glaring at him, her hands on hips framing her dark, bushy triangle. 'Well, least you can do is take your clothes off, come on, there's enough room for two in here.'

Fitzy did not bother replying, there was no fitting answer. He stripped, put his arms around her, and buried his head in her wet hair. She nuzzled his ear and their mouths found each other in an almost violent, passionate clash. His hands slipped down her curves, soaping her back, and ended cupping her buttocks, shower water cascading over them.

She gasped, 'Let's save the foreplay 'till later,' and immediately resumed ramming her tongue into his mouth.

He lifted her slightly up on her toes and she grabbed his manhood. She was a tall woman and had no problem guiding him into her and they bucked and jerked for a few short minutes and then slowly slid down the wall, narrowly missing the taps.

The rest of the night and early hours were spent exploring each other's bodies and catching up on foreplay.

After a period of blissful dozing, she propped her head up on an elbow. 'Well, Fitzy, I've got to go soon, I can't wake up here. Er ... um ... I don't know how to say this but ...'

Fitzy had almost forgotten about his earlier premonition that something was not right between them. Over the last few days there had been a lack of response to his calls and messages as well as her cool manner on the phone and ... and just in the last few hours, he could feel a certain distance she seemed to be putting between them. He looked at her in the dim light from the passage, willing her to continue. *Is she giving me time to say it first?*

She stroked his face. '... I've tried to make it clear, you know, I've really enjoyed our time together, but ...'

He was going to make her go through with it.

'... I tried to be honest with you ... you know, I said we weren't an item, I mean, even though I really enjoyed ...'

He smiled, not unkindly.

'I understand, the boyfriend's back in the picture?'

'No, not that, we've resolved our ...'

'You don't want a permanent ...?' His heart dropped.

'No it's not ... well yes, it is, I want to go places, not that ...'

'It's okay, I get it.' He did really get it.

Up on one elbow she looked at him, head to one side, blood red hair falling vertically over her shoulder.

'Well, it's more than that. I got a promotion to a position with the Australian Federal Police in Canberra. I've kept it quiet, but I really want the job.'

Fitzy grabbed her and kissed her ear.

'When do you go?'

'Within the next couple of weeks, I'm really sorry I didn't tell you earlier but ... I couldn't, the whole thing has been difficult and my boss cracked a fruity when he found out. He was forced to keep it under wraps as well which cheesed him off even further because he couldn't get a replacement. I had to keep it to myself for a range of reasons.'

They lay in each other's arms for a while longer, moved into a gentle pashing session followed by sex once more. Afterwards she dressed quickly, pecked him on the cheek and told him she really did enjoy their time together. She promised to look him up whenever she was in town, then she slipped out the front door. It was over as quickly as it started.

Fitzy lay wide awake as the first rays of sun speared the dust motes across the ceiling. He was mindful a good one had got away, but he was astute enough to know it would not have lasted even if she had not scored the job in Canberra. He had experienced many relationships with women; both in the force and outside, most ended this way. At least it was an amicable separation, not like some where he was demonised because he didn't want a house with a lawn and a heap of children. It was a reminder that liaisons with women as ambitious as him would never really work and he seemed to pick them most times. He was not ready for any serious settling down with anyone anyway, in fact when he looked at all his married friends and their bone jarringly boring lives, he could not think of anything worse. Constable Kaplan *was* ambitious. *Just like you, Fitzy.*

He smiled; thankful for the wonderful experience and realised he did not want things to change anytime soon. Life was okay at the moment, rounds with Fridge at the gym, long punishing runs, drinks with his mates and he was fully aware there were plenty more beautiful women out there in the world. Fitzy was also keen to gain his stripes again. He reset the alarm and drifted into a blissful half consciousness.

He opened his eyes, yes, there was a librarian, and a teacher's aide, who needed to be brought up to date with the status of the cases relevant to them. He punched the pillow and laughed loudly.

Chapter 47

At a run-down rental property in Kedron, a young computer high achiever booted up and slipped a CD into the tray. Jason's lips were dry, and he badly needed a drink. His white pasty hand grabbed a family sized bottle of Coke, dislodging a Jumbo packet of cheese and onion potato chips onto the floor. He did not have time to pick them up. One third of the contents of the coke disappeared and he burped award-winningly loud, and then wiped his lips with the back of a dirty sleeve.

He clicked *view slideshow* with the mouse.

A string of photographs appeared before his eyes.

'Wow, you bet,' he whispered, 'oh, man.'

The photos were explicit shots of Asian children in compromising sexual positions with adult men. The best stuff he had seen ever.

He took another slug from his Coke. A smile crossed his pudgy, pimpled face; his lips were still dry. 'Wow,' he mumbled again as his pants stretched below.

Jason Miles recently commenced a cadetship with the Police Service's Information Technology Section. His security check came out clean, nothing to find there. The medical had been tough; he still had to lose a few kilos. He smiled, his supervisor, Senior Constable Harrison was an easy going bloke and did not suspect anything. How fucking easy was this, eh? He could download anything he wanted from the Q-PED files. Jason had quickly worked out Harrison's security code to enter the system.

'Wow, like too easy, yeah … man,' he said louder. Jason knew he was on to a good thing alright.

The End.

Acknowledgements

To write a book is one thing, to publish it is a different matter. I often wonder how many unpublished manuscripts sit in bottom drawers all over the world.

Without my friends and family, and others who believe in me, the journey to the last page would have taken forever.

Special thanks to Bronwyn Cozens and Denise Miller for the hours you devoted to UNEASY, as well as mentoring and encouragement over the years. You can only imagine what my characters would be like without my secret sensitivity editors.

Also, Bob Goodwin, Robin Storey, Alison Quigley, Michael Doneman and Brian Purdey for feedback and advice.

Pam, Andrea, Sally, Lol, my friends at Haiku Reeds and the rest – you all know who you are - thank you for your support.

Thanks to Jan Forbes for yet another outstanding cover and design as well as general assistance.

Special thanks to Michael Parker for his support and generous assistance with police protocols. Any inaccuracies are entirely my own.

I would like to acknowledge an old friend and mentor, Beryl Muspratt.

Ian Laver

About the Author

Ian Laver is a well-travelled fiction writer living in south east Queensland. His first novel, *CRUCIAL STEP* was published in 2021. He has written several collections of short stories, and many of his stories have been published in anthologies and in magazines. He was editor of a small country association magazine and had a regular column in an on-line publication. He was President of the Sunshine Coast Literary Association, has been active in writing organisations and is currently involved in a Haiku poetry group. Two Henry Lawson Emerging Writer and a Tom Howard Short Story Award are listed among his more than a dozen writing awards.

You can discover more about Ian's writing at-
Facebook: https://www.facebook.com/ian.laver.18
Facebook author page: Ian Laver | Facebook
Website: https://www.ianlaver.net
Instagram: https://www.instagram.com/iwlaver/

www.ingramcontent.com/pod-product-compliance
Lightning Source LLC
Chambersburg PA
CBHW030625120726
47904CB00006B/2041